THE LORD'S RELUCTANT LADY

Sisters of Ember Hall
Book 2

Elizabeth Heights

© Copyright 2025 by Elizabeth Heights
Text by Elizabeth Heights
Cover by Dar Albert

Dragonblade Publishing, Inc. is an imprint of Kathryn Le Veque Novels, Inc.
P.O. Box 23
Moreno Valley, CA 92556
ceo@dragonbladepublishing.com

Produced in the United States of America

First Edition October 2025
Trade Paperback Edition

Reproduction of any kind except where it pertains to short quotes in relation to advertising or promotion is strictly prohibited.

All Rights Reserved.

The characters and events portrayed in this book are fictitious. Any similarity to real persons, living or dead, is purely coincidental and not intended by the author.

AI Statement: No AI or ghostwriting was used in the creation of this story, or any story, published by Dragonblade Publishing. All text, structure, content, ideas, and concept are 100% human generated solely by the author whose name appears on the cover. It is prohibited to use this material, or any copyrighted material, for AI engine training.

ARE YOU SIGNED UP FOR DRAGONBLADE'S BLOG?

You'll get the latest news and information on exclusive giveaways, exclusive excerpts, coming releases, sales, free books, cover reveals and more.

Check out our complete list of authors, too!

No spam, no junk. That's a promise!

Sign Up Here

www.dragonbladepublishing.com

Dearest Reader;

Thank you for your support of a small press. At Dragonblade Publishing, we strive to bring you the highest quality Historical Romance from some of the best authors in the business. Without your support, there is no 'us', so we sincerely hope you adore these stories and find some new favorite authors along the way.

Happy Reading!

CEO, Dragonblade Publishing

Additional Dragonblade books by Author Elizabeth Heights

Sisters of Ember Hall Series
The Scot's Secret Love (Book 1)
The Lord's Reluctant Lady (Book 2)

The Earls of the North Series
Gambling with the Earl (Book 1)
Forced to Marry the Earl (Book 2)
Taming the Earl (Book 3)

CHAPTER ONE

Year of our Lord 1329
Ember Hall, Northumberland

"WHY SHOULDN'T I marry for love? Our parents did—and our eldest sister, as well."

Although delivered with passion, Tristan's pronouncement was met by little more than raised eyebrows and the odd polite nod.

The de Neville siblings were gathered around the long banqueting table at Ember Hall, having just finished a light meal washed down with a wonderfully refreshing wine. Many of them—Tristan included—had imbibed more wine than was wise. The day had been unrelentingly hot and his thirst was not easily slaked after the long ride north from Wolvesley Castle.

Mercifully, the sun had started to set whilst they were eating. But on this midsummer day, a stifling warmth still hung in the air, accentuated by the final rays of dappled sunlight which blazed through the tall windows.

"It's dastardly hot." His brother Jonah made a show of pulling the neck of his finely embroidered tunic away from his neck whilst fanning himself vigorously with the other hand.

A chorus of 'ayes' met this declaration. Little Flora, Tristan's four-year-old niece, slid from her chair and walked boldly over to Jonah.

"You can have this, Uncle Jonah." Her chubby hands held out a small white object studded with white feathers.

"But that's the fan I brought you back from France," Tristan objected, leaning closer to the golden-haired girl.

Flora nodded and wrapped her warm fingers around Tristan's wrist to urge him to lean down closer.

"Mother told me it's kind to share," she whispered in Tristan's ear. With her eyes fixed on her mother, she added in louder tones, "Even with Christopher, who never shares back."

"Especially with Christoper," Frida agreed solemnly. "He is your little brother and as such, you must always look out for him." The eldest de Neville sibling sat at the end of the table, silvery-white hair pinned elegantly atop her head, displaying all her usual poise despite having a chubby toddler bouncing on her knee. Young Christopher pulled at the beads around his mother's neck and burbled happily as his father, Callum, looked on proudly from the opposite end of the narrow table.

They were the perfect, contented little family.

Tristan's heart contracted with envy.

Why is this vision of domestic bliss to be denied to me?

He was about to take another swig of wine when he realised that Flora was still gazing entreatingly up at him, her earnest expression so reminiscent of her mother at that age. Frida was only one year older than Tristan and for much of their childhood, they had been the closest of friends.

Tristan ducked down so his face was level with Flora's again.

"Does Uncle Jonah share back?"

Flora bit down on her lip, a smile playing about her big blue eyes. "Not always," she whispered confidingly, shaking back her long blonde plait.

Callum guffawed with laughter and Tristan sat back, satisfied.

"'Tis just as I suspected." He picked up his goblet and sipped.

"I will try to do better in the future," Jonah declared. Though he shared in the family's golden good looks, he was a head shorter than Tristan and narrower about the shoulders. He led an active life, but he was not a warrior. Being born with a club foot meant he had been spared many of the rigours expected of the heirs to the de Neville line.

Most likely, when the time came, Jonah would be allowed to marry for love.

The delicious wine soured in Tristan's throat at the thought.

"There's no point in trying to change, Jonah," their youngest sister, Esme, chimed in airily. She had positioned her chair strategically so as to catch the faint breeze coming through the open window, and even been so bold as to remove her shoes and stockings. But still the day's heat had flushed her cheeks brighter than her gaily trimmed gown. "We are who we are and that's it."

"How very philosophical." Jonah reached for a red grape, tossed it into the air and caught it neatly in his mouth, prompting little Flora to clap with delight. "Let us follow that thought to its natural conclusion. His piercing eyes roved across the table. "Tristan, therefore, will always be rash and impulsive. And darling Mirrie, here, will forever be waiting upon him." At this point, Jonah reached out his hand to grasp Mirrie's arm before she could take away the now-empty trencher in Tristan's place.

Tristan hadn't even realised that Mirrie had stood up to clear the table. He turned towards the pretty young woman he had known since childhood. She was dressed modestly in a pale grey gown that contrasted with the brightness of her eyes and the shining waves of her long, light brown hair. Tristan had always thought of Mirrie with the same unstinting affection he felt for his sisters. Only Mirrie's nature was so much gentler than either Frida, Isabella or Esme—all of whom exhibited the strong will and steely determination of the mighty de Nevilles.

Sure enough, Mirrie's face was calm and composed even now, when Jonah's words caused everyone to stare. Only her flaring hazel eyes betrayed any sense of irritation. She shook Jonah's hand away and moved from the table without a word.

"I'm sorry," Jonah called after her, his face creasing with regret.

"Is it the heat that makes you so peevish, brother?" Esme enquired, liberally replenishing her goblet of wine from the pitcher.

"Steady with that," Frida spoke up.

"I am not a child." Esme took a long, pointed drink and plonked her bare feet onto the chair recently vacated by Mirrie. "In fact, I am near enough the age you were when you married Callum."

Frida and Callum exchanged another dreamy-eyed smile, which had Tristan swinging up from the table to stride towards the large, mercifully empty fireplace. He half thought of walking after Mirrie, but for the first time he was unsure of what welcome he might receive from her.

It was not true that she always waited upon him.

Was it?

Tristan pursed his lips as he gazed unseeingly into the dark grate, one hand shading his eyes from the glare of the stubbornly bright evening sunlight pouring through the tall windows.

Mirrie possessed a kind and generous spirit. Surely that was the only reason why she so often brought him refreshments and enquired after his wellbeing. They had grown up so closely, with Mirrie as his father's ward, raised alongside them, that it would have been stranger if she *hadn't* been solicitous of him.

"Methinks the heat is making fools of us all," Callum observed as he ushered his family away from the trestle table and towards the tapestried chairs spread out by the fireplace. "Let us sit more comfortably and remember that we are all friends here."

"This year, at least." Jonah shrugged his shoulders as he limped down from the dais, oblivious to—or mayhap even enjoying—the stifled gasps of the ladies.

"Why must you always be so awful?" Esme snatched Flora's fan from her brother and swiped at him.

Tristan spoke up over the hubbub, his resonant voice easily carrying around the vast hall. "Callum and I have put all of that behind us now." He raised his eyebrows questioningly at his brother-in-law, and received a firm nod in reply.

"Aye. What's past is past," Callum said, good-naturedly. He leaned with one hand against a stone pillar as he waited for the de

Nevilles to promenade from the table.

For a moment, their gazes clashed across the room. Callum was dark while Tristan was fair, but both were equally matched for height and strength. To say nothing of their shared experience in feats of arms. As young men, they had trained together at Lindum. But then, five years earlier, whilst working in the service of Robert the Bruce, Sir Callum Baine, a warrior from the Scottish highlands, had received orders to assassinate Lord Tristan de Neville.

What no one could have anticipated was that this quest would bring Callum back to Tristan's sister, Frida, who he had fallen headlong in love with years earlier.

Thus, Callum ne'er made any move on Tristan. However, when Tristan found him living at Ember Hall under false pretences, his retaliation had been swift and severe.

Tristan still felt a twinge of guilt at the memory of Callum, feet and hands bound, laying in a bloodied heap upon this very wooden floor.

He deliberately turned his gaze upwards, to the vaulted ceiling and smoke-blackened beams. They had all come a long way since then. In truth, Tristan couldn't be happier with Frida's match. Callum was a loyal husband and an attentive father. And his long past as a warrior of the highest calibre meant that Tristan could sleep easy without worrying of his sister's wellbeing up here, in a fortified manor so close to the Scottish border.

Still, an awkwardness hung over the assembled party at the memories Jonah had so carelessly evoked. Even little Flora pouted, whilst the usually frivolous Esme had turned away from them all and was talking gently to a panting hound.

Tristan cast around for a change of subject, and landed back on the complaint that had been on his lips for nigh three days now.

"Will none of you support me against Father's new dictates? E'en you, Callum? I would have thought you and Frida would be first to speak out in defence of love." He rolled his eyes good-naturedly. "Are you not living proof of the theory that love conquers all?"

Callum guffawed before looking deferentially towards his wife. "I will not interfere in a family matter." He put an arm on Frida's waist to help her to a chair.

Like Jonah, Frida walked with a limp, although hers was due to a riding accident some years past rather than a defect at birth. Right now, she was further hampered by pregnancy, the swell of her belly visible beneath her deep blue gown.

Tristan felt for a moment the foolishness of raising his grievances in a busy household, to which he had just added the burden of responsibility for his high-spirited sister, Esme. But his ire could not be so easily dampened down.

"You are family," he declared.

"And you are Father's heir, the next Earl of Wolvesley," Frida said, her voice surprisingly gentle. "He asks little of you, considering the import of your inheritance."

"Little of me?" Tristan scuffed his boots on the polished floor, annoyance swirling in his veins. "Only a contract that perchance will last the rest of my days." His pulse picked up speed as outrage took hold. "Only my freedom to live and love as I please. Only my heart and very soul."

Frida's expression passed through disappointment into scolding. She heaved Christopher into her arms, staggering slightly under his weight, and held out a hand towards Flora. "I see you are not to be reasoned with. I'm taking these two up to bed."

Tristan knew he had spoken harshly and good manners demanded an apology, but he couldn't seem to summon it. He took a deep breath and fixed his gaze on the tall window to the side of the fireplace. Beyond these walls, birdsong still filled the blue skies and he itched to be out there, striding over the rolling hills. A brisk walk would burn off this frustration.

He could think of better ways to find release, but none that could be indulged this night at Ember Hall.

At that moment, Mirrie returned holding a heavy tray, which

she carefully lowered onto a wooden table beside Tristan. Too late, he realised he should have taken it from her.

"I have brought in some freshly-baked honey cakes," she said with a small smile.

"Just what we need." Tristan strained to inject enthusiasm into his voice.

"Aye, to sweeten the atmosphere in here." Esme widened her eyes when Tristan shot her a disapproving look. "'Tis true, brother. You should stop this ceaseless complaining."

Tristan bit into one of the soft cakes and allowed himself a moment of pleasure as his mouth filled up with sweetness. "I do not want to find myself in a situation like Isabella," he said, after he had swallowed.

Even Callum chuckled at that. "With a spouse some forty years your senior?"

"In a marriage that has not brought her happiness," Tristan persisted.

Callum shook his dark head, eyes twinkling. "The Earl of Felsham was an old man when Isabella danced at her first ball. An equivalent match, for yourself, would hardly help with your need to continue the de Neville line." He lifted a honey cake in a mock salute. "I do not expect that to be your destiny, Tris."

Esme nodded approvingly at her brother-in-law. "Exactly." She returned her gaze to Tristan. "You know as well as I do that Mother and Father will invite a dazzling array of young heiresses to the midsummer ball. Many a man would welcome such a fate." She swiped another cake from the tray. "Just pick a bride and hurry up about it. 'Tis I who will suffer, being obliged to stay all the way up here, far from anything of import, until you do."

Tristan glanced down at Mirrie, still standing by his side. "What do you think?" he asked her gruffly. "Are you on their side, or mine?"

She straightened up but did not meet his eye. "I think your attention is fixed on the wrong thing."

Her unexpected reprimand was a shock. Mirrie kept her eyes

fixed on the floor, but her sweet voice was firm.

"Your father is ill," she continued, her voice gaining volume and conviction the longer she spoke. "That is, after all, why he is ordering you to marry with such haste. That is why you have brought Esme here from Wolvesley." She looked up pointedly at Esme, who pouted a little in return. "'Tis all so your father can recuperate in peace. And so your mother can concentrate on finding you a suitable bride." Mirrie's shoulders hunched. "It is unlikely you will be given no choice in the matter, Tristan. And in that, you are far more fortunate than I can ever hope to be."

He was winded by surprise. But Mirrie had not yet finished.

"Imagine yourself a spinster without a dowry. Then consider what marriage prospects you may have."

Tristan recovered his wits and waved her concerns aside with what he hoped was a reassuring air. "First of all, my father's health is bound to improve before long. He's the Earl of Wolvesley. He's as strong as an ox." He nodded to give emphasis to his words and saw Esme nodding along with him. Both of them were utterly convinced that their hale and hearty father would soon bounce back to his customary excellent health. "Second of all, what is this talk of you not having a dowry?" He put his hands on his hips and lowered his brow. "You are Father's ward and he loves you like his own. Of course he will see you rightly settled, when the time comes."

"And the time might come soon, might it not?" Jonah interjected, with something of a challenge in his voice. "The new physician in the village has shown quite an interest in our Mirrie."

Mirrie sniffed and turned her face away. Callum was the one to speak up next.

"Methinks dear Mirrie can do better than a blabbermouth who thinks mainly of coin."

"What's this?" Jonah cocked an eyebrow.

"David Bryce became most attentive toward Mirrie when he discovered she was your father's ward," Callum drawled. "'Tis no crime to have an eye to an advantageous match. But no great credit to him either."

Tristan had opened his mouth to agree, but now he found he had lost his train of thought.

Why does the notion of some village physician paying court to Mirrie make me so uneasy?

Mirrie pulled her shawl about her shoulders, despite the heat, and walked closer to the window. "You are wrong about the physician. David Bryce is polite and attentive to everyone, but he pays no special notice to me," she said mildly, alleviating Tristan's alarm only a little. "Your family have always been very kind to me," she added. "I did not mean to appear ungrateful."

"And nor did you appear so."

Tristan glanced over at Jonah who was seated comfortably in an over-stuffed armchair. That was the first sensible thing he had said all evening.

"Quite right," Tristan agreed. He had to get out of this stifling hall and walk over the fields. Some vigorous exercise would surely clear his head.

But Jonah fixed him with his piercing blue gaze. "If you will hear me, brother, I have a suggestion."

In truth, Jonah was the last person Tristan would look to for advice. But he brushed cake crumbs from his tunic and nodded with what he hoped was a genuine-looking smile. "I will gladly hear you." Suppressing his urge to flee, he settled himself in the nearest chair and crossed his long legs at the ankle. "Forsooth, I am relieved to know that at least one member of my family has some interest in my happiness."

He felt, although could not see, Eme rolling her eyes once again. He resisted a childish urge to stick out his tongue at her.

"Speak up, Jonah, and quickly, before Tristan makes another long speech about the hardships he must endure." Esme sashayed past him before plonking herself down in a cushioned window seat, closely followed by the adoring hound. "We are all ready and waiting for you to scatter your pearls of wisdom," she said pointedly, settling her chin on her upturned palm.

Jonah cleared his throat. "You've said it yourself, Tristan. Father's condition is temporary." Jonah waved his hand about in a vague manner. None of the siblings were altogether sure what ailment had struck down their previously invulnerable father. "Your best recourse, surely, is to buy yourself time."

Tristan leaned forward, his interest piqued. "How so?"

Jonah shrugged expansively. "Father is insisting you marry and produce an heir so that his line will be secure into the next generation." His blue eyes glowed with momentary angst, causing Tristan to reflect that for as long as he did not produce an heir, Jonah would be next in line behind him to inherit the Earldom of Wolvesley. "But the need to marry you off has never bothered him unduly before. It seems likely that once he is recovered, some other matter will claim his attention."

Tristan found himself nodding as his fingers drummed impatiently on his breeches. "Aye. But how does that help me now? Mother is planning a midsummer ball with a long line of ladies brought for my perusal." He wrinkled his nose in distaste.

Tristan was not in the least averse to perusing ladies. But he was most uncomfortable with being forced into any situation. Marriage felt like it would be far more of a constraint on him than a blessing. With the wealth of the Wolvesley estate at his disposal, together with his natural good looks and gregarious charm, the heir to the Earl of Wolvesley had grown accustomed to dancing with whomever he pleased, dining wherever he pleased, and bedding whichever willing beauty caught his eye.

He had no intention of settling down and marrying any time soon.

Jonah opened his arms. "Tell Mother and Father you have already found true love. Then their match-making efforts will cease. And once Father is up and about again, your lady can break your heart and leave you free to return to doing as you please."

Silence fell as they all digested this. Tristan repeated Jonah's words to himself, looking for a flaw and finding none. Could it be that Jonah, of all people, had found a solution to his problem?

A low chuckle sounded from the window seat. "'Tis a fine idea." Esme sat back, a faint breeze from the open window ruffling her blonde hair. "But you would need to be convincing, especially with Mother."

"I can be convincing," Tristan declared. His fingers beat out a rhythm on the arm of his chair as enthusiasm took hold. "God's bones, if it gets me out of marrying some empty-headed heiress, I can be utterly convincing." Someone tutted and Tristan swung his head to one side to see Mirrie in the act of bending down to collect the now empty tray. "You do not approve?"

She straightened up, hazel eyes looking directly at him. "I think only of the poor young woman you will enlist for this dishonest venture."

Tristan shook his head, uncomprehending. "What of her?"

A sad smile played about Mirrie's heart-shaped lips. "Exactly that."

"She would have to be in on the plan," Esme piped up, her eyes gleaming with excitement. "Someone we can trust."

"And someone that Mother approves of." This from Jonah, who was refilling his goblet of wine.

Tristan had not lifted his gaze from Mirrie's hazel eyes. The solution was here before him. She was pretty and gentle and kind. A woman well-beloved of both his mother and his father.

And someone that he himself trusted above all others.

"I can think of the perfect person," he said, softly.

A blush stained Mirrie's cheeks as she understood his meaning. She shook her head and proclaimed, "Nay, I could never."

But at the same time, Esme rose from the window seat and rushed forwards to grasp Mirrie's hands. "Perfect indeed," she gushed. Mirrie was still shaking her head, but Esme seemed blind to her hesitation. "You will save us all. Tristan will be free. And I will be able to return home. Not that Ember Hall isn't beautiful," she assured Callum. "But you know how I love the balls and excitement of Wolvesley Castle." She turned again to Mirrie. "As did you, back in the old days before you and Frida moved up here."

"That's right," Jonah agreed. "I know you've missed the dances, Mirrie. You've told me so yourself."

It was indeed the perfect solution. Tristan could not allow Mirrie to say no.

He stood up from his chair and moved into the centre of the circle. Nudging his sister aside, he took Mirrie's slender hands in his and gazed down into her familiar face.

"What do you say?" he whispered, summoning up his most winning smile. "Will you save me, Mirrie?"

CHAPTER TWO

*W*HAT CAN *I say?*

She could not escape the intensity of Tristan's blue eyes, gazing down at her. Nor could she escape the firm grasp of his hands, nor the flush that was spreading up from her chest and neck.

I have ne'er been able to deny Tristan anything.

How could she, when the merest hint of his boyish smile had the power to send her pulse pounding?

But what he asked of her was wrong. She could not lie to Morwenna and Angus; two people who had loved and raised her like one of their own.

Nor could she risk the secrets of her own heart, which she had hidden away so carefully that no one—not even Frida, her closest friend—suspected their true strength.

"Mirrie," Tristan whispered. He lowered his head closer to hers and she resisted the urge to close her eyes whilst inhaling his familiar scent of woodsmoke and pine. "Please."

He tightened his grip on her hands, running his thumbs gently across her fingers and sending a delicious tingle up her spine. Her heart beat so loudly beneath her plain woollen gown he surely must hear it.

Her plain woollen gown. That was what she must concentrate on: the difference between her muted attire and the exquisite embroidery on Tristan's emerald green tunic. Surely

Lord Tristan de Neville, even for a ruse, could not court a woman who sewed her own stockings.

Nor could he publicly proclaim affection for a near-penniless spinster who had already seen as many as five and twenty summers. 'Twas a ridiculous notion, and one that no one would believe.

"There are so many others you could choose," she managed to say. "More suitable than I."

"Ah, but none that I would rather spend time with," he countered easily. "Think of it. We will have to dance together, ride out together, sit together of an evening." He shrugged his muscular shoulders, making Mirrie's breath hitch in her throat. "Forsooth, it will be tiresome. And 'tis a lot to ask of you, to be so much in my company."

Mirrie floundered to find a suitable response. Tristan was offering up her wildest dreams on a platter. But the banquet was just an illusion, and she would be left all the hungrier once it was snatched away from her.

With the greatest effort, she dragged her gaze to one side and focused on the familiar view of rolling green fields glimpsed through the open window. It had been several summers since she had fled—aye, that wasn't too strong a word—to Ember Hall so she could escape the tumult of emotion she experienced whenever Tristan came near. That swirling sensation which even now gripped her insides was so contrary to her otherwise practical nature. It struck at the foundations of the orderly, peaceful life she had toiled to build.

"In truth, the two of you make an attractive couple."

Esme's observation made Mirrie start with surprise. For a moment she had forgotten that there was anyone else in the room with them.

But there was. Not only Esme, but Callum and Jonah too. And Frida would be back at any moment. Mirrie was making a fool of herself before all of the golden-hued de Nevilles.

Tristan turned to his sister with an impish smile. "And why

should we not?" He tucked Mirrie's hand into the crook of his arm. "The lovely Mirabel Duval will wed Tristan de Neville. Who would question it?" He patted her hand with brotherly affection.

Aye. Brotherly affection, while her whole being flamed for him.

Fortunately, Mirrie was well used to hiding her true feelings for the first son and heir of her illustrious guardian.

"I could not countenance deceiving your parents." Her voice wobbled at the very idea. Morwenna, the Countess of Wolvesley, had been kindness itself to Mirrie since she first came to Wolvesley Castle as a frightened orphan. Mirrie could no more look into her intelligent green eyes and utter a falsehood than she could draw a sword against an advancing army.

Tristan glanced down at her. Was that a flash of disappointment across his handsome face? Her stomach twisted at the possibility.

"What if I am the one to handle the deception?" Tristan ruffled a hand through his hair and ignored Jonah's ill-concealed bark of laughter. "You will not have to say anything that is not true."

Mirrie chewed on her lower lip. "But you said that your lady would break your heart." She turned to Jonah, who gazed up at them from his favourite over-stuffed chair by the empty fireplace. "Was that not the plan?"

Jonah shrugged, his face alight with merriment. "The plan can evolve as you see fit."

Drat him.

Since childhood, Mirrie had been Jonah's champion. The only one to have patience with a fragile little boy who walked with a limp and hid his anxieties behind a scowl and a sharp attitude. But right now, she could have cheerfully throttled him. Why was he so intent on bundling Mirrie back to Wolvesley? On Tristan's arm, no less? Suspicion flared within her.

Is he up to something?

Perchance so, but she had little time to ponder it because

Tristan was speaking again, enthusiasm rippling through his deep voice.

"I will speak to my parents of my newly-discovered love for you and our intent to wed." Tristan gripped her arm tightly. "And once Father is well and the danger has passed, I will take the blame for the end of our relationship." He smiled, as if all this were no more than a game to him. "You can return to your life here at Ember Hall. I will spend some days in disgrace, no doubt. But time will pass and soon enough everyone will forget all about it."

Her stomach plunged. Mayhap everyone would forget. Everyone but *her*.

"Seriously, Mirrie, you have to agree to this." Esme danced forward, barefoot and blithely unaware of the pretty picture she made. Her loose-fitting summer kirtle floated above her slender ankles and her golden-blonde hair shone like a halo in the dappled sunlight. She took Mirrie's free hand, the one not held captive by Tristan, and squeezed it entreatingly. "It would be such bliss to return to Wolvesley and, just for once, to not be my parents' most disappointing child."

Jonah tutted from his chair, waving his goblet to attract her attention. "I think you will find me the proper holder of that title."

"Nay, e'er since you took up residence at Ember Hall, Mother can't speak highly enough of you." Esme pursed her lips, dismissively. "She is forever reciting your poetry to anyone who will listen."

"Really?" Jonah leaned forward, spilling a little wine in the process. "Is that true?"

"We are getting away from the subject," Tristan interjected, shouldering Esme aside and taking both of Mirrie's hands in his own. He walked them both a few steps away from the huddle of chairs before gazing down at her entreatingly. "Will you be my betrothed?"

"God's bones, what is happening here?"

Frida had arrived back in the great hall in time to hear Tristan's proposal. She now stood in the arched doorway, both hands pressed to her heart above the visible bump of her belly.

"Did I hear what I think I heard?" Her blue eyes swung from her brother to her friend.

"You did," declared Tristan, at the same time as Mirrie spoke up in denial.

"'Tis all a ruse, Frida. To deceive your parents."

Mirrie breathed deeply, projecting an air of calm whilst inside she was a nauseating combination of nerves, excitement and frustration. For more than ten years she had dreamed of Tristan, tall and strong, holding her hands and gazing into her eyes with such reverence.

Though she had ne'er been so befuddled as to imagine an actual proposal. Mirrie believed in keeping her feet on the ground, even in her wildest fancies.

Which was why she must put an end to this fancy right now, before it caused her tender heart any permanent damage. If only she could find the right words to do so. Mirrie did not excel at thinking and acting in haste.

"My, that actually has the makings of a credible plan. Was it your idea, Tristan?" Frida walked slowly in the room, her face screwed up in consideration.

"'Twas mine," Jonah put in.

"We have all given our approval." Esme sank down to the floor, her brightly coloured skirts gathering elegantly around her as she fondled the silken ears of the hound. "All except Callum, I believe."

Callum was ever the voice of reason. Like Mirrie, he stood out amongst the circle of golden-haired, blue-eyed de Nevilles. Mirrie loved them all fiercely, but sometimes she wondered if being born to the wealthiest parents in the land, and blessed with such luminous beauty, made them blind to the everyday realities most people had to endure. Callum was different. He'd lost his mother at a tender age and latterly faced conflict with his father.

He knew what it was to go through life alone, without a protective barrier of fabled charm and family support. *Will he come to my aid?*

But Callum had no knowledge of her true feelings for Tristan.

Nor had he e'er experienced the sharp sting of unrequited love. He and Frida had been equally smitten with one another from the first time they met.

Mirrie bit down on her lip. She could not expect any help from that quarter.

Sure enough, Callum merely spread his calloused palms and smiled genially at the family group. "'Tis not for me to approve or disapprove."

"There we are then," Esme decreed. "It is settled."

"No, it isn't." Jonah leaned back into the comfort of his chair and crossed his breeches-clad legs. "Mirrie has yet to accept Tristan's proposal."

She must remain composed. She must not allow the treacherous blush gathering beneath her smock to turn her redder than a red apple.

Mirrie flicked back her hair, affecting nonchalance. "There is naught for me to accept, for it was not an honest proposal."

Esme and Jonah sighed dramatically, but Tristan only nodded.

"You are a woman who deals only in truth and honesty. I have always admired this about you."

Merciful heaven, this was no way to steady her blushes.

"Allow me to ask again." He leaned closer, making it wellnigh impossible for Mirrie to hold on to her composure. Her heart beat so hard she thought her tightly-laced kirtle might snap open. "Will you accompany me back to Wolvesley? Will you sit with me at dinner and allow everyone present to believe we are in love?"

Her throat went dry. Tristan's face was so near she could make out the upwards sweep of his thick eyelashes. A pulse beat at his neck, just above the edge of his tunic. He was tanned from long days of riding in the sun. If she allowed her eyes to travel further, she would see the hard lines of his powerful shoulders, dipping down into the arms she had always wanted to hold her.

"Will you dance with me at the midsummer ball?" he added, his voice low and gravelly.

"You always loved dancing at the Wolvesley balls," Esme spoke up, as if this settled the matter.

And mayhap it did.

Aye, Mirrie had always loved dancing. And she had always loved Tristan. Painfully, secretly, constantly. This was her chance to stand in the circle of his embrace. The only chance she would ever have. How could she say no to that? But then…how could she say yes? Her preference was for careful, considered decisions, not this rash choice now being foisted upon her. Yet could she not break free of her self-imposed reserve, just this once?

"I will." She nodded, unable to repress her smile at Tristan's whoop of delight.

"Thank you." He swung her into his arms, lifting her from the floor and spinning her around so her grey skirts flared around her calves. "You are my saviour."

She would do well to remember that. She was his saviour, *not his betrothed.*

But she was still smiling when he settled her back down. Even more so when he bowed before her.

"We will leave at once."

"Don't be ridiculous, 'twould be dark long before you reached the Wolvesley road," Frida pointed out.

"Damnation." Tristan stamped his booted foot on the floor. "I am impatient to put this plan into action."

"Clearly." Frida raised an eyebrow and made a show of whispering in Mirrie's ear. "Perchance my brother has been nursing a secret affection for you all these years."

"I have ne'er made any secret of my affection for Mirrie." Tristan slung an arm around both Mirrie and Frida and gave them a squeeze. His enthusiasm was the same now in the grown man as it had been since he was a mere lad. That boyish energy was something that Mirrie had always found so appealing.

Boyish energy. The sparkle in his blue eyes. The way his thick golden hair hung in waves to his broad shoulders. There were many things about Tristan de Neville that she found appealing.

All the things she had planned to put behind her when she first accompanied Frida to live at Ember Hall. When remaining at Wolvesley, so close to the man she adored, had grown too painful.

"We will leave at first light," Tristan announced. "Unless that is too early? Will you have time to pack and prepare?" His blue gaze held her hypnotised.

Mirrie nodded, unable to look away. Unable to think properly whilst her heart pounded so. "I will have time."

"I would need much longer than that," Esme chipped in.

"And that is just one of the reasons why I have no wish to wed a woman like yourself," Tristan declared. "Too much primping and preening and an obsession with gowns."

Unperturbed, Esme blew him a kiss.

"We will miss you, Mirrie," Frida said. Her beautiful face showed a trace of anxiety.

Guilt washed over Mirrie. They did not live in luxury at Ember Hall and every pair of hands was necessary. "I should have asked if I could be spared. There is the sheep-shearing ahead of us, and the stores to make ready for harvest."

Frida waved away her concerns. "We can manage well enough with that." She lowered her voice and turned them both towards the window, speaking so no one could easily overhear them. "'Tis your happiness I worry over."

Mirrie swallowed. Had Frida discerned the depths of Mirrie's feelings for Tristan?

"Life at Wolvesley Castle is so different to our life here," Frida added softly. "Much will be asked of you. Are you prepared for it?"

Mirrie nodded hesitantly, still worried that Frida had perchance found out her secret. Her gaze drifted downwards and she gasped with awful realisation.

"You are approaching your lying in," she breathed. "It is selfish of me to go."

Frida inclined her head, eyes glinting. "I will have Esme here with me." Her lips pressed together, repressing a chuckle. "What more could I need?"

"Oh, Frida." Mirrie caught at her friend's hands. "I should not leave you."

"What's this?" Tristan was striding towards them, long strides covering the wooden floor. "I trust you are not attempting to change Mirabel's mind, sister."

"Mirabel is more than capable of making up her own mind." Frida attempted to shoo him away, without success.

Tristan folded his arms and regarded them both, bouncing a little on his toes. "Just this morn I was beset by woes, but now I am happy once again. And it is thanks to you." He made another bow to Mirrie.

"It is thanks to Jonah," she said drily, pleased with the steadiness of her voice.

"It is thanks to this beautiful home you have, where peace and love prevail and everything works out for the best." Tristan gestured to the patchwork of fields outside, now darkening beneath the setting sun.

"How very romantic of you." Frida could no longer hide her smile. "I believe you have mayhap imbibed too much wine, brother."

"Methinks we are all a little guilty of that." Callum joined them and claimed his wife with a kiss. "'Tis time to retire. My bed is calling."

"I will come up as well." Frida's hand rested on her ripe belly. "'Tis tiring carrying this little one around all day."

Mirrie's earlier elation was swamped by a wave of sorrow. What she wouldn't give for a loving husband and a baby on the way.

As Callum and Frida departed, Tristan once again took hold of her arm. "I mean it," he whispered. "You have made me a very happy man."

Mirrie tried to smile up at him, aware of Jonah's all-seeing gaze from his usual position by the fireplace.

"As ever, I aim to please the de Nevilles," she quipped, reaching for humour.

Something passed over Tristan's face, making his expression oddly inscrutable. For a moment he drew her close; so close their breath mingled together.

"You could never do anything other than please us," he stated, dropping a kiss on the top of her head before he abruptly turned to leave.

Brotherly affection, she told herself, wrapping her arms about her shoulders as she watched him stride from the great hall.

She must cling tightly to that undeniable truth in the days ahead.

CHAPTER THREE

THE DAY DAWNED bright and clear, with cornflower blue skies and a promise of heat to come. Tristan had slept with the shutters open; he woke with a smile on his lips, bathed in a pool of light. The morning chorus of birdsong filled the air, louder than a peal of bells from a cathedral.

Laying on his narrow but comfortable pallet in a small guest chamber, Tristan felt all of this as a blessing. Yesterday, he had been peevish and cross when he had awakened, but today all had been restored to its natural order.

He was happy.

He had a plan that was sure to work.

He would get his way.

A fly buzzed near his head and as Tristan swatted at it, his hand glanced across an unfamiliar growth of stubble which made his lips wrinkle with distaste. He had ridden from Wolvesley in what could only be described as a blaze of bad temper yesterday, not bothering to take the time to shave beforehand. Now, what he really needed was a good bath and a shave, to remove away the heat and grime of the road, before enduring it all again.

He sat up, groaning at the pain in his head and remembering, regretfully, the strong wine he had drunk with so much relish last night.

A swim in the sea would put much of this to rights.

Tristan heaved himself upwards and took the two steps towards the open window, breathing in big lungfuls of fresh country air tinged lightly with sea salt.

Aye, a swim was just what he needed. He would go down to the cove before breaking his fast.

Whilst Frida had always been drawn to the standing stones during their childhood visits to Ember Hall, Tristan's deepest love was reserved for the deserted cove, with its rearing granite cliffs and sandy beach. It was where he had learned to swim—and where he had first learned to defy his parents, for Morwenna did not like her beloved son to go down to the cove alone, but young Tristan could not stay away.

Sounds reached him from the stable yard; horses being led out and stable hands shouting to one another. He winced at the volume, wondering why there was so much activity at this early hour. A knock came at his door and he bade the person enter before remembering that he wore nothing more than his braies.

Thankfully, it was only Jonah.

"Brother." A faint smile hovered across his sensitively-drawn face as he stood in the doorway. "I see I have caught you before you had a chance to dress. Shall I send up a manservant?"

Still grappling with the last vestiges of sleep, Tristan did not realise he was being baited. "I left Alfred behind at Wolvesley. Frida always tells me there is not room enough for manservants here." He rubbed his eyes. "Has she been lying to me all these years?"

Jonah laughed at him openly. "I am jesting, Tristan. How long is it since you last had to dress yourself? Can you e'en remember how?"

Tristan looked around for something to throw at his younger brother, but the chamber was sparsely furnished and nothing came to hand. He found the grace to smile and waved him in. "Come inside and shut the door, lest I give one of the girls a fright."

Unperturbed by his near-nakedness, Tristan stretched both arms above his head and yawned widely as Jonah closed the panel. The months he had spent in France had turned his skin golden-brown, whilst his regular training kept his muscles honed. Tristan prided himself on his skills with a sword and on his speed and stamina in the saddle. He kept his body fit and healthy. Last night's over consumption of wine was not a customary habit.

He leaned out of the window, once again noting the flurry of activity coming from the stable yard around the corner. However, since his chamber looked out over the paddocks and hills to the west of the hall, he could not see what was causing the disturbance.

"Why all the noise?" he asked Jonah, puzzled.

His younger brother folded his arms and leaned against the plastered wall, an unreadable expression passing over his face.

"As ever, we all rush to fulfil your every command."

Tristan was in no mood for puzzles. "Speak more clearly, brother. I do not have time for this."

"Indeed you do not." Jonah's voice was smooth. "Mirrie is already waiting in the yard. Her bags are packed and her horse is saddled. I came only to see what was keeping you."

Tristan frowned. "My intention is to bathe at the cove and break my fast before setting out for Wolvesley."

"And yet you bade Mirrie to be ready to leave at first light."

Tristan sank down onto the window ledge, his hopes of a swim in the sea plummeting. "I did, didn't I?" He sighed. "Damnation. I was over-eager to be gone."

Jonah inclined his head. "Perchance a little."

Irritation swirled in his gut, firstly at himself, for speaking so rashly yesterday eve, and latterly at those who so unthinkingly followed his instructions. Was it too much to ask for a little peace? To clean the dust from his skin before embarking on another day-long journey?

"There is no need for such haste," he declared. "Tell Mirrie to rest awhile. I will not be overly long." Jonah's face remained impassive, but Tristan was a quick reader of expressions, and he could see a flicker of *something* behind his brother's blue eyes. He rose to his feet and opened his arms. "What is it?"

"'Tis naught." Jonah offered a slight bow. "I will take your orders to the yard."

"Nay." Tristan raised a hand to stop him. "Has Mirrie been ready a while?"

"Since first light." Was there a hint of sarcasm in Jonah's voice?

Tristan bit down on his lip. His irritation had been joined by another emotion, which he belatedly recognised as guilt.

"No one woke me," he muttered.

"'Tis a hard life indeed, without a manservant." Now the sarcasm was undeniable.

Tristan stamped down on his displeasure. "You have made your point, Jonah. I will join Mirrie directly." He glanced about the chamber and scowled. "Is there no bowl of water with which to wash?"

"Warmed water is available in the kitchen. But I will fetch it for you." Jonah paused in the act of leaving the room. "For Mirrie's sake," he added.

Aye. Just as it was for Mirrie's sake that Tristan would forgo his longed-for dip in the sea.

But it was for *his* sake that dear Mirrie was leaving her home and entering into a subterfuge which went against her honest nature. He must curb his impatience and remember this.

Jonah returned soon enough with a bowl of tepid water, much of which had been slopped over the stairs on the journey from the kitchen. Again, Tristan silenced the complaint before it reached his lips.

Much longer at Ember Hall and he would turn into a veritable saint.

He expected Jonah to leave whilst he washed, but instead he walked with his uneven stride towards the window, averting his eyes from Tristan's ablutions.

"May I make a request?"

Tristan had splashed water onto his face and was now rubbing at the grimy skin on his arms with a washcloth. He did not pause.

"Aye."

Jonah cleared his throat, his gaze still fixed on the fields outside. "Will you be good to Mirrie?"

Tristan stopped and lowered his brows in confusion. "Of course, I will be good to Mirrie. When am I anything but?"

Jonah pursed his lips, as if there was something he wanted to say but could not find the correct words. "She has a sensitive side. She is not like—"

"Not like me?" Tristan finished for him, water dripping down his chest.

"Mayhap I should not have suggested this plan." Jonah gripped the window ledge in frustration. "We are sending her off to Wolvesley with little thought for her wellbeing."

Tristan put his hands on his slim hips and stared, his ablutions forgotten. "What the devil do you mean by that?"

Jonah rubbed at his temples, his eyes squeezed shut. "For one thing, she is not a confident horsewoman."

Understanding dawned. Tristan tossed the washcloth into the bowl and strode forward to clap Jonah's shoulder. "Your concern does you credit, brother. Have no fear. I will ride close beside Mirrie. God's Bones, we have had riding accidents enough in this family already."

The warm water had done much to restore Tristan's usual good humour. He flung open the small closet and picked out his tunic and breeches, humming all the while.

"I suppose I cannot persuade you to take the carriage?"

Tristan paid this little heed. "The journey is so much slower by carriage. And I have faith in Mirrie, even if you do not." He threw his brother a look. "As I said, I will ride close beside her."

Jonah sighed. "That is all I can ask, I suppose."

"Have no fear." Tristan was emphatic. "All will be well. Our Mirrie will have the time of her life at Wolvesley. I will make sure of it."

Though he still did not appear entirely convinced, Jonah left the chamber, muttering something about victuals in the great hall. Tristan had never seen him so domesticated.

As he pulled on his tunic, a thought occurred to him that left him almost winded.

Could it be that Jonah has feelings for Mirrie?

Tristan straightened his clothing, his eyes wide in contemplation. That would certainly explain his profound concern for her wellbeing.

But it would not explain why Jonah himself had concocted the plan for Mirrie to masquerade as Tristan's betrothed.

Tristan pursed his lips, casting his mind back to the precise events of last night. Perchance Jonah had not been the one to suggest Mirrie's name. But he certainly had not spoken up against it. Nay, it was most unlikely that Jonah would harbour anything but brotherly affection towards the young woman who had grown up alongside them. And, viewed in a fraternal light, his diligence in regards to Mirrie's safety did him credit. Although Tristan did not think this diligence was necessary. He had long ago perceived depths of courage and determination in Mirre, that others did not see.

Dressed and ready, Tristan scanned the chamber for a looking glass but found none. He had to content himself with pulling a wooden comb through his tangled locks and ruffling his hair into a style he hoped would be presentable.

He clattered down the narrow wooden stairs, to find his whole family assembled around the dining table in the great hall. Esme started a languid round of applause as soon as he strode through the archway.

"Hail, he appears at last."

"Do be quiet," he countered with a smile. He scanned the long table, which fairly groaned with food. Then his eyes travelled over the assembled faces. He paused when he noticed one was missing. "Where is Mirrie?"

"Outside with the horses," piped up little Flora, her hands

clutching a slice of bread spread with honey. "She said the fresh air would steady her nerves."

Frida shot her a look between Christopher's flailing arms. "She said that in confidence to you and I, Flora. I do not think Mirrie wanted it repeated."

Flora shrugged, her big eyes round with innocence.

Tristan had hoped to sit a while and satiate his hunger while ridding himself of what remained of his wine-induced headache with this tempting spread. But it appeared that duty called him elsewhere.

"I will go out to her." He leaned over Esme and tore off a heel of bread, inhaling the freshly baked aroma and trying to ignore the rumblings in his belly. "May I beg a skin of ale for the journey, Frida?"

"Mirrie has it all taken care of." His sister smiled benignly. "We will follow you out and say our goodbyes."

"We don't need a leaving ceremony," he protested. But it was all in vain. The whole family followed him down the stone-flagged entrance hall and out into the courtyard, where Mirrie stood waiting, along with the small party of armed guards who had ridden with them from Wolvesley. The hilts of their swords gleamed in the morning sunshine and their emerald green cloaks looked overly formal against the background of barns and scratching chickens.

The horses had been waiting for some time, judging by the way they pawed at the ground with impatience.

Tristan summoned a smile for Mirrie.

"I apologise for my tardiness."

He thought for an awful moment that she might bob into a curtsy, which would imply some difference in their status that he would prefer to ignore, but she only lowered her head. "It is no trouble." She wore a pretty straw bonnet, tied beneath her chin with ribbons bright enough for Esme. Her riding habit was a light sage green.

Tristan's heart constricted as he realised this was a deliberate choice. Mirrie had worn Wolvesley green to travel home.

His mood lifted and he crossed the ground between them, laying his hands upon her small ones. "Frida tells me you have arranged food and drink for our journey. Pray tell me this is indeed so, for I am famished."

She met his eyes for the briefest second, long enough for him to see a dart of excitement in their hazel depths.

'Twas good to see she was happy about the adventure ahead of them. Jonah's doubts were without foundation, just as he'd thought.

"I have," she confirmed.

"Of course she has," Esme chimed in breezily. "We were all raised to anticipate your every whim."

"If only that were true." He clasped his youngest sister in a warm embrace. "Be good, Esme. Do not cause too much trouble for Frida."

"I will be the opposite of trouble. I will be a great help. Callum is going to teach me how to shear the sheep."

Tristan raised his eyebrows at his brother-in-law. "I wish you luck."

"And I wish you luck in return."

The two men clasped hands as the ladies embraced in a flurry of swirling skirts.

"Do not be gone long," Flora demanded of Mirrie.

"I shall not." Mirrie bent her knees so she was closer to the little girl. "Do not grow overly tall while I am gone."

"Do not become such the grand lady that you don't wish to return," Frida put in.

Mirrie straightened up as something like regret flickered across her pretty face. "There is little danger of that, Frida." She smiled with determination. "I shall be back in good time for harvest."

Tristan nodded emphatically, stepping forward to help Mirrie into the saddle. "If all goes well, I might even come back myself and help."

A few chuckles met this proclamation. Tristan lifted Mirrie high into the air, forgetting, in his enthusiasm, that she was not a natural horsewoman. At the last moment, she flung out her leg and caught her balance, but she had come dangerously close to tipping over the other side of the little chestnut horse. He gripped her thigh to hold her steady, laughing out an apology.

Mirrie's cheeks flushed red as she fished for her reins and Tristan remembered his conversation with Jonah.

"I will look after you," he said in a low voice, his head tipped back to look at her whilst one hand remained on her leg. "You don't need to worry about anything."

When she met his gaze, he realised she was battling a torrent of emotion. Mayhap Jonah was right after all? Mirrie might prove to be more sensitive than he had realised. Deep down, Tristan had always sensed that Mirrie was brave and capable. But even the bravest individuals suffered a crisis of confidence every now and then.

Tristan gave her leg a reassuring pat as he called for his own horse to be brought forward.

He would ride close beside her, every step of the way.

He would keep his promise to Jonah. And he would make sure Mirrie had an experience she would never forget.

CHAPTER FOUR

MIRRIE HAD RIDDEN the little chestnut mare a couple of times before. She recalled that the horse's stride was steady and her manner sensible, but that didn't stop her from clinging onto the reins for dear life.

Unlike Frida and Esme, she was not a natural horsewoman.

"You are doing well." Tristan's deep voice broke into her thoughts. His manner was soothing and if the man didn't make her pulse pound simply by being nearby, Mirrie might have found his presence something of a comfort.

They had already left behind the well-trodden tracks leading down from Ember Hall. Gone was the familiar scent of woodsmoke and the contours of the land that she loved so well. Soon even the local village would be but a memory.

This is my last chance to turn back.

"Give the mare her head and lengthen your legs down her sides."

She could feel his eyes upon her. His unfamiliar attentiveness did little to calm her anxiety.

"I am trying," she replied through gritted teeth.

"You are succeeding," he corrected her. "And if I am being a bore, please tell me. My only aim is to keep you safe and happy."

She silently digested this as they passed a group of villagers who stood aside and bowed. Usually she would have smiled and spoken in greeting, but her concentration was solely on the horse beneath her. After a while, greatly daring, she allowed a section of rein to slip through her fingers. The little mare, happy to gain a sense of freedom, strode out with more conviction.

"There you are," said Tristan.

She glanced up at him. He was riding close, but his height atop his bright bay warhorse meant that he towered above her.

"I am sorry for being such a coward."

"You are no such thing." His horse skittered at a clump of gorse but Tristan held him steady.

Mirrie found her lips turning up into a smile. They were passing through open moorland. Above them, the sky was a deep blue. Bluer even than Tristan's eyes. Aside from the steady beat of their horses' hooves, all they could hear was the occasional call of a curlew.

Mirrie remembered her determination to snatch at happiness whilst it was within her reach. Here was a lovely day, and the man she loved was by her side. She would allow herself to enjoy it.

"I oft wish I had learned to ride as early as you and the others."

"Before we could walk, you mean?" Tristan's grin was almost enough to make her forget she was perched atop a horse, at the mercy of its whims.

She nodded. "Before fear and reason had chance to set in."

"Well, none of us had a choice in the matter." He held his reins loosely with one hand, the other arm hanging down by his side. "As you will know, having met my mother."

They shared a smile. "Your mother is the only reason I can ride at all."

Lady Morwenna, Countess of Wolvesley, loved horses almost as much as she loved her husband and children.

"Did she have you up on a horse the first day you arrived in Wolvesley?"

Tristan's tone was light, but Mirrie's answer was serious.

"Nay. The first day I arrived in Wolvesley, I had hardly the confidence to speak my name, let alone ride a horse."

Tristan shook his head, his lips pressed together regretfully. "I hardly remember, though I know I should. We had both of us seen near enough ten summers at that time."

"Eight," she corrected him.

"To me, it is as if you were always there." Tristan treated her to one of his widest smiles, but when she found herself unable to return it, contrition filled his eyes. "Forgive me, Mirrie, 'twas a thoughtless thing to say. You must have had a full life before you came to live with us."

She had. One with loving parents and a happy home. But she had had years to grieve the life she had left behind, and to come to terms with the one she'd been given instead. Her voice was quite steady as she replied.

"I was blessed with kind and caring parents. When they died, I was blessed again to be taken in by your family."

The small of her back was aching. Mirrie summoned all her courage and placed her reins in one hand so the other could rub at it. The chestnut mare scarcely altered her stride, but her furry ears flickered back and forth, showing she was aware of her rider's movements.

"Good girl," Mirrie tried.

Tristan smiled again. "See this? You are becoming a horse-woman before my very eyes. Jonah doubted that you could manage the journey on horseback, but I was sure that you would succeed. Just as you do in all things."

"You must not flatter me so. I am not used to it." Mirrie would have loved to disguise the blush now staining her cheeks, but there was nowhere for her to hide up on the moors.

"I am more accustomed to the company of ladies who expect to be flattered," Tristan quipped.

Of course he is.

Ladies who had been raised to make a match with a wealthy noble. Ladies who knew how to make charming conversation even whilst sitting atop a horse.

Mirrie fought against her habitual self-flagellation. If she and Tristan were to succeed at this ruse, she must take hold of her courage with both hands.

"Well, you are not conversing with them, you are conversing with me," she retorted, employing the tone of voice Frida sometimes used with Flora. She took a deep breath and added, "Furthermore, you are not on the cusp of declaring your love for them, but for me."

Tristan chuckled with delight.

"True enough, Mirrie. I thank you for the reminder. From this point on I will pay court to you and you alone. Methinks that will be rather fun." He ruffled at his golden hair, his eyes dancing with mischief. "God's blood, it is hot. And it seems we are the only ones here for miles about." He grinned down at her from his warhorse. "My men have ridden ahead to source a spot for luncheon, but that is some time away yet. What say we stop for a while, just you and I?"

Mirrie felt as if all the air had left her lungs. *What is he suggesting?*

Some of her confusion must have shown, for Tristan released a great, bellowing laugh which sent birds squawking up from the trees.

"I meant only that we could rest awhile in the shade." Tristan composed his face with seeming difficulty. "You are quite safe with me, Mirrie, I give you my word."

She inclined her head, attempting to hide her scalding cheeks.

"I know that." She huffed out a breath, desperately reaching for her composure. "You are like a brother to me, Tris."

How smoothly the lie trips from my tongue.

She was only glad that neither Frida nor Jonah was present to witness it. Though neither of them had confronted her on the matter directly, she suspected they both had some inkling of her long-held attraction to the eldest de Neville boy.

"And you are like a sister to me." He waved a hand. "In truth, some of the time I like you better than my sisters."

"Now I know that is untrue."

The moment of danger had passed.

Still smiling, he twisted in his saddle to look at her. "I will ask again. Would you like to stop and rest? There is plentiful shade nearby, and this may be our last opportunity before luncheon."

Mirrie's legs and back were aching, but she knew they had many miles ahead of them and did not wish to delay them by requesting a pause in their journey this soon. And besides, her heart still fluttered too quickly for proper conversation.

"Nay, let us continue awhile yet." Her horse caught up and they rode for a while in companionable silence, but Mirrie was aware that Tristan's eyes kept turning down towards her. "What is it?" she demanded, hoping fervently that he would make no further reference to his *brotherly* affection.

"Since we are on the cusp of such intimate acquaintance, I wonder if I might ask you a question?"

Holy hell.

She would have preferred brotherly affection.

But she kept her gaze straight ahead, looking between her horse's bright chestnut ears. "Go ahead."

Tristan cleared his throat. "'Tis a little indelicate. If you do not wish to answer, you do not have to."

Her heart threatened to leap out of her chest. "I will keep that in mind."

Tristan reined in his long-striding horse so they fell into step together. "Just now, you mentioned the death of your parents. I recall there being some scandal around your father's passing." He had dropped his voice to a whisper, even though there was little chance of them being overheard. "I always wondered about it, but Father was emphatic that it should not be mentioned."

"And here you are, disobeying him."

"'Tis wrong of me." He bowed his head. "If it pains you to speak of it, then please pretend I said nothing. I've no wish to upset you."

"I am only teasing." Mirrie smiled, to demonstrate the truth of this. "There is no cause for shame or secrecy. I am proud of what my father did."

"Which was?" Tristan watched her closely.

"He stood against the King, in favour of the Earl of Lancaster. 'Twas the time of the old King, Edward II. Many men spoke against him, but few were brave enough to take a stand."

Tristan nodded slowly. "But your father was."

"Aye." She twisted her fingers in her horse's thick mane, keeping herself rooted to the present moment. "He was executed for it. And my mother died of grief soon after."

"And then you came to live with us." Tristan's voice was caring, as if he could sense the weight of her memories.

"My father was a law-maker."

"Like mine," Tristan interrupted.

Mirrie nodded. "That is how they met. Father knew that what he was doing was dangerous. He arranged with your father that if anything should happen—" Mirrie's voice faltered.

She fixed her eyes on the distant horizon of rolling hills. Somewhere, miles ahead, stood the might and grandeur of Wolvesley Castle, where against all odds she had spent the latter part of her childhood. She remembered how utterly terrified she had been to stand in the vast, echoing entrance hall with servants scurrying this way and that. The earl had been like a giant to her; his castle like something from a fairy story. She thought she might get lost in the maze of torch-lit chambers and spend the rest of her days trying to find the way out. It was all so different from the modest homestead she'd known before.

She didn't need to glance up at Tristan to know that his face would be creased with compassion. He could be rash and self-centred, but beneath it all ran a rich seam of good sense, courage and kindness.

He cleared his throat. "I am sorry that you came to Wolvesley under such sad circumstances. But I'm mighty glad to have grown up beside you. We all are."

She smiled, thankful for a faint breeze which lifted her hair from her neck and took some of the heat from her face. "As I am glad to have known all of you. Though at first, I was very much in awe of the mighty de Nevilles."

Tristan guffawed at this. "I am sure that didn't last long."

Her horse stumbled, jolting Mirrie forwards over her neck. She righted herself with some difficulty. "I sometimes feel that way still," she admitted, as surprised as Tristan by her confession. "Mayhap you have to be born to the wealth of Wolvesley to accept it as the norm."

He shot her a piercing look. "I hope you are no longer in awe of me?"

How to answer that?

She managed to shake her head.

"Or anyone else?" he added.

In truth, Angus de Neville, the Earl of Wolvesley, still inspired more than a little awe in Mirrie. But she knew that Tristan would not want to hear that.

"The compassion of your parents soon outshone all else."

Tristan nodded his understanding, his eyes also roving over the horizon. The sun blazed brightly above them, but 'twas as if a cloud had settled over his handsome features.

They rode in silence for a little while before Mirrie found she could not resist asking her next question. "What rift has occurred between you?"

"No rift," he answered readily, making her exhale with relief. "Just a…disagreement." He waved a hand vaguely. "To be honest, Father and I have been railing at each other for some years now. I want to bring new ideas to the estate. To try new things. Surely that is our duty, is it not? To improve the lot of our tenants?"

Mirrie frowned. "Your mother would always take food and clothing to the poorest of your tenants or to those suffering from illness or hardship."

"Aye, and she does so still. But what if we could bring more prosperity into the area? Then they might not need to rely on our charity."

Mirrie was moved by the passion in his voice. "What ideas do you have?"

"I have heard of castles that host a covered market, so folk can barter and trade all year-round, in one place. Whatever the weather. Even in the midst of winter." Tristan spoke quickly, his words almost following over one another. "We have room enough for that and more at Wolvesley." With one hand holding his reins, he lifted the other upwards, entreatingly. "Father has always been first and foremost a law-maker and with our land yielding reliable crops, he has never had to expand his circle of knowledge. But there are new farming practices in the south. A three-field system, with less land left to fallow each year. More crops can be grown. More can be sold." He shrugged his shoulders as if it was obvious.

Mirrie considered this. "And Angus does not wish to try these ideas?"

"Father does not like to try anything new." Tristan's horse, picking up on the tension in his voice, began to jog forward. Unthinkingly, Mirrie nudged her horse to catch up. "Honestly, Mirrie. These things bother me less in times of unrest. But if we are to know peace, oft times I think I might follow in Jonah's footsteps and hide away at Ember Hall."

"Really?" She felt her eyebrows shoot upwards as she balanced with one hand on her horse's withers.

Tristan did not appear to hear her. "Wolvesley has known decades of peace and prosperity under my father's rule. He is well-respected."

"Well-loved, I would say," Mirrie interjected, relieved when both horses slowed back to a walk.

"Aye, true enough." Tristan smiled at her ruefully. "He asks me why I am so intent on bringing change to an estate that is already flourishing."

"He has your best interests at heart." Mirrie was staunch in her defence.

"Father has what he *thinks* are my best interests at heart,"

Tristan corrected her, before shaking his golden head. "Forgive me. I am talking too much. You must tell me when I am being a bore."

You could never be that.

"I certainly shall," she said out loud.

Around the next bend they found Tristan's men waiting with a picnic rug spread out in a grassy clearing and a hamper of food being unpacked. They reined in their horses beneath the shade of an oak tree and Tristan bounded to the ground with enviable ease.

"Let me help you down."

He held up his arms for Mirrie, leaving her little choice but to lean into them as she slid from her horse's back. Tristan's grip was strong and steady, he smiled down at her, haloed by the sun.

"Thank you," she managed.

It felt like years earlier that Mirrie had arranged bread, cheese, apples and skins of cider for their lunch. The Wolvesley guards seated themselves near the grazing horses, talking companionably between themselves as they ate. Tristan flung himself onto the rug and tore into the bread, chewing hungrily. Mirrie lowered herself down with as much dignity as her stiff and aching legs would allow. Trees provided dappled shade, a relief from the noon-day sun. What she really wanted to do was lay back and close her eyes, to fix this moment in her mind forever.

Birds singing. A faint breeze. And Tristan. All to myself.

"Are you not eating?"

She reached for some bread and cheese, overly aware of Tristan's proximity as she bit into it.

'Twas difficult to be delicate and ladylike whilst sitting on the ground, her long skirts twisted uncomfortably beneath her.

"I am famished," he declared. "But I did not break my fast before we left because I did not wish to keep you waiting."

She stilled her inner voice, which wanted to tell him that he should have prioritised his own comfort. That she would have waited for him. Because she *would* wait for him *endlessly*. But if

Tristan really was her brother, and she really thought of him as such, then she would be more inclined to scold him. And since that was what he doubtless expected from her, she should craft her response accordingly.

Once again summoning her best imitation of Frida, Mirrie retorted, "All because you slept in too late."

He glinted at her. "Aye, milady."

It cost too much effort to hold his laughing gaze without blushing. Mirrie turned her attention to a rosy red apple, enjoying the burst of sweet juice on her tongue.

"'Tis good to have you with me," he said, unexpectedly. "Speaking the truth and keeping me on my toes. Like Esme, perchance, but better."

"Better how?" Mirrie raised her eyebrows. "Because I do not demand your opinion on bonnets and ribbons?"

"That would be reason enough, to be sure, but your greatest charm is that you allow me to finish my sentences and most times listen to what I have to say." Tristan brushed crumbs from his tunic and leaned back on his elbows, tipping back his head to look into the canopy of leaves above them.

Mirrie averted her eyes so as not to be caught staring at the chiselled perfection of his cheekbones. She made herself remember that Tristan thought of her with nothing more than brotherly affection.

In short, he was not for her.

But oh, how her heart wanted him.

"I must tell you again how grateful I am for your help with this particular situation."

Mirrie stifled a gasp when she realized that Tristan had rolled onto his side and was now mere inches away from her. He idly plucked a strand of grass from beyond the edge of the rug and let it fall through his long fingers.

"You thanked me most effusively last night."

"Ah, but I was far from being at my most eloquent, given that I had imbibed more wine than was good for me last night." He threw her a radiant smile. "And yet, while my words might have been clumsy, I am grateful for the wine, for I likely would ne'er have conceived such an audacious plan if I were not well into my cups."

Mirrie inclined her head. Now would be the time to claim that she had also imbibed too much strong wine yesterday evening. For why else would she have agreed to it?

But in truth, she had not overindulged. Well, not in wine. Given in to Tristan's whims—for the reward of his smile—had always been an indulgence of hers.

"You do not need to keep thanking me," she said primly. "I understand the situation well enough."

Tristan rolled back onto his back, with his hands behind his head. He was utterly relaxed, whilst Mirrie had never been so entirely aware of everything. The rise and fall of his muscular chest beneath the exquisite embroidery on his tunic. The sweep of his golden hair across his brow. The fact that his elbow brushed against her skirts.

"I am glad to hear it, for I begin to think that I do not understand anything at all." Tristan twisted his head to look at her properly. "I thought only of my own happiness in persuading you to agree to this ruse."

Mirrie's heart began to gallop beneath her kirtle. "That is not true. You reminded me, quite fairly, of how I used to enjoy the Wolvesley balls."

Tristan pursed his lips. "Much as I would like to take credit, I believe it was Esme who recalled your fondness for dancing."

Mirrie hugged her knees. "Well, it was true, either way."

"You are kind and beautiful and we would all be lost without you."

His voice was a soft murmur, his words were like a caress. She could hardly believe she had heard him correctly.

Whilst she floundered for a response, Tristan propped himself onto an elbow so his face hovered just inches away from hers.

"Mayhap you will find a husband during your stay in

Wolvesley."

Her mouth opened and closed like a fish. "That is not my intention at all."

"Why ever not?"

"Because I do not wish to marry." She was becoming unaccountably hot. A burst of laughter from the nearby guards only increased her embarrassment. "That is, after all, why Frida and myself left Wolvesley for Ember Hall."

"Ah, but Frida married Callum soon after that."

"Aye, but that was hardly her plan at the time. And besides, my own resolution still stands."

Surely he could hear how her heart pounded against her ribs?

Still leaning unbearably close, Tristan's mouth twitched. "That is a shame…"

Time stood still. Mirrie's eyes widened at the crazy, wonderful idea that he might be about to kiss her.

"…for all of the eligible young men at Mother's Midsummer Ball," he concluded, raising himself up to a sitting position and shading his eyes from the sun. "We should get going if we want to arrive home before dark."

Mirrie felt as if she had been doused with cold water. Dumbly, she accepted his hand as he pulled her to her feet.

"Do not forget what I said, Mirrie." He took her elbow in a friendly way as they walked towards the horses. "You would make someone a wonderful wife."

Mirrie couldn't stand much more of this.

She pulled her elbow away and fixed him with her best attempt at a stern stare. "Tristan, do shut up. You are becoming a bore."

He was still chuckling as they mounted their horses and resumed their long journey to Wolvesley Castle.

CHAPTER FIVE

TRISTAN HAD NEVER passed such a pleasant ride home.

The bright summer sun that had hurt his eyes and caused so much irritation just yesterday, now seemed a joyful benediction on all that lay ahead. With Mirrie looking increasingly confident astride the little chestnut mare, Tristan allowed his attention to wander, noting the pleasing expanse of purple-hued moorland and overhead, the sweet song of a ruddock. Tristan remembered his mother taking him to one side when he was a boy and pointing out the red-bellied bird which sang so loudly for a creature so diminutive in size.

"You don't have to be the largest or the grandest to stand out," she'd said.

Young Tristan had smiled, blithely unheeding of her wisdom. He was heir to the largest estate and grandest castle in the land. He would always stand out. It took many years before he realized that that was not always a good thing.

"What has you so deep in thought?" Mirrie enquired.

He glanced down at her and decided to tell the truth. "I was enjoying the call of the ruddock and reminiscing about my mother."

Mirrie squinted up at him. Her bonnet had slipped backwards and her long hair fanned across her shoulders. "That sounds almost poetic."

He laughed. "You see, Jonah is not the only one of us capable of deep thoughts."

She nodded gravely. "I shall remember that." Her horse trotted a little to keep up with the long stride of his warhorse. "What was it about the ruddock?"

He strained his ears but the little bird was no longer anywhere near. "It is but a tiny little thing, yet the melody he creates is as beautiful as the throstle."

This time her smile was wide. "I believe Jonah has penned a poem on the very subject."

He rolled his eyes. "I might have guessed."

"Mayhap you should attempt the same, then we can compare the merits of the two."

Tristan glanced again at the woman riding by his side. "Do not attempt to convince me that your assessment would be fair. You would favour my brother, every time."

"What is this?" Mirrie's eyes danced as she looked him fully in the face. "Is this insecurity that I can sense in the great Tristan de Neville?"

Aye, it was. At least a little. But he would ne'er admit to it.

"I am content to let Jonah be a man of letters, whilst I am a man of action."

Mirrie pursed her lips. "Jonah is quite skilled with a sword." She broke into a laugh as she saw the expression on his face. "I speak in jest, Tris."

"Nay, you speak the truth. Jonah and I were trained by the same knight."

"But Jonah does not share your natural abilities," she pointed out.

His lips twitched upwards into a smile. It was nice to know that his talents were appreciated.

"Nor I his with a quill," he added generously. They were riding so close that her knee knocked against his calf. The sunlight danced across the ripples in her light brown hair, adding highlights of gold. Tristan knew a lightness of heart that this clever, capable young woman would be at his side in the days ahead, helping him with such an important matter.

Albeit, one that no one else deems important.

"Are we nearly there?" Her voice drooped a little with tiredness and Tristan was immediately contrite.

"Over the next hill we will be able to glimpse the castle battlements, but the light will hold for many hours yet. If you would like to stop and rest, we can do so."

"Nay." She shook her head. "I would rather press on and get there all the sooner."

"I too." He nodded with conviction. "I long to set the wheels of our plan in motion."

Mirrie's mouth tightened. "You will tell your parents straight away?"

"Why wait?" He lengthened his reins, giving his horse his head, and looked down at her in puzzlement.

She didn't answer for a long moment. The only sound came from the clumping of their horses' hooves over the moorland track and the distant buzzing of flies.

"Tell me what troubles you," he prompted, noting that the expression on her pretty face had become rather fixed.

Mirrie shrugged. "I merely imagined you would wait until you'd received the latest news of your father's health."

Now it was Tristan's turn to be quiet.

It was not the first time that Mirrie had floored him with her straight-talking.

"You are right, of course," he allowed. "His health is my first concern, and I am eager to hear news of how he fares. But I have little doubt that the news will be good. Surely Father will regain his strength soon. I would wager he will be up and dancing for the midsummer ball."

"Even so." Mirrie's voice remained clipped.

"Even so," he agreed. "Mayhap I am overly enthusiastic to claim you as my betrothed." He smiled widely, though he was more than a little baffled by the blush that rose up to stain her cheeks. "Forgive me, Mirrie. You know that patience has never been a particular virtue of mine."

Her expression softened. "I know it."

He had to be satisfied with that, for the track narrowed and Mirrie reined her horse back to fall in step behind his. The flies were buzzing nearer in the still air, causing him to wave them away. As an experienced knight, Tristan was well used to long days in the saddle, but even he was beginning to feel stiff. It was a relief when they reached the top of the hill and spied the jagged top of granite stone battlements rearing into the blue sky.

Wolvesley Castle.

Though Tristan had travelled far and wide, he had never visited anywhere half so grand as his childhood home. He had always been proud of his family's lineage and the peaceful, fruitful lands they ruled over. 'Twas only in these last weeks, when the demands on him as first son and heir took such a sudden turn, that a small spiky ball of resentment had lodged itself in his stomach.

"There it is." Mirrie's face was transformed by a smile. "I had not realised I missed it so much."

Her positive words banished his gloom. "I knew you would be glad to be home." But it was the wrong thing to say, for Mirrie's expression closed off all over again. "I do not mean to imply that Ember Hall is not your home," he added hastily.

Mirrie reached down to pat her horse, hiding her expression. "Wolvesley was my childhood home and will always hold a special place in my heart."

Her voice wobbled and it pierced something inside him. Mirrie had always seemed so content. He had never thought of her as being vulnerable or fragile. He had given little thought to her childhood circumstances, or how it would have felt for her to come and live with them so soon after the death of her own parents.

Was Jonah right? Was he rash and impulsive? Was that why they were here?

Nay, for Mirrie had made that choice of her own free will.

"What of me, Mirrie?" he asked impulsively. "Do I hold a special place in your heart?"

For a moment she looked disconcerted by the question, but then she rammed her straw bonnet more securely onto her head and met his gaze squarely. "Of course," she answered. "Have you not always known that?"

He inclined his head and met her impish smile with one of his own. "I have always hoped, to be sure."

"And now we will meet our destiny as a betrothed couple." She nudged her horse forward and preceded him down the hill.

"It is all I wanted and more," he called after her.

His horse fell in behind and Tristan reflected on his good fortune in finding such a lovely young woman to join him in this ruse.

Forsooth, he hadn't had to find her. She had been right there all along.

Minutes later, they reached the wide, smooth road that led right up to the castle. Tristan longed to urge his horse into a trot but, mindful of his companion, he lengthened his reins and sat easily in the saddle as the familiar landmarks came into view. There was the lake where they had all learned to swim, laughing and splashing in the shallows. There was the grassy noll where his mother would spread a picnic rug for the six of them to gather on. The landscape was filled with happy memories from their shared childhood; but when he went to comment as such to Mirrie, he saw that her gaze was fixed straight ahead and her mouth once again set in a grim line.

"What is wrong?" he asked.

"The lie we are about to tell." Her answer was short.

"We will get it over with straight away," he declared, nodding for emphasis. "I shall do the talking. You will not have to say a word that is not true." She nodded slightly, but still looked unconvinced.

There was no time for further discourse as they had already reached the high outer gates. The marshal stood back to let them through with a sharp salute. Tristan heard the shout, and a long line of armed guards stood to attention as he and Mirrie trotted past, the small group of men-at-arms who had travelled with them filing in behind.

He could not deny that it felt good to be home. To know that a hot bath awaited him and that he would not have to fetch his own water, nor bribe any of his relations to do the same.

Mayhap sharing his enthusiasm for home—or at least, for the prospect of a hearty meal—his warhorse broke into a canter for the final stretch to the stable yard. They burst under the archway then skidded to a halt in a cloud of dust. His horse exhaled with relief and pricked his ears, looking this way and that for his familiar groom.

"Welcome home, milord."

Gerrault, the stable master, came striding out of the workshop. He was a tall man with silvery hair who had worked at Wolvesley for most of his life. His grey eyes rested only momentarily on Tristan before going to the horse he loved.

"How is he?" he asked.

Tristan swung his leg over the horse's back and jumped to the ground.

"Ready for a good feed," he told Gerrault before reaching out his hands to catch at the bridle of Mirrie's chestnut horse.

"Let me help you down," he urged, placing his hands around her waist and lifting her easily towards him. But Mirrie held herself stiff and taut, not relaxing into his arms as he had expected. He steadied her on the cobbles. "We made it," he added, wanting to soothe her anxiety. "The hard bit is over."

Mirrie gave a small shake of her head. "I fear it is only just beginning."

Before he could respond, a flurry of grooms approached to untack the horses and lead them away. Tristan nodded in response to their greetings and when he next looked over at Mirrie, she was better composed; her hands folded neatly before her.

"'Tis good to see you again, Miss Mirabel."

Gerrault's sincerity brought a proper smile to her lips.

"You too, Gerrault. I am glad that naught e'er seems to change at Wolvesley."

A flicker of anxiety passed over the stable master's face, but he nodded smartly.

"Where is my mother?" Tristan asked. She was usually to be found somewhere about the stables or the paddocks.

Gerrault hesitated. "We have not seen the countess for nigh on two days."

That seemed troubling. Tristan held out his arm for Mirrie and nodded his head towards Gerrault. "We shall look inside."

The path from the stable yard to the castle keep was as familiar as the back of Tristan's hand. They walked quickly under the high stone archway and passed through sweeping, well-tended lawns before reaching the sparkling fountain which arched into the deep blue sky. Mirrie paused for a moment, tugging on his arm as she gazed, entranced, at the foaming waters.

"I had forgotten how beautiful it is," she breathed.

Aye. It was beautiful. But Tristan was impatient to move on.

"It will still be here on the morrow." He smiled to take the sting from his words.

Mirrie was behaving more like a visitor to Wolvesley than a young woman who had grown up within its walls. She gazed at the intricately carved stone lions which guarded the steps to the keep with her hazel eyes open wide.

"They will also be here on the morrow," he reminded her.

"'Tis all too easy to become immune to this grandeur when you see it every day." She nudged him sharply with her elbow. "You should take the time to appreciate what you have."

He *did* appreciate what he had. But one thing war had taught him was that everything could change in an instant. And right now, he had no wish to moon over fountains or lions when he had the nagging sense that something was wrong. All he wanted was to get to the bottom of it. The sooner the better.

Eventually, she allowed him to lead her into the keep, their boots rapping against the marble tiles in the entrance hall which was surprisingly quiet. Usually Wolvesley hummed with activity and servants running this way and that, but today just one guard stood to attention by the front steps.

Tristan placed his hands on his hips and gazed about. "Where is everyone?" His words ricocheted off the frescoed walls and reverberated up to the vaulted ceiling, high above their heads.

Mirrie was wide-eyed all over again. "This is most unusual." She caught at his arm. "Tris, we should take heed."

But he had already set off, taking the polished wooden stairs two at a time in his haste. He wasted no time in going to his own chamber and headed straight to the ladies' solar where he expected to find his mother. But the familiar figure of his mother's maid, standing to attention by his father's chamber, stopped him in his tracks.

"Molly." He strode over to her, his heavy footsteps making the wall torches flicker. "Why are you keeping watch here?"

Molly bobbed into a curtsy. Her chestnut hair was tidily pinned beneath her servant's cap as usual, but her warm brown eyes were tinged red, as if she had been crying.

"Your mother's orders, milord."

Tristan was aware of Mirrie coming to her side and laying a hand on his shoulder. "Are they in there?" he demanded. "I wish to speak with them."

Molly pressed her lips together in distress. "They are inside with the physician but Lady Morwenna said I was to admit no one."

This was growing more and more concerning.

"Come, Tris. We should wait downstairs." Mirrie's voice was soft against his ear.

Tristan wanted to demand answers, but Mirrie's calming influence prevailed.

"Very well," he muttered.

"I will tell my lady that you have arrived," Molly called after them.

Tristan only grunted in reply.

"Will we wait in the great hall?" Mirrie asked.

The great hall at Wolvesley was a vast, public space, usually filled with minstrels and knights and castle servants. Tristan shook his head. The idea of being in full public view did not sit well with him.

"I have no desire for company," he declared. "Not until someone will tell me what is going on. Let us go to my father's solar."

"Will your father not mind?" Mirrie's eyebrows disappeared beneath her hair.

Tristan made an impatient gesture. "He claims to want to hand the running of the estate over to me. In theory, he already has. Some of it anyway. I have as much right to the books and ledgers in the solar as my father. And besides, he will not be using it right now."

Shaking off a complicated swell of emotion, Tristan marched down the passageway and flung open the carved wooden door to the solar. A fusty smell met him, as if the door had not been opened for several days. The chamber within was stuffy; the shutters fastened closed. Mirrie wasted no time in stepping past him and flinging them open, bringing light and fresh air into the masculine space.

Tristan had been coming in here since he was a boy. He would sit on his father's knee whilst the earl worked at his polished wooden desk, making his own painstaking marks on old pieces of parchment. Later, he would sit in one of the over-stuffed chairs by the fire, listening attentively as his father explained the running of their vast estate to his eldest son. The chamber was filled with books and precarious piles of parchment. It had always smelled of leather; the scent he associated with his father. Today, it was merely hot and airless, and a feeling of loss washed over him.

"I shall go and fetch refreshments from the kitchen." Mirrie was practical.

"Nay." He shook his head decisively. "You should not be running back and forth to the kitchens like a servant."

Her reply was gentle. "But there are no servants about."

"And why is that?" He flung his arms wide. "What is happening here?"

"Your father is clearly unwell. Perchance your mother bade the servants to stay away from the family quarters today." With a meaningful look, she turned away from him and walked from the room.

Tristan balled his hand into a fist. He knew what she was trying to say, but he would not, could not accept it.

His father was not about to die. Not today. Nor the morrow. Nor any time soon.

To kill the time until his mother was available to come speak to him, he wandered over to the desk and lowered himself into a sturdy wooden chair with elaborate carvings on the arms and legs. The chair evoked yet another childhood memory; the face of a roaring lion was carved into the back and young Tristan had spent many happy hours tracing the curving lines with his fingers. Now he drummed his fingers onto the unsettlingly tidy desk as pinpricks of worry broke through his previously impenetrable barriers.

It was the silence that unsettled him so. Wolvesley was not meant to be a quiet castle. He had never known it so devoid of life and laughter. The absence of sound allowed his fears to fester.

He must do something. Talk to someone. Brimming with impatience, he stood up, causing the chair to scrape loudly against the wooden floor—at the same moment the chamber door swung open. Mirrie started in surprise and some of the wine she was carrying slopped over the sides of the pitcher.

"I'm sorry," they both said at once.

"Here, let me help you." Tristan rushed forward to relieve her of her burden.

He poured the wine, passed her a goblet and they both drank deeply.

"Forsooth, I needed that." He wiped his lips with his hand. "Food would make us feel even better. I will go to the kitchens myself and ask for bread and cheese."

Mirrie tried and failed to hide her smile. "Do you recall your way to the kitchens?"

"Of course." But she was right. It had been some years since he had last been there. And then it had only been to swipe freshly baked cakes from the store.

A commotion by the doorway made them both turn.

"Mother," he exclaimed.

His mother was a small, slight woman with silvery blonde hair and beautiful green eyes that had always been able to read the secrets of his soul. He had never before seen her face so drawn, nor her body sway with grief and weariness.

"Welcome home, my boy." Despite it all, her smile was still warm. "And Mirrie too. What a lovely surprise." She took Mirrie's hands in her own and kissed them before stepping into Tristan's embrace. He was shocked at how frail she felt in his arms.

"What is happening here, Mother?" He pulled back to better look at her. Morwenna, Countess of Wolvesley, had always been more at home in the paddocks than in a ballroom. She loved to be out-of-doors, and usually her cheeks shone with the bloom of good health. Today, she was pale and fragile.

She pressed her lips together and looked at him sorrowfully. "I'm afraid it is your father."

He heard Mirrie exclaim and was dimly aware that she had lowered herself into a chair.

"What did the physician say?" he demanded. Surely the man could prescribe some curative potion that would see the Earl of Wolvesley regain his strength and vigour.

"Oh, Tristan." His mother's eyes grew glassy with tears. "He said that we should prepare for the worst."

CHAPTER SIX

MIRRIE HAD NEVER seen a change come over someone so quickly.

All of Tristan's confidence disappeared in an instant. Despair washed over his handsome features as he staggered away from Morwenna. At first, he put his hands to his face but then he gripped the back of his father's chair like a man on the verge of falling.

Morwenna fixed her steady green gaze on the floor, as if she could not bear to witness such anguish in her son.

"I am sorry," Mirrie said aloud, wishing there was something to do to help. "Shall I attend to Angus for a while and give you the chance to rest?"

The countess looked as if a gust of wind might knock her sideways, but she summoned a smile and shook her head slowly. "Thank you, dear Mirrie. But I do not like to be long away from him."

Mirrie put a hand to her heart. The deep love shared between Angus and Morwenna was something she had admired since childhood. It had brought them much happiness and now that would inevitably turn to pain.

"Is there really nothing that can be done?" Tristan's voice broke on the question and Mirrie knew another stab of sympathy for him. "I did not think him so very ill when I left."

"Your father took a turn for the worse the day before you

departed for Ember Hall, but I did not like to burden you with it. Of course, we all thought the setback was temporary and he would soon recover." Morwenna rubbed at her arms as if warding off a chill. The dark smudges under her eyes caused Mirrie to wonder when she had last slept. "Your father has been bled so much, I fear he has little left in him."

Tristan made a choking sound and Mirrie joined Morwenna in gazing at the dark knots in the polished floor beneath their feet. But something niggled at the back of her mind. Before she could think better of it, she found herself speaking into the silence.

"Frida has always been against the act of bleeding to cure illness," she declared. In the next moment her cheeks flushed hot. Who was she to question the castle physician? "I am sorry," she added quietly, hoping her pronouncement would be ignored.

But Tristan was gazing at her as if she had handed him fresh hope. "Frida is a skilled healer." He motioned towards his mother. "You have always said so."

Morwenna gave a little shrug. "Frida inherited the skills of my grandmother, it is true. But I cannot claim that either of them ever treated an illness of this sort."

Tristan leaned over the back of the chair, almost entreatingly. "What are Frida's arguments against the practice?"

Mirrie's mind raced as she tried to remember. "I only know that she would not allow it for Flora last winter. She turned the physician away and nursed the child back to health using only herbs and potions she mixed herself."

"We must summon Frida." Tristan's pronouncement echoed around the solar.

"Nay." Morwenna spoke with equal force. "She is near her time and the upset could harm the babe. I will not allow it."

Mirrie thought for a moment that Tristan would argue the point, but he only nodded. "Mayhap you are right." He rubbed at the growth of stubble across his suntanned cheeks. "But there are other healers. Other physicians, even, who have more in their arsenal than bleeding." He strode from the desk and came to stand beside his mother, towering over her diminutive frame. "Has anything else been tried?"

Morwenna's eyes widened. "At the beginning, of course. Before calling the physician. We tried hot broths and applied henbane to his joints. But the new physician trained in Italy. He said our potions were outdated and ineffective."

"And began with the bloodletting?" Tristan raised his eyebrows.

"Aye." Morwenna nodded. "He is the best in the land," she protested. "Your father put his faith in him."

"And that faith has been ill rewarded." Tristan looked as if he might run upstairs this instant and take the man to task. "How long has this bloodletting been going on?"

"About a sennight." Morwenna sighed shakily. "I did not think to question it."

Mirrie bitterly regretted planting this idea that the physician was not trustworthy in Tristan's head. Once again, he was concentrating on the wrong thing. Instead of admitting his feelings of grief and sorrow, he was determined to try to fix a situation not in his control.

Because Tristan cannot bear to be not in control.

She dragged a hand over her eyes and heaved herself up from the chair. She ached from top to toe, although the long ride from Ember Hall already seemed part of another life entirely. "Should you not go to him?" she suggested gently, daring enough to take Tristan's hand in her own. "This time may be precious."

You should not waste it arguing with your mother, she wanted to add.

Tristan's piercing blue gaze clashed with hers for a brief moment. "That is true." He bit down on his lip. "There is not a moment to lose."

He still held her hand, but she could tell from the far-away expression on his face that he was not thinking of this time in the solar, nor of the dying man on the floor above. Tristan's sharp mind had gone elsewhere.

Morwenna took a few steps over to her husband's desk and ran her fingers across the polished surface. "The times I would berate him for poring too long over his books..." she said sadly.

Tristan folded his arms and walked to the other side of the desk. His heavy brows drew together as if he was puzzling something out.

"I will return to him." Morwenna sighed deeply. "You will come with me, Tris." It was a statement, not a question. Then she smiled at Mirrie. "And you too, Mirrie, dear."

Mirrie opened her mouth to protest. This was time for family and she did not want to intrude on their grief.

"What was the name of Frida's friend?"

Morwenna and Mirrie both started in surprise at the question. Tristan gazed from one to another, clearly expecting an answer.

"Which friend?" Morwenna asked with a shrug. "She had many over the years. None so close to her as Mirrie, though."

But Mirrie had divined the path of Tristan's thoughts. "You mean the girl called Juliana," she injected, quelling the sharp-edged emotions that threatened to surface at the memory of her name.

Tristan snapped his fingers and smiled in triumph. "That's the one. Juliana. Dark hair. Tall."

Morwenna shook her head in confusion, her weary face showing even greater signs of strain than before. "We have not seen the girl for years. Whatever can you want with her?"

"She was a healer," declared Tristan, as if it was obvious. "One of the druids, if I remember correctly." Shafts of evening sunlight fell through the open window and cast golden highlights all around him.

A brightness so at odds with the darkness of their situation.

Mirrie stood quietly. On the one hand, she could see the possible wisdom of Tristan's idea. On the other, she knew that Morwenna would never yield to it.

Morwenna had a deep-seated fear of sorcery. Even her own daughter's youthful Sight had caused her some distress; Mirrie had always privately suspected that the countess felt relief when Frida lost her gift after her accident.

Juliana was as much a Seer as Frida had ever been. She had been raised amongst the druids. Perchance her gift may even have strengthened over the years.

Mirrie tightened her lips. In her experience, women like Juliana usually grew stronger over the years. More beautiful. More skilful. *More powerful.*

Rendering her more likely to attract the attention of those who thought witchcraft was a crime that should be punished.

Which was all the more reason not to bring her into Wolvesley Castle at a time when the respected judiciary, law-maker and peace-keeper, Angus de Neville, was fading from life.

Only Tristan would concoct such an audacious plan. She shook her head in disbelief.

But he caught her movement and now she found herself a prisoner of his piercing stare.

"You do not think it a good idea?" he demanded.

"I do not." She stood up to him, telling herself that it was for Morwenna's sake and nothing to do with her own, closely-guarded, feelings about Juliana. "It would only cause more distress," she added quietly.

"Should we not try everything possible to bring about my father's cure?" His voice grew louder.

"We have already tried everything that is *reasonably* possible." Morwenna stood tall in the face of Tristan's visible frustration.

"So now is the time to try something bold," he retorted.

"I forbid it." Morwenna lifted her head proudly. "This is my home and I will not have you bring sorcery into it."

Tristan did not falter for a moment. "Juliana is most likely long gone from these lands. But thanks to Father's protection, the druid camp remains and I have no doubt there will be healers within their midst. I will instruct them to use only what herbs and potions can be found in the natural world. No spells, no incanta-tions." He shrugged. "Think on it, Mother. If your physician's pronouncement is correct, then I shall be the Earl of Wolvesley within days. I believe that gives me the right to invite whomever I wish to the castle."

Morwenna stifled a sob and even Mirrie flinched.

"It appears you will do whatever you wish," the countess stated, her voice hard. "I will return to my husband's bedside."

"And I shall dispatch a messenger to the druid camp."

Mirrie watched both of them stride out of the solar before sinking back into the tapestried chair she had recently vacated.

She put her head in her hands and squeezed her eyes closed, willing her heart rate to slow and her breathing to steady. Family relationships at Wolvesley Castle were usually loving and easy. She had never before seen mother and son at so at odds with one another.

To think that just hours earlier, she had been concerned only with hiding her true feelings for Tristan. The preoccupation that had haunted her every waking thought since the previous night had now paled into insignificance. She wanted only to offer comfort to the people she loved. Tristan included.

He had been wrong about his father's imminent recovery.

She only hoped he was not wrong about this as well.

SHE AWOKE IN her old bedchamber at Wolvesley and enjoyed a few blessed seconds of peace before remembering the terrible reality they faced.

Angus, Earl of Wolvesley, was dying.

For many years he had been the closest thing she had to a father. He was wise and fair-minded, his fierce charisma and majestic stature a charming contrast to the gentle nature of a man who loved his family above all else.

Angus was a giant of a man with a big booming laugh and a handshake that could leave knights anxiously flexing their fingers for hours afterwards. He would have made a mighty warrior, but preferred to wield his quill, rather than his sword, to ensure peace and prosperity for his estate and all who lived within it.

Mirrie allowed tears to brim in her eyes as she recalled him swinging her out onto the dance floor at her first ball. They spilled down her cheeks as she remembered how he had praised her studious efforts in the school room. Her achievements could never eclipse those of the bright and brilliant de Neville siblings, but Angus had always made her feel wanted and welcomed.

Aye, she was in awe of him still. Only a fool would not be at least slightly in awe of such a man. But he had never been anything other than kind to her. To everyone.

And now he had sickened, and he might soon pass from this world. Long before his time.

She could understand Tristan's violent desperation to try something, anything, that might keep Angus tethered to life for a while longer. 'Twas only respect for Morwenna's deeply-held feelings that had prevented her from saying as much last night.

That and her long-buried dislike of the woman called Juliana. Mirrie had only known her for a few days, many years past, but those days had been long and hard. Feelings of envy, spiky and hot, had lodged in her stomach the very first time she beheld the beautiful woman that Frida had welcomed to Wolvesley as her new best friend.

Envy which intensified when Mirrie beheld the admiration shining in Tristan's eyes.

Juliana was gifted as well as beautiful, that much was undeniable. Beside her, Mirrie felt as plain and ordinary as a dormouse.

Mercifully, Juliana had stayed little more than a sennight at Wolvesley before being "called elsewhere" as she insisted on saying.

Mirrie had ne'er been so glad to see the back of anyone.

Now Tristan was in search of her. Hopefully the woman had wandered far from here and another healer could be summoned in her stead.

Mirrie sat up in bed, the covers falling away from her. She wanted to find Tristan and express her support for his plan. She wanted to find Morwenna and ask what she could do to help. And she wanted to venture into Angus's bedchamber and find the words to thank him for all he had done for her, before it was too late.

But she was no longer at Ember Hall, free to pull on a crumpled robe and wander the house at will. She was in Wolvesley Castle, where a myriad of rules of manners and decorum applied—not all of them at the forefront of her memory.

She swung her legs to the floor, enjoying the softness of the rug beneath her toes and wincing at the ongoing ache in her thighs and back after yesterday's long ride. She would have liked a hot bath before retiring last night, but after the drama of the evening—and with the household so disrupted—she had been content to strip down to her chemise, crawl under the covers and close her eyes.

All of which meant that the dust and grime of a hard day in the saddle still lay upon her skin. Even her hair felt dirty. But what could she do about it?

Her chamber was beautifully decorated with mouldings on the ceiling, a stylish writing desk and a large wardrobe to hold the many gowns she had once needed as the ward of the Earl of Wolvesley.

How many gowns would I need as Tristan's betrothed?

Pushing the thought to one side, Mirrie padded over to the window and swung open the shutters. Her chamber looked out over the rolling paddocks and the winding lane down which they had ridden just yesterday. The large oval lake glinted invitingly in the morning sunshine. If only she were a man, able to throw caution to the wind and do as he pleased, she could have taken a dip in the lake that would have left her clean and refreshed, ready for the challenges ahead. But strict rules of etiquette applied to the ladies of the household, and Mirrie had never wielded the breezy confidence of Esme or Isabella when it came to flouting those rules.

Rules which would be even stricter if she was announced as Tristan's intended bride.

Mirrie put her palms to her flushed cheeks. Would Tristan go ahead with their intended subterfuge, in the light of his father's failing health?

Nay, she decided, their ruse would likely be abandoned under the circumstances.

She fixed her eyes on the distant treeline, unable to decide if her relief outweighed her disappointment.

A knock sounded on the door, breaking her reverie.

Conscious of her state of undress, Mirrie called out, "Who is it?"

"'Tis Molly."

"Come in." She self-consciously crossed her arms over her chest and moved to the centre of the room.

Molly opened the door and bobbed into a curtsy.

"Good morn, Miss Mirabel. I thought you might wish to bathe before going down."

"You are quite correct." Mirrie smiled, but she felt awkward about being waited upon after so many years of self-sufficiency at Ember Hall. "Thank you."

Her feelings of awkwardness increased as several chambermaids followed Molly into the chamber, two of them dragging a gleaming copper bathtub and the others carrying pitchers of hot water. Soon steam began to rise and as the maids took their leave, Mirrie abandoned her scruples in the anticipated pleasure of sinking her aching limbs into hot water.

Molly pulled forward a screen and Mirrie wasted no time in pulling off her chemise and stepping into the tub.

Bliss.

She rarely had time for a warm bath at Ember Hall. A quick dousing with cold water had become her norm. What luxury it was to stretch out in the heat, her hair floating up around her. When Molly perched behind her on a low wooden stool and began to lather her hair with soap, Mirrie closed her eyes and submitted to the pampering without a word of complaint.

Much more of this and she would find herself ready and waiting to be named as Tristan's betrothed.

Her eyes flew open just in time to catch a bubble of soap sliding down her forehead. Mirrie sucked in a gasp of stinging pain and Molly chuckled.

"Best to keep still, Miss Mirabel, until I've finished."

Mirrie settled herself more comfortably in the tub with her eyes firmly closed as Molly rinsed her hair and gently rubbed it dry. At the maid's urging, she stood up, dripping wet, and was warmly wrapped in a linen cloth and led over to a stool so she may sit down whilst Molly combed out the tangles in her long hair.

"I can sense your impatience, miss. But I can tell you that Lord Tristan has not yet returned and Lord Angus is none the worse this morn. My lady is sitting with him still." Molly spoke through a mouthful of hair pins.

Mirrie thought she had been doing a good job of disguising her eagerness to have these preparations over with. She pressed her lips into a smile in acknowledgement of Molly's insight.

"What do you mean, Lord Tristan has not yet returned? Did he ride out this morn?"

"Nay, miss. 'Twas last night that he called for a fresh horse to be saddled for him."

Mirrie twisted round, causing Molly to grip her hair tighter to secure the complicated braid she was in the process of tying. "Where did he go?"

"That I don't know."

"But he's been gone all night?" Mirrie could not keep the edge of concern from her voice.

"Alfred, his manservant, has been sitting up for him since dusk." Molly grimaced around the hairpins. "The poor man dozed off whilst sitting in a hard chair."

But Mirrie had no thoughts to spare for Alfred. Where had

Tristan gone in such a hurry? He had spoken of dispatching a messenger to the druids. Did he go himself after all?

"I must go downstairs." Anxiety was rising in her chest.

"There is naught you can do to bring him home any sooner." Molly gave a final pat to her hair. "But let us get you dressed and ready."

Molly crossed to the wooden closet and brought out a simple gown in pastel colours. Mirrie stood as quietly as she could whilst the maid helped her into it. The gown smelled of lavender and was a relic from a former time. Mirrie was just admiring the familiar folds, when Molly audibly tutted.

"The fashions have changed since you last wore this, Miss Mirabel. We had better arrange for some new gowns to be stitched for you."

"Please don't go to any trouble." Mirrie was on the cusp of saying that she could stitch her own gowns, but in truth her needlework was not fine enough for a Wolvesley wardrobe. She was comfortable mending her clothing at Ember Hall, where a dropped stitch or an uneven hem would not be noticed. But standards were far higher here.

Molly stood on her tiptoes to straighten the neckline of the gown. "I shall ask one of the maidservants to attend you for the rest of your visit. Mayhap Lady Esme's personal maid. Would that please you, Miss Mirabel?"

"It certainly would not." Mirrie answered before she could properly gather her thoughts. "I mean to say, thank you, Molly, but I have grown accustomed to life without a lady's maid." She clutched her hands together, not wanting to cause offence, but unable to countenance the prospect of Esme's experienced maid tutting over the state of her wardrobe. Her stomach turned somersaults of anxiety at the very idea.

Molly looked unconvinced, but thankfully something outside caught her attention. "Hark at that." She nodded towards the window. "I fancy that's his lordship I can see returning."

Mirrie rushed over and placed her hands on the sill, leaning out as far as she dared until she could make out a large bay-coloured horse approaching the gatehouse. She could discern nothing about the rider, save the glint of a sword in the dazzling sunshine.

"I think it must be Tristan," she agreed, unable to keep the excitement from her voice. "I shall go down and meet him."

"Very good, miss." Molly dropped into a short curtsy.

"Thank you for all you have done," Mirrie added.

Molly inclined her head. "It's the least I can do to tend to a daughter of the household."

Mirrie wanted to run, but conscious of her long skirts, she bade herself be satisfied with a scurrying walk down the sweeping staircase into the marbled entrance hall. Once again, there was but a lone guard standing by the front doorway. He bowed smartly as she passed.

A warm breeze caressed her freshly-bathed skin as soon as she stepped outside. The day had dawned warm and perfect once again, with not a cloud to be seen in the deep blue sky. The manicured lawns ahead of her were a far cry from the wild beauty of the lands around Ember Hall, but Mirrie found comfort in the familiarity of the splashing fountain and the proud stance of the stone lions. Yesterday, the grandeur of Wolvesley Castle had struck her as if she was seeing it for the first time. But happy memories from her youth were gradually banishing her social anxieties. She remembered one hot day when, unwilling to walk all the way to the lake, Jonah had jumped into the fountain instead. And the midsummer ball, not so very long ago, when Esme had tied two straw bonnets, replete with ribbons, onto the stone lions.

She picked her way down the path to the stable yard, shading her eyes from the bright sunlight and realising, too late, that she wore neither gloves nor a bonnet. The steady clop of a horse's hooves was closer now, and she wanted to speak to Tristan before he entered the keep and was rightly claimed by his mother.

Her pulse beat faster as she neared the stone archway, knowing from the shouts she had heard that it was indeed Lord Tristan drawing near. She had long since given up berating herself for the swell of anticipation she always experienced before seeing Tristan. Her attraction to him was simply part of who she was—a woman with a moderate singing voice, a dislike of needlework, and a heart that would forever beat for Tristan de Neville.

Now at least she could hope to speak to him without the usual audience of his siblings, friends and numerous visitors to the castle. It would just be the two of them. She could offer comfort, a friendly ear and support for his ambition of a second medical opinion.

Taking a deep breath, she walked through the archway with as much grace as she could manage. Gerrault stood waiting to receive the horse and he tugged his forelock as soon as he saw Mirrie. But before she could frame a greeting, Tristan's horse trotted into view.

Mirrie shaded her eyes once again as she tipped her head backwards, wanting to see from Tristan's face if his mission had been successful. But what she saw made her flesh grow hot and cold at the same time. Her heart took a deep dive downwards and she all but staggered to one side in shock.

Tristan's mission had clearly been a success. She could tell from the beaming smile on his handsome face. And from the smug expression of the woman perched on the saddle in front of him; her slender body pressed up against his. The woman had long, glossy black hair, dark eyes and the reddest lips Mirrie had ever seen. Tristan's arm curved protectively around her waist while her head rested against his clavicle.

It was Juliana.

CHAPTER SEVEN

TRISTAN COULD SEE that Mirrie was shocked to see Juliana riding in front of him. In truth, he was as surprised as she was. And he wanted to shout his victory from the rooftops. Against all the odds, he had succeeded.

He'd galloped through dense woodland towards the druid camp, fuelled more by desperation than any real hope for success. He knew not if any healer of renown still resided amongst the druids, nor what welcome he might receive from people who were, by nature, private and secretive. His way was lit only by the light of the moon and with every springing step his horse took, a mantra beat through his mind. *You will fail. You will fail.*

But you have to try.

He wasn't ready to live without his father. Not yet. Not for many years. That was why he rode through darkness and exhaustion and the sharp sting of his mother's disapproval. Because Angus himself had taught him to never give up.

Tristan wasn't sure how he would be received by the druids. Angus allowed them safe passage throughout the Wolvesley estate and turned a willing blind eye to the home they had created some miles from the castle, but Tristan had never had dealings with them. He guessed they might not take kindly to his sudden arrival, mud-splattered and frantic, in the dead of the night.

So be it. I'll beg, if I have to.

A healer to visit his father. That was not too much to ask of those who would have been persecuted without the protection of a man who now needed their help.

As it happened, he did not have to even enter their camp. Juliana was waiting for him, calm and unperturbed, in the centre of a wide grassy path. She carried a torch which called to him like a beacon, flickering light banishing the black of night. Her pale skin glowed and he wondered if she was a figment of his flailing imagination. But then she smiled and spoke his name.

"Tristan de Neville," she said, and his horse slowed as if of his own accord.

For a moment he had stared at her, recognising the glossy black mane of hair and shrewd, all-seeing green eyes that hid their intelligence behind a veneer of amusement.

"How did you know I would come?"

He half expected her to claim second sight, but she merely shrugged. "We have lookouts. You were spotted some time since. We do not encourage visitors, especially in the dark of night, but the Elder said you should not be harmed."

Tristan told himself not to smile at this. He did not fear ambush by the druids. "I thought you had left these lands long ago."

"And yet you came in search of me?" She lifted her eyebrows and stepped forward to run her hands over his horse's head. The animal heaved out a sigh and leaned against her, willingly accepting her touch.

"I came in search of a healer," he corrected her and then thought better of it. "But I hoped I would find you."

"Your mother all but banished me from Wolvesley Castle," she countered smoothly.

"And now my father is grievously ill." His words burst into the warm night air and immediately, he wanted to call them back. To speak of his father's fading strength was to utter a heresy.

Her eyes showed a flicker of distress, but whether this was for the earl's wellbeing or for some other reason, Tristan could not guess.

"The Countess of Wolvesley is a wise woman. I would not go against her wishes." Juliana rhythmically stroked his horse's neck.

"I am here with my mother's blessing." It was a lie, but only a small one. Morwenna knew his intentions and had given no order against them. "Her consent, at least," he amended, seeing Juliana's sceptical smile.

The druid healer pressed her dusky pink lips together. "How goes your sister, Frida?"

"Well, thank you." He did not wish to speak of Frida now.

"Frida welcomed me to Wolvesley as a kindred spirit, but the countess correctly divined that my presence there would bring turbulence to the lands and people she holds dear."

Tristan gritted his teeth. "My mother would move heaven and earth to save my father."

It was the right thing to say. He saw something shift in her face. "The earl is a just and fair man. I have been instructed to help you in any way I can."

"Then come back with me to Wolvesley. He has been bled near to death by the castle physician."

"If that is so, it may already be too late." Her soft words sliced him like the sharpest blade.

"I will pay you for your troubles." His horse sensed his mounting distress and shied to one side. Juliana raised her torch so her whole face was illuminated.

"I do not seek your coin, Tristan de Neville."

"I will pay in cattle or cloth or anything your people need." There was no price that was too high.

Juliana nodded slowly. "Then help me up, my lord. We have no time to lose." She put out the torch in a bucket of earth before reaching up to clasp his arms.

Her long hair smelled faintly of woodsmoke and wild flowers, and the warmth of her body pressing against him seemed to lull him into a state of relaxation. By the time they glimpsed the granite battlements of home, Tristan's earlier fears had all but evaporated.

All would be well, now that Juliana was here.

But Mirrie's stricken face was a reminder there was much still to be done, and he sprang from his horse's back before lifting the healer down beside him.

"You remember Juliana?" he asked, brushing down his breeches and ignoring the sharp ache in his calves. He had spent the greater part of the last three days in the saddle, but now was not the time to admit to weakness.

"I do." Mirrie's voice was unusually tart.

He recalled her opposition to his plan and shot her a beseeching look. "She is here to heal my father."

"I am come to see if I am *able* to heal your father," Juliana corrected him. She scarcely glanced in Mirrie's direction before taking his arm and urging him forwards. "Let us go to him."

They walked under the archway and through the gardens, with Juliana notably uncowed by the grandeur of her surroundings. She looked neither right nor left, not even at the sparkling fountain or the uniformed guard who stood to attention as they ascended the front steps. She had seen it all before, he recalled, but not for a number of years.

Inside the marbled entrance hall, Tristan paused, conscious of his dishevelled appearance. He turned, wanting to ask Mirrie her opinion on entering his father's chamber before changing his attire, but he and Juliana were all alone. Mirrie must have remained in the stable yard.

Juliana seemed to sense the path of his thoughts. "I must wash the dust from my hands before visiting a sick room," she said.

He looked at her properly. The filtered light streaming in through the high windows showed the precise needlework of her dark-coloured gown and a small satchel tied about her waist. About her shoulders, she wore a thin woollen shawl. Her clothing was clean and neat, but her appearance was altogether different to the usual ladies of his acquaintance. The difference lay in the cut and tailoring of the fabric, as well as in her hair, which was long, loose and unadorned.

He cleared his throat. "I will have someone show you to a guest chamber."

"I would prefer to go straight to your father."

Tristan considered this and then nodded to the guard. "Fetch us warm water and towels."

Juliana raised the shawl over her head and threw him a small smile. "I will show modesty in your mother's home."

"There is no need to hide," he said, his eyes drawn to the fullness of her pink lips.

She inclined her head. "I am an uninvited guest."

"You are here at my invitation," he countered quickly. She stood tall and proud, but he could not shake the idea that she may yet flee like a gazelle.

Juliana took a step closer to him, her eyes locking with his so he was drawn into their smoky depths. "But you are not Earl of Wolvesley." She paused. "Yet."

A commotion at the door released him from the spell. Mirrie stood at the top of the steps, looking unaccountably cross.

"Tristan, will you appear before your father in such disarray?" she demanded, sounding so like his elder sister Frida that Tristan's lip quirked.

At that moment, Alfred hurried forward with a basin of water and a folded towel. Behind him tripped Molly, carrying the same utensils and looking up at Juliana with wide eyes.

Tristan splashed water onto his face, realising only then how thickly his cheeks were coated with stubble. He should go upstairs to change his clothes and drag a comb through his tangled hair, but the thought of such tasks made his skin prickle with impatience.

"Enough dallying." He waved the servants away and switched his gaze to Juliana, who was drying her hands with all the poise of a visiting lady. "Are you ready?" Renewed urgency flowed through his veins. His father was just steps away and Juliana's presence could change everything.

She smiled in reply and preceded him up the wide stairway as if she knew exactly where she was going. Tristan was aware of Mirrie behind him, but then her tentative footsteps ceased.

He looked back. "Will you not come with us?"

She shook her head as she pulled away from him, into the shadows. "I was going to, but now I think not. We should not crowd him."

He opened his mouth to argue, but changed his mind. Wolvesley was Mirrie's home and she could make her own decisions, but part of him bristled with some unspecified annoyance.

I want her by my side at this difficult time.

There, it was not unspecified. He knew exactly the root cause. What he did not understand was why Mirrie, usually so sensitive to his thoughts and needs, should choose this moment to abandon him.

But there was no time to examine this. Juliana was already sweeping down the torch-lit corridor, pausing by the correct door and turning to him with a half questioning face.

"Is this your father's chamber?"

He gave his head a little shake. "How did you know?"

"I can sense the sickness within."

Before he could react, Juliana had raised her hand, knocked once and pushed open the sturdy wooden panel.

Tristan stood frozen by surprise, before scurrying after her into the large, high-ceilinged room.

At once, three things assaulted his senses. One was the thick, nauseating scent of illness. Then came the unsettling darkness, such a contrast to the bright morning outside. The shutters, he saw, were so tightly closed that not a chink of light came through. Only half a dozen candles cast a feeble glow into the room. Then came the worst of all: the sight of his father.

Tristan let out a sound that was half a sob and half a growl of anguish.

Angus de Neville had always been a large-framed, powerful

man, and his personal strength and unrelenting vitality gave his height an extra dimension. Whenever he walked into a room, heads turned towards him. Whenever he spoke, people listened. But the man on the bed was not a giant amongst men. He seemed small, diminished, only just recognisable as the mighty Earl of Wolvesley.

His father's eyes were closed. His hair, still more golden than silver, spread lankly over the pillows. His breathing was faint. Too faint.

Tristan put a hand over his heart, needing a moment to recover. His mother, who had been kneeling by the bed seemingly in prayer, turned tired eyes towards them.

At once, her gaze narrowed and Tristan sought the right words to defend his decision. But Juliana was unfazed. She swept into a low, graceful curtsy and remained there until his mother spoke.

"You may rise."

Juliana kept her gaze turned to the rushes on the wooden floor. "I will not presume to come closer, my lady, without your permission."

Morwenna waved a hand. "Come. Sit. You can do no harm now, I suppose."

Tristan went to embrace her, once again humbled by how small and fragile she felt in his arms. "I'm sorry, Mother," he whispered against her blonde hair. He saw now that she was right. The night that had passed would have been better spent in here, with his father, than in some wild chase through the woods.

My father is dying. It was impossible and yet it was true.

As the fight went out of him, he fought an urge to lean against her, like he had as a boy. But he was the future earl and the one who should offer comfort and strength to those that needed it.

"There is naught to forgive." Her face was wet with tears. "I do not hold your efforts to save him against you." She smiled weakly. "Even if I disapprove of your methods."

They both turned to the man on the bed, who they loved and revered above all others. Juliana was leaning over his prone form, her dark eyes scanning his face.

"I must examine him," she declared.

Morwenna gave a strangled sound and turned away. "I cannot watch."

Tristan nodded to give Juliana his permission, then led his mother to a tapestried chair pulled near the bed. The heat of the room was oppressive, muddling his thoughts. He dropped to his knees and clasped Morwenna's hands in his own. "What can I do?"

"Just be here," she whispered. "Do not leave me again."

Salty tears stung his eyes and he blinked them away. "I will not go anywhere."

"I thought of sending for Jonah and your sisters." His mother's hands trembled. "But Frida should not travel in her condition and the news is bound to distress her. I worry it will harm the babe."

Tristan processed this. There was no method by which they could bring Jonah and Esme home without alerting Frida as to the reason.

"And Isabella cannot leave Westchester with her own husband so unwell." Morwenna's voice cracked and Tristan thought this added burden of responsibility was about to break her.

"Let us wait just a little while longer," he urged. He wanted to add that such alarm may yet be unnecessary, but he could not form the words.

Rustlings from the bed indicated that Juliana was pulling away the covers. Like his mother, Tristan felt he could not watch. To see his father so incapacitated caused him actual physical pain. He fixed his gaze on a flickering candle and tried to steady his breathing.

Time slowed down so he knew not whether minutes or hours had passed before Juliana came to stand before them.

"I believe I can save him," she said, simply.

Her words fell into silence. After finally accepting the awful inevitability of his father's death, Tristan found that he could not easily abandon it.

Morwenna straightened her back. "The physician was quite clear. He told us there was no hope." Her voice wavered but remained strong.

"There is always hope, my lady." Juliana bowed her head respectfully. "But I will not act without your say so."

Still holding his mother's hands, Tristan felt a tremor pass through her. He stayed where he was, but tilted back his head so look up at Juliana. He had not had a chance to warn her away from mentioning anything that could be construed as witchcraft.

"What will you do?"

"I brought a salve with me that I thought would help. And a tincture that was mixed at dawn just yesterday."

"How did you know what was needed?" Morwenna's question was sharp.

Juliana did not flinch. "Word has spread about his lordship's condition," she said, carefully.

Tristan rubbed at his forehead. "And what is in the salve?"

"'Tis merely herbs. The tincture is an old recipe." Juliana paused. "An effective remedy."

Morwenna stood up abruptly. "Do what you will."

Tristan reached for her. "Mother—" he began.

But Morwenna motioned him away. "I will wait for news in my solar." With her head held high, the countess swept from the room.

For a moment, Juliana's gaze met with Tristan's. "I require some assistance," she said.

"I will send for Mirrie," he replied without thinking. "She is an excellent nurse."

But Juliana pursed her lips, her hands resting on her hips. "I do not believe I am a favourite of Miss Mirabel."

"Mirrie likes everyone," he stated, frowning.

Juliana paused. "As you wish, of course. But I prefer to work in a chamber free of tension."

She walked over to the bed and Tristan found himself following her. When she raised her eyebrows pointedly, he reached into the leather satchel and withdrew a glass jar filled with a dark green ointment. Juliana nodded and held out her hand for it.

"The tincture is in there as well. Pour two drops into some wine and try to make him drink."

Like a well-trained servant, Tristan did as he was bid. A flask of wine stood on his father's nightstand. He poured some into a goblet and added two drops of the clear tincture.

It occurred to him then that he had placed his whole trust in Juliana. At her word, he could be about to administer poison to one of England's most powerful men.

Midway to his father's lips, his hand faltered.

"This will help him?"

He meant it as a warning, so that he might look into her eyes as she answered and discern the truth of her intentions. But it came out as a plea.

She nodded once, meeting his gaze without hesitation.

Tristan falteringly slid a hand beneath his father's heavy head and urged him a little off the pillows.

"Drink this," he spoke encouragingly. Not hoping to stir him into consciousness, but to appeal to the part of his brain that might respond to such common instruction.

The earl did not answer, but his dried lips parted enough for Tristan to tip some of the liquid into his mouth. He held his breath until his father swallowed, then repeated the action. At last, the goblet was empty.

Juliana gave him a half smile of approval. She had rubbed the green salve into his father's muscular chest. It smelled faintly of mint and Tristan felt reassured that this was something akin to his sister Frida's curative potions.

"What now?" he asked.

Juliana put her hands on her narrow hips and fixed him with a stare. "What happens now is up to you, my lord."

His father made a sound, somewhere between a gasp and a groan. Tristan leaned over anxiously, but he seemed to settle again.

"What do you mean?" he asked. "I already said you should do whatever it takes to save him."

"Are those your orders, that I do *everything* in my power? Or should I restrict myself to the tincture and the salve?"

He looked at her, confusion clouding his brow. "What else is there?"

A draught must have entered the stuffy chamber, for the slender candle on the nightstand began to dance and splutter.

"'Whatever it takes'?" she echoed.

At last, understanding dawned. Tristan gripped the carved wooden headboard for support. "Magic?" he whispered.

Juliana tightened her lips. "You could call it magic. You could call it prayer."

Strength left his legs at such heresy. "My mother would never—" he began.

"Your mother was on her knees praying to your God when we first came in. The Gods of the old religion can be called on in different ways. Are you strong enough in your faith, Tristan de Neville, that you confidently assert the dominion of the new?"

In his state of exhaustion and grief, Tristan did not even fully understand the question. His mind whirred with contradictions. He should order Juliana to restrict her healing to the use of herbs found in the natural world.

But what if Father then dies?

Would he ever forgive himself?

Tristan took a deep breath, his knuckles growing white as he gripped the headboard. He wanted Mirrie by his side; her calm, practical mind would assess the situation and deliver a sensible verdict. But she had walked away from him as soon as Juliana entered the keep.

He was on his own.

He looked down into the beloved, familiar face of his father.

The earl was tanned golden-bronze by the summer sun. Faint laughter lines creased the corners of his closed eyes, but he was not an old man. He deserved every chance at life.

Whatever it takes.

Without lifting his gaze, Tristan nodded his head. "Do what you must," he said. "But I cannot be a part of it."

"I would not ask that of you." Juliana's voice was smooth. "Will you wait with your mother?"

Tristan's stomach churned as if he might be sick. *Did I make the right decision?* He shook his head, one hand going to his mouth as if to keep his emotions locked inside. "Nay, she would ask questions that I cannot answer." He staggered over to the shuttered window, feeling like he was on board a ship in a storm.

"You may open the shutters," Juliana said. "I do not require darkness."

He turned to question her, but she had already positioned herself at his father's head, her palms outstretched and hovering inches over his face. Tristan whipped himself back to the window and slowly, quietly, began to draw back the shutters.

The change in the room was instantaneous. Bright sunlight flooded in along with fresh air and the melody of birdsong. He rested his hands on the window ledge and breathed it all in. Down below in the castle gardens, the big, blowsy heads of pink roses reached towards him. He fancied he could catch a trace of their scent, carrying its promise of vibrancy and renewal. Faint shouts came from the stable yard, together with the wicker of ponies in the paddocks. Life went on at Wolvesley, despite the gloom and sorrow of his father's chamber.

He tipped his face towards the sun, closing his eyes and allowing his busy mind to slow. The rigidity in his face and shoulders began to ease. He felt almost as if someone, his mother mayhap, was standing behind him, running calming hands over the tense muscles in his back, encouraging him to relax, reassuring him that all would be well.

All will be well.

It was an idea potent enough to make him weep.

His knees sagged with the sharpness of his grief. Suddenly, he no longer cared what ancient healing arts Juliana was practising on his father, he wanted to see. He couldn't waste another moment of his father's life, looking in the wrong direction.

He turned around to see the druid healer standing away from the bed. Her head was bowed and her hands were folded neatly before her. As if conscious of his gaze, she lifted her face to his.

"All will be well," she said. "Your father will live."

CHAPTER EIGHT

T HE WEIGHT HAD fallen from his shoulders. Relief made him feel vital and alive. He wanted to swing the druid into the air and kiss her, but instead he stepped forward and grasped her hands in his.

"Truly? He will live?"

Juliana nodded, her intelligent green eyes glinting to show she understood how he felt. "He will sleep a while longer yet. When he awakes, he should eat. He needs to recover his strength."

Tristan looked across to his father's bed. Angus slept on, much as before, but his breathing was stronger and colour had returned to his face. He looked like a man who slumbered, rather than a man inches from death.

"I should tell my mother." He didn't want to walk away from Juliana, but duty called.

She gave him a slow smile. "Indeed, you should. I will leave so she can visit with her husband in peace."

"Nay." Tristan was emphatic. "You are our honoured guest. You may leave this chamber, of course. But please, you must dine at Wolvesley with us this night." He was already walking towards the door, plans brimming in his mind. At the other side, stood Molly, just as he had hoped. "Show Miss Juliana to the best guest chamber," he ordered. "And have the kitchens prepare a broth for when my father awakens."

Molly's small hands flew to her cheeks. "Milord will awaken?"

Juliana appeared by his side, smiling with soft reassurance. "Before midday, I would wager."

Molly dropped into a curtsy. "Praise be," she muttered, wonderingly.

Tristan left the two women together and strode off towards his mother's solar. Exultation was battling weariness now, for he had not rested since rising at Ember Hall the day before. The keep was still a strange, quiet place. He should tell his mother that a celebration feast was in order.

He flung open the door and stood blinking, for a moment, at the brightness within. His mother and Mirrie sat side by side on the cushioned window seat, haloed by light. They had their sewing on their knees, but neither of them applied themselves to it. His mother's face was pale and drawn with fatigue. Mirrie's eyes were red-rimmed. She was the first to stand when she saw him.

"What news?" she asked, uncaring of her sewing which had fallen to the floor.

He nodded briefly. "My father will live."

His mother made a strangled sound, her hands going together as if in prayer. Mirrie looked from one to another.

"The druid?" she began.

"Has accomplished what I brought her here to do." Tristan drew himself up to his full height. Both of them had doubted him.

Mirrie smiled, transforming her into the young woman he knew. "I'm so pleased." She dropped to her knees beside his mother. "The worst is over." She gripped Morwenna's hands. "Your prayers have been answered."

His mother's lips shook and tears shone in her eyes. She opened her mouth as if to speak but no words came out.

"Go to him," Tristan urged. "Go and see for yourselves." He threw them a smile. "We shall have feasting and revelry at Wolvesley this night."

His mother drew herself to a standing position, though her

whole body still trembled. "'Tis a little early for feasting, my boy."

"Go to him and see for yourself," he repeated.

She crossed the room towards him and took his hands. "I will. And if all is as you say, I shall thank you from the bottom of my heart. But I shall attend no merry-making until my husband is at my side."

He inclined his head, conscious of the long days she had spent in the sick room. "You will at least take some rest." He raised his eyebrows.

"Aye, if I am persuaded of his recovery. And I must get word to your brother and sisters. Though it seems you were right, Tris, in your decision to wait before sending for them. 'Twould have caused unnecessary alarm."

Tristan turned to Mirrie. "Go with her," he urged. "See for yourself that all will be well. Then dine with me, please."

Mirrie reached up and patted her hair, a little self-consciously. She looked especially lovely, he realised, in a more formal gown than she was wont to wear at Ember Hall. He hadn't noticed, earlier in the stable yard. Too many concerns had crowded his mind. But now, he wanted her by his side once more, his lifelong friend. His ally.

A smile flickered across her lips. "I must attend your mother for as long as she needs me," she replied, carefully.

"Of course." He waved his hands dismissively. "Do what you must, both of you. But go, now. Before my father awakens and finds himself alone."

That was enough to make both of them hurry from the chamber, skirts trailing behind them. Tristan heaved a deep sigh and eyed the window seat speculatively. It called to him, soft and comfortable. He could curl up there and rest. His eyelids seemed to droop at the very idea.

Someone cleared their throat behind him and Tristan spun around to see Alfred, his manservant, hovering in the doorway.

"Milord." He bowed in greeting.

"Alfred." Tristan crossed his arms. "'Tis mighty good to see you."

"Can I fetch you refreshment?" Alfred's eyes lingered on Tristan's travel-stained tunic. "Mayhap a bath and a change of clothes?"

Tristan clapped him on the shoulder. "All of the above," he declared. "But first of all, what I need is sleep."

SOME HOURS LATER, Tristan was dressed and refreshed, presenting his usual golden-hued self to the world—or at least to the now-bustling keep of Wolvesley Castle. It was a relief to hear booted feet treading the stone steps and see the green flash of liveried servants once more about their work. He had slept deeply before bathing, shaving and forcing a fine-toothed comb through his thick and curling hair. Energy hummed within him. After three days of hard-riding and distress, he was ready for some fun.

"Is Miss Mirabel about?" he asked Alfred, as his manservant finished straightening his fresh tunic of dark blue.

"I have not seen her, milord. I believe she is resting."

"And my mother?"

"Still with his lordship." Alfred bowed his head. "Though I understand Lord Wolvesley recovered enough to speak some words to her."

"That is good news, Alfred." Tristan watched him through the looking glass. "And what of Miss Juliana?"

Alfred cleared his throat. "The healer who was once friends with Lady Frida?"

Tristan nodded.

"I glimpsed her some time past, walking by the lake."

Where else? It made sense that a druid would feel compelled to be out of doors on such a glorious day. Tristan looked towards the window. The noon day sun had begun its descent and shadows were beginning to lengthen across the lawns, but it would not be dark for a long while yet.

He clapped Alfred on the shoulder. "I shall go and walk with her."

"Very good, milord." His reply was rather stiff and it occurred to Tristan that his loyal servant had no great fondness for Juliana.

So be it. The woman had cured his father. That fact alone was enough to elevate her in Tristan's opinion. And in his well-deserved mood of celebration, he didn't allow himself to question how much of his approval rested in the woman's handsome face and arresting smile.

With a final nod of thanks to Alfred, Tristan left his private chamber and tripped down the wide staircase into the sunlit entrance hall. Unlike earlier, the usual low hum of conversation echoed down the corridor from the great hall, where he fully expected fires to be lit and tables laid ready for a celebration tonight. He emerged into the warmth of the afternoon, newly energised by the balmy air which carried the scent of summer grass.

He put his hands on his hips and looked about him. The fountain had never looked grander, the lawns never greener. He was home, in every sense of the word. His keen eyes travelled over the flower beds, which were blue with the cornflowers specially cultivated at Wolvesley as they were a favourite of his mother's.

And a favourite of Mirrie's too, if he recalled correctly.

And there was Juliana, more striking than ever as she walked delicately along the gravel path from the lake. She looked every bit the visiting lady, with her glossy hair pinned atop her head. If only his mother could put her age-old fear of sorcery to one side and show a more fitting welcome to the woman who had saved his father's life.

Morwenna had long-dreaded the finger of suspicion being pointed at them, especially given Frida's one-time gifts, but that danger had now passed. Frida no longer talked to people who weren't there, nor did she prophesise the future with unerring accuracy. The de Nevilles had nothing to hide—with or without the might of the Earl of Wolvesley to protect them.

All of which meant that Morwenna had no reason to fear Juliana's presence amongst them. It was habit and exhaustion, he decided, which had caused her to react with such alarm.

A genuine smile creased his face as he walked towards her. "I am glad to have found you," he greeted her, simply.

Juliana curtsied low. "My lord."

"Tristan, please," he corrected her. "Will you walk with me?" he offered his arm.

"I have just come from the lake." She hesitated a moment before placing her slender hand on his elbow. "'Tis a place of great peace and beauty."

"'Tis a marvellous place to swim on a hot day," he countered, catching her flash of a smile before she hid it. "Do not tell me, Juliana, that you have ne'er known the pleasure of immersing yourself in cool water under the summer sun?"

She put her head to one side, her eyes glinting like a bird. "For myself, my lord, I prefer to bathe under the light of the stars."

A laugh rumbled through him. God's bones, it was good to be carefree. "That is a better plan by half." He pretended to mull it over. "Will you join me there, after dark?"

Juliana laughed as well, quiet and low, before nudging him correctively with her elbow. "That would hardly be proper."

"And are we to bother ourselves with such things as proprie-ty?"

He was flirting, he knew it. Flirting came easily to him and he liked to see an answering smile on the face of a pretty girl. But usually, his flirtation was harmless—nothing more than talk with no intention on either side of following through. It occurred to him that with Juliana, he did not know where it might lead. And the fact of his not knowing was both exciting and somehow daunting.

"Do you question my integrity, Tristan?"

The question was lightly asked, but wounding nonetheless. He turned with an apology on his lips, only to meet Juliana's laughing smile.

"Should I?" he countered.

"Only as I question yours. Ah, but you are a man. And heir to a mighty earl at that. Of course, you can do entirely as you please."

He instantly sobered at the reminder of the difference between them. "Whereas you meet with suspicion wherever you go," he guessed.

They had skirted the fountain and were walking through the rose garden. Juliana paused and lowered her head to the soft petals, inhaling their rich perfume—as Mirrie also loved to do. "'Tis the fate of my people."

Tristan found he could not take his eyes from the slender young woman. The dark pink of the rose petals contrasted so becomingly with the sleek darkness of her hair.

"You still have not told me how I should repay you for coming here and helping my father."

She turned her shrewd gaze to his. "It was a kindness I offered, not a service requiring coin. I still think of your sister as a friend."

"And what about me? Am I not a friend?"

"You are Tristan de Neville," she stated, rising up from the roses. "A man who has not yet come to realise the full extent of the power he wields."

There was a challenge in her words. A smile flickered across his lips as he decided to meet it. "And what power might I hold over you, Juliana?"

He expected an answering smile or mayhap a toss of that silken hair. But Juliana closed the gap between them and answered seriously. "Only that which I choose to grant you."

She was near enough for him to smell the sweetness of her breath, and to see the rise and fall of her chest beneath the bodice of her gown. If he lowered his lips, he would find hers. "Which is?" he breathed.

Juliana was a tall woman, but Tristan had inherited his father's height and muscular breadth. She had to stand on her tiptoes to whisper her reply into his ear. "None whatsoever."

After a moment of startled surprise, he laughed again and tucked her arm into his. "That is only because I have yet to dazzle you with the full extent of my charms."

Juliana ran her free hand through her hair, pushing it away from her face. Her lips, he saw, were struggling to restrain a smile. "I speak in jest, my lord. Forgive me. Your father wields power and influence over all my people and we are forever grateful for his protection."

He shook his head. "Do not hide behind the façade of a dutiful subject, Juliana. I see beyond that. I *want* to see beyond that." He paused and turned to face her, a copse of holly shielding them from the open lawns. "I wish to repay you for your kindness, however freely it was given. And I wish for you to dine with me tonight."

"Very well." She ducked her head so her veil of hair swung forward. "I am honoured to accept."

"In fact, I see no reason to tarry." His stomach was aching with hunger and he realised he had not eaten all day. "Let us go now and see what refreshments might be found for us."

They walked together into the keep. A lone musician strummed a lute in the far corner of the hall, but otherwise Tristan and Juliana were alone in the vast room. He looked about in some dissatisfaction. Usually the great hall at Wolvesley was alive with bustle and activity. Men-at-arms would wander in and out all day, servants would keep the fires stoked and conversation would flow as freely as the wine. Clearly the keep had not fully returned to life as usual since his father's illness.

Tristan waved Juliana towards an elaborately carved high-backed dining chair, usually his mother's. He, in turn, sank into the chair usually reserved for his father before beckoning to a pink-cheeked serving wench. "Bring us food and wine," he ordered.

Juliana looked about her, her gaze lingering on the bright frescoes and marbled pillars. "You have a beautiful home," she observed.

"'Tis usually a home with more life in it than this." He inclined his head. "Mayhap you could liven things up with a song?"

She shook her head. "I do not sing." She paused. "Do you?"

"Only when I am well into my cups."

The young serving wench returned with a flask of wine and a tray of sweetmeats which she carefully placed on the table before them. She bobbed a curtsy, but Tristan held up a hand to stop her from leaving.

"Will you carry a message to my mother and Miss Mirabel?"

The girl nodded.

"Tell them we await their company in the great hall."

"Aye, milord," she whispered, before scurrying away.

"They will not come," Juliana observed, lifting a goblet of wine to her lips.

He lifted his own goblet and cradled it in his large hands. "Why would they not?"

"Because they do not like me." Juliana drank again, her eyes fixed on his.

"You are very upfront about this."

She settled the goblet on the table and sat back in her chair. "I tell the truth as I see it. Your mother is grateful to me and regrets her initial show of displeasure at my arrival. But she will be happy to hear of my departure. Mirabel has never trusted me."

The ways of women were mysterious to Tristan. He pursed his lips and gazed into his goblet "Surely she will trust you now that you have healed my father. He is, to all intents and purposes, her father too."

Juliana's eyes laughed at him as she reached forward for a sweetmeat. "Nay, she will not. I spoke to her earlier, whilst you were resting in your chamber. She was polite. In fact she has the makings of a great lady. But she could not hide the fact that she does not trust me."

Tristan shook his head, puzzled. "She does not trust you with what, exactly?"

Her reply was swift. "With you."

Once again, a laugh rumbled through his belly. "Juliana, you have this all wrong. Mirrie is like a sister to me."

She met his gaze with her eyebrows raised in challenge. "I am very rarely wrong."

"Believe me." He lifted his goblet in a toast. "You have naught to fear from Mirrie."

"Oh, I do not fear anyone," she assured him, raising her goblet to meet with his.

He leaned closer towards her. "Nor do I."

Aye, he was flirting again. And he had met his mark, he was sure of it. Her body language, the path of her eyes, the way she leaned towards him, all told him that Juliana would be ready and willing to share his bed this night.

And why should he not avail himself of such warmth and pleasure?

But despite the heady temptation, something was troubling Tristan, and after a moment's thought, he realised what.

It was that the path of his thoughts kept circling back to Mirrie.

Unaccountably so.

Mayhap this was due to Juliana's continued insistence that Mirrie did not like her. Did not *trust* her. How could that be, he wondered, when Mirrie always looked for the best in everyone?

But when he next raised his eyes from the platter of sweetmeats, he saw that Juliana, for all her foresight, had been wrong on at least one point. Mirrie had come down to the great hall and was even now making steady progress towards them. Her hair was pinned elaborately on the top of her head and she wore a beautifully cut gown of pale blue laced with tiny pearls.

His heart lifted with pleasure.

With a beaming smile, Tristan pushed back his chair and extended his hand to help Mirrie up the steps of the dais. Her hand in his felt cold, despite the warmth of the evening. And her own smile was tight. *But she is here.*

"Sit," he urged, realising as he sank back into his chair that his slightly blurred vision was most likely due to rich wine on an almost empty stomach. Small cakes and sticky pastries would not suffice. He was dimly aware of Juliana leaning towards Mirrie, and of Mirrie's answering nod. But a wave of tension wove up around them both.

Holy hell, he needed food. *Proper food.*

And as if summoned by his thoughts, the double doors of the hall swung open and a line of liveried servants entered holding steaming platters of meat and vegetables. Tristan's stomach growled audibly and Juliana's twitching lips showed that she had heard. It took all his reserves of patience and good manners not to urge the maids to hurry.

The hall had filled up. Not to its usual level, but men-at-arms occupied the trestle table near the fireplace and the hum of their conversation together with the tempting aromas of roast venison helped him to feel that life was getting back to normal once again. When he had torn off a hunk of freshly baked bread and scooped up some of the tender meat in its rich sauce, his temper was almost entirely restored.

He glanced to his right, where Mirrie sat toying with her trencher, and was seized by the desire to see her smile. *Properly* smile.

"Have you passed a pleasant day?" he enquired, spearing another hunk of meat.

Mirrie did not look his way, but she answered readily enough. "Seeing your father awaken was a blessing."

He could not resist replying, "And all thanks to Juliana's intervention."

She nodded, though her lips were pressed into a thin line. "We owe you a debt of gratitude, Juliana." She drew the name out over four syllables.

Juliana herself smiled widely. "My people will rejoice to know of his recovery."

"And that he will reign for many years yet," Tristan said, sanguine with his wine and good meal.

Mirrie fixed him with her hazel eyes. "We cannot claim to know the future, Tris."

"Not always, at least," Juliana interjected.

Tristan looked from one to the other, equally surprised by both statements.

"You still doubt my father's recovery?" he demanded of Mirrie.

"Nay," she frowned. "Not explicitly, but it is sensible to accept we cannot know what is ahead of us."

Juliana tossed back her hair. She was a striking figure on the dais, with her waterfall of dark hair tumbling over her shoulders. Several men-at-arms dining below them could not help but stare in her direction.

Tristan placed a hand on her elbow. "What say you to that?"

Her laughter rang out like a peal of bells. "I would not be so bold as to issue a contradiction."

"But you can see the future?" His curiosity was piqued. "What does it hold for me?" He held out his palm for her inspection.

"You think me a wise woman at a country fair?" Juliana raised her eyebrows as Mirrie looked pointedly away from them both.

"I think you a woman of many talents." He inclined his head. "Am I wrong?"

Tutting, Juliana took hold of his hand and pulled it closer. He could feel the warmth of her breath as she leaned over to trace the faint lines with her slender fingers.

"I see that you will live a long and happy life," she said, blandly.

"I think you can do better than that." He bit down on his lip, thinking hard before asking the question that had been foremost on his mind these last days. "What of marriage?"

"Oh yes." Juliana nodded sagely. "There is marriage and children in your future. And soon, I would wager."

His breath came short. "Soon?"

It was not necessarily what he wanted to hear.

Juliana's expression changed and she brought his hand closer to her eyes, peering downwards with unexpected concentration until Tristan grew perturbed.

"What can you see?" he demanded.

"I see that a betrothal has already been arranged," she said softly. She placed his hand down on the table and gave him a long, puzzled glance before looking past him towards Mirrie. "With someone you already know very well."

"You don't mean—" Tristan began, but Juliana stopped him with a shake of her head.

"You should have told me," she reprimanded.

"What should my son have told you?"

So engrossed had Tristan been in Juliana's actions that he had not noticed his mother's stately entrance to the hall. She stood behind them now, one jewelled hand resting on the back of the ornate chair that was rightly hers. The Countess of Wolvesley was robed in rose-coloured silk, her silvery-gold hair braided about her head. Her face was still drawn but her eyes had never been sharper as she looked down at Juliana.

"Speak," she commanded.

Juliana's eyes flickered sideways but she answered steadily. "Lord Tristan should have told me that he is betrothed to Miss Mirabel."

CHAPTER NINE

MIRRIE DIDN'T KNOW whether her chief emotion was anger or disbelief. Either way, it took every ounce of self-restraint for her to remain seated up on the dais.

It had been bad enough to enter the great hall and see Tristan and Juliana clearly flirting with one another, in full public view. That Tristan had risen from his chair and been so attentive towards her had appeased her irritation for a while, before the bunkum with the palm-reading began.

Mirrie had never seen such a poor excuse for physical intimacy.

And now this! Had the exchange been pre-planned, like a spectacle arranged for the Twelfthtide revels? At first she thought that Tristan must have brought Juliana in on the ruse, thus rendering an awkward situation almost unendurable.

Then she saw the wideness of his eyes and realised that Tristan had also been taken unawares by Juliana's announcement.

What is she about?

Mirrie dared not lift her gaze to see the countess's expression. She gripped her fork and gazed down at her unwanted trencher of food until the items blurred and became one. The smell of venison clogged her throat and made her nauseous, but she did not trust herself to move away.

Morwenna was the first to speak. "Is this true?"

"Aye, Mother," Tristan answered. "It is. I was going to tell you. We were going to tell you, but when we arrived…" His voice trailed off.

"Mirrie?" Morwenna's voice was gentle. "I would hear it from your lips too."

Fearing her voice may shake, Mirrie lifted her chin. "'Tis true," she confirmed, but when Tristan made to speak, she raised her voice again. "But this is hardly the time for such an announcement."

Morwenna put both hands to her face and Mirrie jumped to her feet, fearing the woman who had raised her as one of her own was sobbing.

"I am sorry," she exclaimed, daring to put an arm around the countess. "Pray, do not cry."

"These are tears of joy, my dear." Morwenna lowered her hands to show her shining eyes. "This is joyous news."

"Joyous news," Tristan echoed, nodding his agreement.

Mirrie shot him a look. "The joy of this night is all rooted in the earl's recovery. Let us concentrate on that."

"Nay." Morwenna gripped her wrist. "You and Tristan are to be married. This is cause for celebration."

Mirrie's heart thudded against her restrictive bodice as her face flooded with heat. Morwenna's voice had carried throughout the hall and now the nearby men-at-arms had turned to face the dais.

"Congratulations, milord, milady," called one, lifting his mug of ale in a salute.

Soon the refrain was taken up and repeated. Tristan had no choice but to rise up from his chair, close the distance between them and embrace her as a resounding cheer went up. His men stamped their feet and shouted their approval, whilst Morwenna beamed from ear to ear and Juliana looked firmly at the floor. Mirrie saw all this as if it was happening to someone else. She knew Tristan was beside her, his muscular arm laying across her shoulders, her head hovering close to his own pounding heart. But she didn't care.

For the first time in her life, she didn't want to be close to Tristan. This whole charade felt wrong, and she regretted having ever agreed to it. But she couldn't disavow it now, in front of everyone. The most she could do would be to draw this performance to a close.

She stepped forward, precariously close to the edge of the dais but finally free of Tristan's grasp.

"Thank you, all of you." Her voice rang out over the hubbub. She curtsied low as the men cheered once more, then pointedly returned to her seat. Slowly the chatter resumed its usual level. Now it was Juliana's turn to rise from the table.

"Pray, sit," she urged the countess.

Mirrie observed she at least had the decency to keep her voice and head low.

Morwenna hesitated, then gave a regal nod. "Very well." She sank gracefully into the carved chair as Tristan poured her a fresh goblet of wine.

Juliana stood as if she did not know which way to turn. Mirrie almost felt sorry for her, before noticing the druid's eyes resting on Tristan.

She still wants him. She knew a rush of frustration. *Even now.*

"Pull up a chair," Tristan suggested, waving his hands behind him.

Under usual circumstances, some hovering servant would have already fetched a chair for Juliana, but these were not usual circumstances. Wolvesley was not running at full strength.

Juliana shook her head. "I believe this is a family celebration." She dropped into a curtsy. "I will retire for the evening."

Good riddance, though Mirrie. But she smiled politely at the druid's departing back.

"There is much to plan, much to discuss," smiled Morwenna. "I can't tell you both how pleased I am." She laid a hand on each of them, her heartfelt joy so evident that Mirrie thought she could not bear the deception a moment longer.

"You are much too kind." She shot another glance at Tristan, but he hardly seemed to notice her discomfort. "But I insist that we let the matter rest for tonight. We have endured much these last days. These plans and discussions can wait a while longer." She leaned forward to fill the countess's trencher with meat and vegetables, wondering how long it had been since she had last eaten a proper meal. "Here." She pushed it towards her.

"I am not overly hungry, my dear." Morwenna put a hand to her heart as she surveyed the offering.

Tristan spoke up. "You must eat something, Mother."

At least she could count on him for this—he always looked after his family.

"Something small," Mirrie agreed.

"You are in unison, as you have been for much of your lives." Morwenna twisted her head so she might smile at them both. "I should have seen this marriage coming."

Mirrie could think of no suitable response to this. Her smile became fixed as she gazed at the far end of the hall where tables stood empty and pushed against the wall.

"I have long admired Mirrie." Tristan's voice was husky.

Her heart beat grew faster, but not with pleasure. This all felt like too much. Morwenna's words made everything seem too real.

"And I have long loved and admired all of you de Nevilles," she retorted. "You welcomed me into your home when I was but a child, Morwenna, and now you welcome me again. I am more grateful than I could ever express." Shaking with emotion, Mirrie once again pushed herself up from the chair, but this time it was she who dropped into a low curtsy at the countess's feet.

"My dear." Morwenna put a hand on her cheek and urged her up. "We are family. You do not have to curtsy before me."

"I fear the events of the day have overtaken me." Mirrie knew her voice was trembling but hoped it might help her cause. "I have a headache and must retire to my chamber. Forgive me."

"There is naught to forgive," said Morwenna.

Tristan rose up from the table. "I will escort you."

"Nay." The word came out more harshly than she had intended and she summoned a hasty, insincere smile. "Pray, do not trouble yourself, Tristan. You should stay here with your mother."

Never had she spoken to him so firmly. Never had she denied herself his company. But just now, she did not think she could bear it.

Mirrie feared her knees might give way beneath her as she descended the steps from the dais and picked her way through the trestle tables. The men-at-arms stood to let her pass, nodding their heads and clearing her path of discarded sword belts and slumbering hounds.

These same men usually treated her with respect, but this show of deference was reserved only for the earl, countess and heir to Wolvesley.

But of course, they now thought her Tristan's intended bride.

By the time she reached the sanctuary of her own bedchamber, Mirrie's cheeks were burning with embarrassment.

How foolish she would appear when everyone learned she no longer held such status.

Why did I not think of this before?

She knew the answer to that well enough. She had been caught up in Tristan's web of charisma and unerring self-belief. And she had wanted this chance to stand by his side, even within the circle of his embrace. Even though she knew it all for a ruse.

What an idiot I have been.

Mirrie pulled the pins out of her hair with force, taking perverse pleasure in the twinges of pain as strands of her own hair came away with them. What she wanted now, more than anything else, was to return to Ember Hall. Where life was simple and honest. Where people said what they meant and meant what they said.

And where she could stride from the house and walk over the rolling hills without causing a stir.

Here at Wolvesley Castle she dared not even appear out of

her chamber in the incorrect attire.

Tears brimmed at the corner of her eyes and she dashed them away. Mirrie had never been one for self-pity. She was far more apt to push concerns about herself aside and focus on some task before her. She had learned many summers since that hard work and exercise could banish most demons. But neither of these outlets were available at this moment. The boiling tension inside her belly had nowhere else to go. She thought she might scream as she paced over the thick rugs on her chamber floor, clenching and unclenching her fingers.

When a knock sounded on the dark-wood door, she imagined it must be Molly.

Mirrie had no patience for the idea of a maid fussing around her. But there was little chance she could wriggle out of this tightly-laced kirtle without assistance. Not without tearing the expensive fabric. Swallowing her complaints, she pulled back the panel.

The last person she wanted to see was Tristan.

He stood with one arm hooked over the doorframe. His shoulders were so broad that he blocked almost all the light from the torch-lit corridor, making it hard for her to read his expression, but she could see that his heavy brows were lowered.

"What is it?" she asked, without preamble.

"May we talk?" His usual charming smile was absent, and he looked painfully earnest.

Mirrie knew a moment of weakness before giving her head a firm shake. "We can talk in the morn. 'Tis not proper for you to come to my bedchamber."

Tristan folded his arms, his movements allowing a beam of light to illuminate his cleanly-shaven face.

"What have I done to anger you?"

Mirrie knew such a swell of frustration that she wanted to slam the door in his face. But this man had been her friend since childhood. She could not bring herself to treat him so harshly. She contented herself with another shake of her head.

"Please, Mirrie," he pressed. "I can't bear it when you're cross with me."

"Urgh." She brought her hands up before her, clenching them together to prevent herself from swatting at him. "This is inappropriate, Tristan. What if you are seen at my door at this hour? Do you not realise how this will appear?"

She looked nervously past him, up and down the plastered corridor, but there was no one in sight.

Tristan, however, seemed to consider her words. "Forgive me." He bowed low, forcing her to step backwards into her chamber. And that was when he darted forward, closing the door behind him.

She was so surprised she could do no more than glare at him, wide-eyed.

"What are you about, Tristan? This is madness."

Her chamber was lit by several flickering candles, positioned on chests and in wall sconces. Tristan stood in a pool of golden light. He held up his hands in a gesture of surrender and leaned back against the smooth wall.

He is still half drunk, she realised.

"You have been angry with me all day," he said, "and I do not see why. All I have done is find a cure for my father and rejoice in his recovery."

"You could not wait to bring that woman here." The words burst from Mirrie before she could call them back, but releasing them into the night air helped sooth some of the fire in her belly and she held Tristan's gaze, ready and willing for a fight.

"What woman?" Tristan took a step closer to her. "Juliana? The woman who helped to heal my father?"

"The woman you wanted in your bed." Mirrie was shocked at her forwardness, but she did not allow any repentance to show on her face. Instead, she raised her eyebrows in a further challenge and met Tristan's glare with one of her own.

He shook his head, seemingly in wonderment. Silence stretched between them until Mirrie could bear it no longer.

"You do not even deny it." The fire inside her was dying. Now she was merely tired and resigned.

"My decision is made. She will not come to me. And I will not go to her."

"Why not?" Mirrie flung back her head to look at him again, her loose hair flying out behind her. "I could see it was what you both wanted."

"Because I do not like to see you so upset." Tristan gazed at her as if she was an impossible puzzle he was keen to solve.

"Just go," she said. "Please."

"Not until you believe me." He stepped forward and rested a gentle hand on her shoulder. "I will have nothing more to do with Juliana, if that is what you want."

"What I want is not important." To Mirrie's horror, her voice was trembling. "This betrothal between us is but a ruse, as we both well know." She took a deep breath and straightened her back. "But your mother believed it. As did all your men. It will not be long before everyone knows of it. Which is why you must leave. You cannot be seen coming out of my chamber." Her voice rose in emphasis. Mirrie had no fortune of her own, but she at least had her reputation.

She would not allow anyone to take that from her.

"I will go." He nodded, ducking down to her level. "But I hope you know that although our betrothal is fake, my deep affection for you is very real. And it always has been."

He dropped a kiss onto the top of her head and left. Mirrie stayed still until the sound of his footsteps had faded. Then she carefully closed the door and leaned back against it.

She had been wrong to come back to Wolvesley Castle, believing she was equal to withstanding the emotions she would experience as she pretended to be Tristan's betrothed.

Their plan had seemed so simple back at Ember Hall. But it was becoming more complex by the day.

CHAPTER TEN

TRISTAN WOKE TO bright morning sunlight and a nagging feeling that something was wrong. His head ached, a sure sign he had imbibed too much fine wine the night before. But his shoulders also felt stiff and sore, and shooting pains ran up and down his calves when he swung his feet down onto the floor. In a few seconds, as he rubbed the sleep from his eyes, his mind supplied the reasoning for all of his ills.

Too much wine, aye, that was at least the half of it.

Too much hard riding explained some of the rest. First to Ember Hall, then back here, then to hunt for Juliana at the druid camp.

But also, he suffered from tension over his father's health.

And worry over Mirrie.

The last point unsettled him, for Mirrie was fit, healthy and about to attend the Wolvesley midsummer ball—an event which she had always looked forward to.

But Mirrie was displeased with him. He recalled the flash of anger in her hazel eyes as she looked at him over his mother's greying head, and his belly shrivelled into a tight ball.

It felt wretched to have upset her.

He padded over thick rugs to the shuttered windows, extending a finger to widen the slats rather than flinging them open as was his habit. This morn, he was not quite ready to meet the brightness of the day.

It would not do to continue like this. Mirrie's friendship and support was as vital as his mother's smile and his father's wellbeing. Whatever harm he had caused, he must put it right.

Alas, he had moved too quickly. His tidy chamber heaved from side to side as Tristan leaned his hot forehead against the slatted shutters. His stomach rolled and he imagined last night's wine swilling around inside him. It took all his concentration not to cast up his accounts onto the finely-stitched rug beneath his bare feet.

A knock sounded at the door but Tristan could only grunt in reply. He sensed rather than saw Alfred's concern as he entered the chamber.

"My lord, are you unwell?"

With one arm extended above him, Tristan clenched his hand into a fist and leaned his head on his forearm.

"'Tis only that the sun is too bright," he managed.

"I shall fetch the physician."

From the corner of his eye, Tristan saw his manservant turn to leave.

"Nay," he shot out, even though the effort made his head spin all the more. "Bring me something to drink. I am parched."

Tristan closed his eyes against the lilting of the walls, but could hear by his footsteps that Alfred was approaching.

"I have a small ale for you, my lord."

Tristan reached out. "Put it in my hands."

His fingers closed around the smoothness of a cup and he drank deeply, knowing from experience that this would sooth the ravages of his head.

"I do not need the services of a physician, Alfred," he croaked. "My ill health is a result of my own bad decisions and the passing of the hours shall be my healer." Feeling slightly better already, he straightened his spine and tentatively peered at his manservant. "But if I did need a physician, I would counsel you to look elsewhere than he who bled my father half to death."

Alfred bowed his dark head. "As you wish."

Tristan took another swig of ale. "I must seek another castle physician. But first, tell me, how fares my father this morn?"

"The earl has already broken his fast." Relief shone through Alfred's words. "The countess is with him. She has ordered the next service at chapel should be one of thanksgiving."

"Aye." Tristan nodded his approval, ignoring the stab of pain in his temples. "I shall go to him myself, once I am dressed."

"You are sure you would not prefer to spend the day at rest?" Alfred raised his eyebrows questioningly. "These last days have been most taxing, my lord."

"I thank you for your concern, but I am my father's heir and there are jobs to be done." Tristan's vision was clearing. He placed his cup down on Alfred's silver tray and realised, for the first time, that he was still wearing yesterday's tunic. "Pray, fetch me water with which to wash and a change of clothes. Then I shall be about my day."

Not long later, Tristan was striding along the echoing corridors to his father's chamber, averting his gaze from the beams of light pouring in through a series of high narrow windows carved into the plastered walls.

He was not prepared to meet the dark-haired maiden waiting for him at a turn of the stairs.

"Milord." Juliana dropped into a curtsy.

"Juliana." He touched her elbow to raise her up, ignoring the frisson of connection that rippled through him. He had not seen her since quitting the great hall last night. Did he owe her an apology for all that had occurred?

Juliana smiled as if she could read the maze of thoughts in his mind.

"I have come to wish you farewell."

"You are leaving?" He steadied himself against a wall, drawing her closer to him to avoid a servant carrying an armful of linens.

"It is time."

He cleared his throat. "I shall ensure you are properly rewarded for all you have done here. And, of course, one of our guards will see you safely back to the camp."

Juliana raised her dark eyebrows as if something had amused her. "I do not require a guard."

"But you will require a horse," he countered. "Speak with the grooms and all shall be arranged."

"You are a good man, Tristan de Neville. I know you will do what is right."

"Will I see you again?" As soon as he had asked the question, he regretted it. Hadn't he sworn just moments ago to mend his relationship with Mirrie?

Juliana dipped her head. "Who can say, milord? I hope we might see one another in the fullness of time. But for now, our paths must diverge."

He bowed over her hands. "Thank you."

She smiled, her dark eyes flashed, and then she turned away and was gone.

Tristan gave his head a little shake. Juliana had represented temptation. Would he have succumbed if she had not taken matters into her own hands?

He didn't know.

Pushing such thoughts from his mind, he knocked sharply on his father's door, holding his breath for what he might find within.

His father's manservant pulled open the door and bowed to Tristan. "Good morn, milord."

"Good morn." Tristan nodded his head in return. "Is my father in sufficient health to receive visitors?"

"Come in, my boy."

It was unmistakably his father's voice that boomed from the bed. Thinner than usual, but still carrying sufficient force to make a smile tug at the corners of his mouth.

Tristan walked into the chamber, noting the open shutters and the prevailing scent of summer grass. His father sat up in bed, propped up by pillows, his golden hair framing a face which looked tired and drawn but was no longer ravaged by illness.

"Father." He bowed, hiding his emotions by turning his face to the rushes on the floor.

"Tris. Come closer so that I might see you properly."

He rose to find himself caught in a piercing blue stare. His father always had the uncanny ability to make Tristan feel he could see all the way into his soul. He pushed himself to close the distance between the doorframe and the large, canopied bed. When he was close enough, Angus reached out to grasp his hand in a steely grip and Tristan's vision clouded with salty tears.

"'Tis good to see you so much recovered, Father," he managed.

"Aye." Angus released his hand, but his all-seeing gaze did not lift from his son's face. "I thought my time had come, Tris. But I am spared. And I am told 'tis all thanks to you."

Tristan inclined his head to the side, uncomfortable with the praise. "I merely sought a second opinion, sir. As you always taught me. 'Twas your own guidance I followed."

Angus gave him a small smile. "Your mother has gone to her chamber to rest. I believe she has scarcely left my side these last days."

"She has not," Tristan confirmed. His large hands rested on the clean coverlet.

"I am most blessed." His father settled more comfortably against his pillows. "And I understand that you are soon to enjoy such blessings in a union of your own."

It took Tristan's dazed mind a few seconds to piece together his father's meaning. He then had to take a breath to prevent himself from stuttering like a fool. Instead, he slowly nodded.

"You speak of Mirabel?"

"Aye, this match has your mother beaming from ear to ear. 'Tis joyous news, Tris."

A flush heated his cheeks. He told himself 'twas the warmth of the chamber.

"I am glad you think so," he managed.

"Bring her to me." Angus gripped Tristan's hand once again. "Let me see the both of you."

"I will." Tristan nodded, recalling his resolution to speak to Mirrie and mend the rift between them.

"Before noon." Angus released his hand. "I would like to witness this love that has sprung up from friendship."

Tristan's mouth went dry. Did his father doubt him? The Earl of Wolvesley had always been able to read the truth in a man's eyes. It was one of the many reasons he was such a great leader.

But when he dared to meet his father's gaze, Angus's eyelids were drooping.

"I will let you rest, Father," he whispered.

Angus half raised his hand. "Come back soon, my boy. With Mirabel at your side."

Tristan walked quietly from the chamber, closing the panel behind him.

His father was recovering. This much was certain. And Tristan's heart was much lighter for it. Were it not for the risk of being spotted in a moment of weakness, he might have put his hands on his knees and wept with relief. As it was, he held his head high and marched back along the corridor and down the wide wooden staircase to the great hall. There, his hungry senses were met with the tempting aromas of freshly-baked bread, glistening ripe fruit and soft cheese cut into wheels.

"Tris!"

Whilst he was perusing the offerings of the long table, his name was hollered across the bustling room. Tristan turned to see Jakob, a red-headed knight who had trained alongside him at Lindum, waving frantically from a small table set below the dais.

Grabbing a fistful of red berries, Tristan walked over to the group of men. Jakob was dining with two recent recruits. He did not know their names, which meant he must learn them at the first opportunity. Tristan did not like to be at a disadvantage, even amongst his own men. And he had always believed that soldiers would more willingly follow a leader who gave them the time of day.

"Good morn," he greeted them.

"Especially for you, I hear." Jakob grinned up at him cheekily. Tristan remembered Jakob's many teasing taunts in their more youthful days. He was always the first to laugh and quick to celebrate any trifling success.

Tristan picked an empty cup from the table, sloshed ale into it from a nearby jug and raised it in a toast. "Well said, Jakob. I am just come from my father's bedchamber. He is on the road to recovery."

The men readily raised their cups to his and voiced their pleasure at this news.

"That is indeed something to celebrate. Although I was not at first talking of the earl," Jakob added, unexpectedly. "Congratulations on your betrothal. You did not tell me you were courting Miss Mirabel."

Tristan took a breath, telling himself that the length of his and Jakob's friendship would forgive the impertinence of such a statement.

Usually it would not be impertinent at all to compliment a man on his betrothal to a beautiful woman.

But he had not yet readied himself for such dialogue. Events seemed to be spiralling out of his control, which was ridiculous as this ruse was entirely of his own making.

"Thank you." He took a mouthful of ale to negate the need for further conversation.

"I am only sorry I missed last night's announcement." Jakob's gaze was trained on Tristan. A lesser acquaintance would have thought the exchange to be innocent, but Tristan could see the calculations taking place behind the man's eyes.

Jakob was wondering if this sudden betrothal was brought about *by necessity*. He would wager a bagful of coin that the knight was counting back the weeks since Tristan's last visit to Ember Hall.

Tristan recalled Mirrie's insistence that he leave her chamber last night before they could be seen together. Until she had spoken up, he had not spared a thought to how careless he was being with her reputation.

A reputation that was already being questioned. *Because of him.*

He grimaced behind his cup, before banging it back down on the table. "Fear not, Jakob, you will have full opportunity to celebrate with us at the midsummer ball. And perchance thereafter, for we are in no rush to set a wedding date." Whilst Jakob's jaw worked to formulate a response, Tristan looked for a change of subject. "How is your new squire working out? The lad that I sent over to you at Beltane."

Jakob flashed him a genuine smile. "As you know, I had my doubts, but he is progressing better by far than I predicted. He is a quick study, good with the horses and brave to boot. I readily admit that you were right about him."

Tristan was pleased. "I sensed the lad's potential." He turned his attention to Jakob's companions. "I do not believe we have been introduced."

"Edward Byers, milord," spoke up the oldest of the two; a muscular youth with freckles across his nose. "My father served yours, under Sir Henry de Gaunt."

Tristan nodded in recognition of the loyal knight who had led the Wolvesley army for more than two decades. "Sir Henry was a great man."

Edward Byers nodded enthusiastically, while the young man at his side turned a shade of beetroot red.

"I am new to Wolvesley, milord."

"And what is your name?" Tristan was instinctively cautious of newcomers, although 'twas far from easy to join the ranks at Wolvesley. No man could claim so much as a trial without a seal of recommendation.

"'Tis Thomas. I travelled here from Darkmoor, milord."

Tristan was reassured. Darkmoor was the province of one of his father's oldest friends. Otto Sarragnac was unlikely to send spies into their midst.

"You are both welcome." He smiled widely at them all, even Jakob. "Forgive me, I have business to attend to."

All three rose up from the table as Tristan swept away.

He must find Mirrie. If only he'd taken the time to pick up more than berries to break his fast. His stomach growled audibly, but he did not want to waste another moment in the great hall.

The front door to the keep stood open, inviting the warm breeze to bring the melody of bird song into the marbled hallway. He stood for a moment, looking out at the deep blue sky and the hues of sunlight reflected in the sparkling fountain. It was another beautiful day. If only he could spend it at leisure.

But Tristan had spent enough time watching his father at work to know that ledgers of accounts would need attention, including matters that were over and above the jurisdiction of his young steward. The castle court was sitting in two days and Angus must give word if proceedings would go ahead. All of this and more Tristan had decided to take to his father's bedside. It was time to show the Earl of Wolvesley what his eldest son was capable of.

Which meant he must find Mirrie, for he had no hope of concentrating on such mundane tasks if he still itched to make things right with his oldest friend.

First though, the cornflowers by the wall of the keep were calling to him. Tristan strode over and plucked a handful, being careful not to crush the petals in his large hands. He waved to attract the attention of a passing maidservant.

"Would you be so kind as to put these in a vase in Miss Mirabel's chamber?"

The maid curtsied politely and took the flowers, but Tristan could see that she was puzzled by his choice of bloom.

So be it. He was certain Mirrie had a fondness for the little flowers that were as blue as the sky. Seeing them in her bedchamber would please her, and that thought pleased him in turn.

Something caught his eye down by the fountain—a familiar figure he would recognise anywhere. Tristran wasted no time in running down the steps, heaving a sigh of relief when he rounded the corner to find Mirrie standing by the carved stone and gazing up at the high jet of foaming water. On the occasions he had visited Ember Hall, Tristan had grown accustomed to seeing Mirrie in worn work clothes with her shining hair tied into a rough plait. The Mirrie he knew at Ember Hall was usually found working in the fields or chopping vegetables in the kitchen. She was capable and kind, quick to bring a blanket or a bowl of broth to anyone in need.

He had forgotten how lovely she could look, simply standing still.

"There you are," he greeted her. Her hair had once again been expertly braided and pinned about her heart-shaped face. Her slender hands, usually so busily occupied, rested against the damp stone of the fountain's outer wall.

Mirrie did not break her gaze. "I have always wondered how it can rise so high into the air, with naught to support it."

He followed the line of her hazel eyes. "The water?"

"It amazes me now, just as it did when we were children."

Tristan pursed his lips. "'Tis all about the speed with which it ascends."

She threw him a look that would have been scornful from anyone else. "I did not believe it was the work of fairies."

He gave a bark of laughter. "I much prefer that idea." Mirrie was working to hide her smile, he could tell as much from the brightness of her eyes. "Walk with me," he entreated, holding out his elbow. When she hesitated, he merely moved nearer. "Come, 'tis a shame to waste this beautiful morn being angry with me."

"I am not angry with you."

"Then take my arm."

Mirrie huffed, sounding annoyed, but she took his arm with an outward display of grace and they began to promenade through the rose gardens. He reached over to pat her hand, carefully keeping his eyes straight ahead of them to ensure no one was near enough to overhear.

"I'm sorry. About last night. You were right."

"About what, exactly?" She arched her eyebrows.

"About me coming to your chamber. 'Twas not proper and it will not happen again."

"I am glad to hear it."

He paused to glance down at her pointed face. "Are you sure you are not angry with me?"

Mirrie let out a sigh. "I am exasperated with you, Tris. I am exasperated of this entire situation. I do not enjoy deceit. And it would seem that I no longer enjoy being laced into fancy gowns which threaten to trip me at every step."

Laughter bubbled up inside him. "Then pick up your skirts and run," he dared her.

"Whatever do you mean?" She shaded her eyes from the sunlight and tilted her head to look up at him.

"Let us race to the lake. I seem to recall a time when you oft would beat me there."

"I am glad you recall such a time." Her tone had softened. "But those days are gone. You have rather the advantage over me now."

Of course he had. But he was enjoying teasing her. "In what way?"

"Your height, for one, you buffoon." She gave him a little push, but merriment had chased the crossness from her brow.

"I will give you a head start." The idea had seized him and he was reluctant to let it go.

"I cannot go racing about the grounds of Wolvesley Castle." She lowered her voice. "Whatever will people think?"

"They will think it an example of our young love and exuberance."

She shook her head at him. "'Twould be more proper for us to stroll around here and admire the roses."

"Proper be damned," he let out. Mirrie's lips twitched and he knew at once what he must do. "Unless, of course, you fear the challenge?"

She folded her arms and fixed him with a level stare. "I have ne'er feared any challenge from you, Tristan de Neville."

"Then race me to the lake." He lowered his face to hers. "I'll give you ten seconds head start."

"Ten!" Her eyebrows disappeared under her hair.

Tristan took a step back and started counting. "One, two—" He got no further before Mirrie picked up her skirts and launched herself down the path.

She had always been quick, like a leggy colt just let out in the paddocks. Young Tristan could easily out-run his older sister Frida, but Mirrie would beat him every time, no matter how hard he tried. He recalled their last race down to the lake. They had been running so fast he thought he might stumble and fall. Mirrie had been pink-cheeked and euphoric in her victory.

"You will never be faster than me," she had crowed.

But by the next summer, he was a whole head and shoulders above her and by unspoken agreement, they no longer raced one another around the grounds of Wolvesley.

Overcome with nostalgia, Tristan had forgotten what he was about and Mirrie had disappeared between the trees before he came back to himself and began to give chase. He had thought he might let her win, for old times' sake. But so fast did he have to move to make up for his mistake, that the boyish spirit of competition entirely took him over. He pounded down the slight incline towards the lake, his eyes fixed on the slight figure of his target, moving at a blur of speed towards the shimmering expanse of water.

Tristan's arms pumped and his long legs ate up the ground, but he could not catch her. Laughing, he congratulated her on her victory.

"You have beaten me again," he wheezed, putting his hands on his knees as he caught his breath.

"'Twas never in doubt," she replied airily. But Mirrie could not cloak the fact that she was also panting for breath, and soon she was laughing in turn as she leaned on the upper rung of a wooden gate.

"I gave you too great a head start," he reflected, running a hand through hair that had become damp with effort.

The morning sunshine shone down like a blessing on the blue lake whilst the tall trees around them provided welcome shade. Down here, they were screened from the castle and Tristan felt the same way he had as a child, that they had escaped all rules and had claimed the authority to do exactly as they pleased.

If only that were true.

He stood by Mirrie at the gate and together they gazed over the water. Birds called and tentative waves rolled onto the shingle shore. His heart was strangely full and he busied himself by rolling up his sleeves.

"My father is much recovered," he announced.

Mirrie put a hand to her heart. "I have never been gladder of anything."

Tristan kept his eyes fixed on the lake. "He has asked to see us, together, before noon." He cleared his throat. "He was pleased to hear of our betrothal."

Seconds passed before Mirrie swung around to face him. "Do you not feel guilty, Tris?"

It was a simple question that demanded an honest answer. He nodded. "Aye. Right now, I do."

"Good." Mirrie scuffed at the soft earth with her boots. "So do I."

He did not want her to feel guilty. She did not deserve that burden when the whole betrothal farce had been at his urging.

"Seeing my father so close to death was a shock. If I had known how ill he was, perchance I would ne'er have conceived of this plan."

Aware of her searching gaze, Tristan lowered his head.

"It is not too late to tell them we have changed our minds," she suggested, softly.

"But the root problem still exists." His hand curled into a fist. "My parents see me as little more than an instrument for breeding."

Mirrie made a strange sound and when he looked down, he found her shoulders shaking with laughter.

"Like a stallion?" she suggested. "Or a prize bull?"

"It is not funny," he said reproachfully.

"Oh, but it is." She shook her head. "What's funnier is that you have no notion of the power you have."

Tristan frowned but Mirrie ploughed on before he could say anything.

"'Tis in your power to change the way your parents see you. You've already shown all of England that you are a skilled warrior and more besides. Now you need only prove to your parents that you can do more than fight and—" she ground to a halt.

"Provide heirs?" he suggested.

"Exactly." Mirrie made a visible effort to recover her composure. "You spoke to me about introducing a covered market. Why not put that plan in motion? You are quick, I believe, to take the initiative in battle. You could do the same at home."

"Aye." He nodded slowly, as his mind turned over her words. "You are not wrong." He recalled Juliana's words from just yesterday.

"A man who has not yet come to realise the full extent of the power he wields."

"What is it?" Mirrie was watching him closely.

"Juliana said much the same thing to me," he answered carelessly. But when Mirrie turned away from him, he reached out to grasp her wrist. "You cannot blame me for speaking to the woman when you shared details of our betrothal with her."

Mirrie gaped at him like a fish. "I ne'er spoke of that to Juliana."

He released her wrist. "Then how did she find out?" He frowned. "I thought you told her."

Mirrie shook her head. "I thought *you* did."

For some reason this struck Tristan as funny. "Mayhap she looked into my palm and foresaw our actual wedding?"

"Do not be a fool," Mirrie answered calmly. "You are the

future Earl of Wolvesley. You cannot marry me."

Tristan pushed at the gate and was pleased to find it unbolted. He held it open and ushered Mirrie through. "I think you will find I can do exactly as I please—as I intend to prove right now."

"Where are we going?" She looked up at him with wide, hazel eyes.

Tristan grinned. "We're going bathing."

CHAPTER ELEVEN

*B*ATHING!

Mirrie followed him down to the lake, though she knew she shouldn't. It had felt good to run through the grounds of Wolvesley, as if she were a child again, shaking off the mantle of responsibility and gloom that had dogged her for so long.

It felt even better to beat him!

There had been a time when Tristan was her worthy opponent in many childhood games. Out in the fields and up in the school room, they would endlessly challenge one another. Then Tristan went away to the knights' training college at Lindum, and when he returned to Wolvesley, he had been a man.

Gone was her childhood friend. In his place stood a squire with broad shoulders and stubbled cheeks. The new deepness of his voice made butterflies flutter in Mirrie's stomach. Naught had been the same again.

Now, more than ten summers later, he paused by a low, flat rock and removed his boots and stockings. When he rolled up his breeches to reveal muscular calves, she felt her breath catch in her chest. But when he swivelled around to catch her eye, he found her gazing at a gull.

"Let's paddle," he said.

Mirrie affected nonchalance. "I thought you were going to bathe?"

"Aye, but I had forgotten the rules around betrothed couples and what they are permitted to do in the broad light of day."

He was teasing her. And if Mirrie wasn't careful she would begin to blush again.

"You may paddle if you please. I shall sit here and watch." She smoothed her skirts and arranged herself cautiously on the rock.

"You used to be more fun than this," Tristan complained. "Don't you want to feel the water rush between your toes?"

Aye, I do. But she wasn't going to permit herself the pleasure of it. "Go on." She flapped her hand at him.

With a shrug of his shoulders, Tristan turned away from her and walked the few steps to the shore. He whistled sharply as the water came up around his ankles. "It's cold." For a moment, he smiled at her over his shoulder. A vision of height and strength, haloed by light.

He is too handsome by far.

And he has always known it.

Mirrie allowed herself to drink him in. His golden hair, brighter than the sun overhead. The graceful power of his broad shoulders. The sculpted strength of his bare calves as he kicked at a piece of driftwood. She sat on her hands to stop them from trembling.

She must get a grip on herself.

"Come in, Mirrie," he urged, turning to face her.

"I shall not." Her voice was prim. "And it is high time you stopped talking to me as if I were your childhood playmate."

"But you *are* my childhood playmate." He put his head to one side and shaded his eyes from the sun.

"We are both grown with responsibilities." Mirrie sniffed. "I know why you have never met a woman you wanted to marry."

"You do?" She had his attention now. He walked back up the shore, water dripping from the lower half of his legs.

"You do not take life seriously enough."

He snorted. "I can assure you, I do. I've served on battlefields, Mirrie. They're no place for childishness."

"No, I know that," she conceded. "I'm well aware that you take your duties seriously. But when it comes to your dalliances…'tis another story entirely." She sat up tall. "You are a terrible flirt. In fact, you treat women as if they were playthings."

"*Playthings?*" His voice throbbed with incredulity.

"Playthings." She nodded firmly. "Have you ever struck up conversation with a woman, without thinking of taking her to bed?"

He put his hands on his hips. "That is most unfair. I talk to Esme most days, heaven help me. Whene'er I come to Ember Hall, I particularly enjoy conversing with you and Frida."

"I mean apart from me and your sisters." She pressed her lips together, keeping her emotions locked up inside.

Tristan thought for a moment, then brought his gaze back to hers. "Mirabel, I have never forced myself on anyone."

"You have never had to," she retorted. "Your flirtations and persuasions are equally dangerous."

"Dangerous?" His eyebrows rose with his voice.

"For the state of your soul," she replied, primly.

"I see." He scratched at his shoulder, a smile playing about his lips. "Then what would you have me do?"

"Stop flirting," she demanded. It was the only way she could possibly deal with Tristan and the wealth of feelings she had for him.

He bowed his head. "As you wish."

Did he mean it? She didn't think he would lie to her, but flirting was something he did so automatically, she was not at all certain he could bring himself to simply stop. Still, only time would tell—and perhaps it would go better if she helped him.

"Come and sit beside me." She made space for him on the rock. "And I shall coach you in the art of proper conversation to nice young ladies."

"But nice young ladies are so dull." He plonked himself down, bringing with him the scent of fresh water and clean sweat. "I'm joking," he added, nudging Mirrie with his shoulder. He cleared his throat. "Might I say how very pretty you look this morn?"

"No." She jabbed him sharply with her elbow. "That is flirting."

"Then how should I proceed?" He opened his arms entreatingly.

"Begin by telling me something true." She arched her eyebrows at his silence. "The truth is so much harder, isn't it?"

"I was telling the truth before." His voice dropped low enough to bring goosebumps out on her arms. "You do look very pretty in that dress, with your hair pinned up so elegantly. But then, you always look pretty."

She pressed her lips together and shook her head, not trusting herself to speak.

"Very well. If you will not accept compliments, I will find a new truth to tell." Tristan leaned back on his hands and stretched his long legs out in front of him. Gulls called overhead and a gust of wind rustled through the trees. He thought for a long moment before speaking again. "It was terrible to see my father so weakened."

Mirrie turned to him, her lips parted in surprise. "It was," she murmured in agreement.

"Truly, I had not expected his condition to worsen so quickly. 'Twas an unwelcome reminder that death awaits us all," he finished quietly.

Mirrie bit down on her lip and allowed several beats to pass. "That is very sombre."

"And very true?"

She nodded. "Undoubtedly so."

"I have seen death up close on the battlefield. I have lost good friends. Young men who should have had all their lives ahead of them." Tristan sighed. "But my father, I somehow thought, would live forever."

Moved by this glimpse of vulnerability, Mirrie reached out and took his hand. It was the impulsive action of a friend, or e'en of the sister that he saw her as, but as soon as his warm fingers interlinked with hers, she began to regret it.

"I'm sorry for being so gloomy." He threw her a smile.

"Do not be sorry for telling me the truth."

He cupped her hand inside both of his, caressing the inside of her index finger with his thumb. She told herself it meant nothing. That Tristan would do the same to Flora, his niece. But it did not stop a thrill of pleasure travelling all the way up her arm.

"I know how you see me, Mirrie."

For a moment she feared her heart had stopped beating. "You do?"

"Aye." He smiled gently. "To you I am irresponsible. Perchance you imagine that I do not understand the myriad advantages I enjoy as the son of an earl. But you are wrong."

Relief came over her in a hot wave. "I am glad to hear it," she managed.

"I have faced assassins in my own home." He gripped her hand more tightly now. "I have dined with my enemies and risked my life. All for the good of my country. And I would do it all again, without question. I do not shirk from my duty, with or without a sword in my hand."

She knew this. All of it. Frida's husband, Callum, was one of the assassins once sent after Tristan. "I see you, Tris," she whispered. "Good and bad."

"I will serve my country and honour my parents, whatever that takes. But I do not wish to be pressured into marrying a woman I do not love."

She could only nod.

"Can I tell you something else that is true?"

"Aye," she whispered.

"I do not like it when you are cross with me."

She swallowed. "Then you should stop doing things that make me cross."

He shifted a little on the rock so he was facing her. His blue eyes shone with sincerity. "I shall make that my mission over the coming days."

Her heart beat so loudly she feared he might hear it. "Then we shall be friends once more," she said, as lightly as she could.

Tristan kept his eyes trained on her face. "Ah. We shall have to be more than friends. We are a betrothed couple, do not forget."

Mirrie reached for her composure, but it was difficult to find beneath Tristan's all-seeing gaze. "I am unlikely to forget," she managed. "Even your men treat me differently now."

"They treat you with the respect you deserve." His hands travelled to her arms, holding them lightly. "As I shall try to be the husband you deserve."

Mirrie's throat had constricted so it was difficult to breathe. She concentrated on the ripples on the lake, visible over Tristan's shoulder. She thought of the sharpness of the rock, pressing into her thighs. She noticed the sun on the back of her neck and the distant coo of a woodpigeon. But none of it was enough to distract her from the man she loved, sitting so close.

"You're flirting again," she breathed.

Tristan laughed, but it only served to weave the spell closer around her.

"Honestly, that was not my intention." He leaned a little nearer. "I was still telling you the truth. Methinks the practice has grown addictive, or perchance it is you, sweet Mirrie, bringing out what is good and honest in me."

Her heart threatened to jump out of her chest. Mirrie fought for words, but Tristan mistook her silence for denial.

He cleared his throat. "In these last days I have learned that I would do aught within my power to see you smile."

Mirrie would never know what made her do it. But before her rational self could intervene, she closed the gap between them and kissed him.

Tristan's lips were soft and warm. She felt him stiffen with surprise, then came a delicious moment of unity when their mouths melded together and his hand came lightly against the small of her back. She breathed it all in—his face, his touch, his scent; then she pulled back, before she lost her mind entirely.

She wanted to move away, but Tristan's hand on her back did not shift. He kept her close, his searching eyes mere inches from hers.

"Well, that was a surprise." His voice came out as a croak.

Mirrie took a breath. "I wanted to show you that nice ladies can be surprising sometimes. We are not always dull."

"Lesson learned." A devilish smile flickered around his lips, making her heart pick up speed all over again. "Is there anything else you would like to teach me?"

Mirrie rapped her palm against his chest, closing her mind to the hard ridge of muscle she encountered beneath his shirt. "You are flirting again."

"Under the circumstances, you shall have to forgive me."

She must bring this wild interlude to a close. It was not at all what she should have done. In fact it was everything other than sensible. If coming to Wolvesley as Tristan's pretend betrothed would risk her heart, this was a sure way to break it completely.

But oh, how good it felt.

She shot him a severe look and firmly pushed him away. "We should return to the keep." Mirrie rose up from the rock, praying that her knees would not give way beneath her. The sun was hot on the top of her head and she was conscious that she wore neither a bonnet nor a headdress. She had intended merely a short walk in the gardens, but it seemed a lifetime had passed since she left her bedchamber.

I kissed Tristan. Broke the boundaries that had always existed between them. Mirrie fixed her eyes on the lake and bit down on her bottom lip. Everything had changed, and yet naught would differ. For he was still the man she loved.

And he loved her. *Like a sister.*

Which meant she needed to hold her head high and go about her day without showing the turmoil she was feeling. The story she had conjured, about *nice young ladies*, would hold true.

Tristan came to stand by her side, stretching his arms above his head and rotating his shoulders.

"You are sure I cannot tempt you to paddle?"

The question made her smile. Aye, naught had changed between them. She told herself that she was glad of it.

"Did you not say that your father wished to see us?"

He grimaced. "I did. You are right, as always, Mirrie. We should return to the keep."

Mirrie stood calmly whilst Tristan pulled on his stockings and boots. She would present an unruffled demeanour to the de Nevilles, to the world at large.

This subterfuge could only continue for a certain amount of time. Then she would return to Ember Hall and pick up the pieces of the life she had forged for herself.

She had kissed Tristan once.

The memory will have to last me a lifetime.

CHAPTER TWELVE

F OR TRISTAN, THE world had tilted on its axis.

Ye Gods, it had felt good and right to kiss Mirrie.

How did I spend so many years in her company, without seeing her at all?

They walked together back to the keep and it took a great effort of will to keep his hands away from her. It would be the easiest thing in the land to take her arm, to offer gentlemanly assistance over the uneven ground. But Mirrie had always been a competent and capable girl, not the type to trip and plead some feminine weakness.

He had always liked that about her.

Earlier that morn, he had drawn her to his side without a thought. Now he was hyperaware of her every movement. How her long stride matched his. How she walked tall and proud, with no hint of hesitation or artifice. How her hazel eyes shone in the shafts of noontime sunshine which fell through the tall trees.

She had always been there, in his life. Like one of his sisters. He had noticed her beauty, of course, in the same objective way he observed the charm and good looks of Frida, Isabella and Esme. But never before had he felt that loveliness imprint itself on his soul.

And she had once been one of his closest confidantes. With that in mind, he wanted to halt their progress; to declare this new confusion in his heart. But what words could he use to describe it?

Tristan appreciated the irony. He had never been lost for words around women before.

As they emerged out of the woods into full view of the castle, he summoned his courage and came to a stop. After a few steps, Mirrie also paused. She turned to face him, her heart-shaped face creased with an emotion that looked like fear.

"What is it?" he asked, immediately concerned.

She put a hand to her heart, also seemingly gathering her courage. "I think I am a little afraid of what you might be about to say."

He had always admired her straightforward honesty.

She spoke the truth.

"Truly, I don't know exactly what I am about to say. I only wanted another moment with you. Alone."

Mirrie gave her head a little shake. "We can't do this, Tris."

"Do what?" He stepped closer. If it were any other woman, he would have taken her hands in his. But right now, Mirrie was making him unaccountably nervous.

"Whatever this is." She flung out her hands in a gesture of confusion. "The task ahead of us will be difficult enough without adding further complexity. We both know who we are. Let us not forget it."

It took a moment for her words to make sense to him.

"You mean, you are a nice young lady. And I am—"

"You are Tristan de Neville." She rolled her eyes good-naturedly. "Nay, I mean that you have always thought of me as a sister. You told me so just days ago."

"I did." He dimly remembered doing so. A sentiment from a different time.

"You must marry an heiress," she said, as if she were reciting lines. "A woman of good, *noble* family."

"Must I?"

Mirrie huffed out a breath. "That is, after all, why I am here." She folded her arms, mirroring his posture. "I begin to think the sun has affected your thinking."

"Ah, Mirrie." He couldn't help but chuckle, ruefully. "If only I could find an heiress who puts me in my place as well as you do."

"Mayhap you will find her at your mother's midsummer ball."

He made a noncommittal sound before he reached out and ran a finger softly over the curve of her cheek, noting the way her eyelashes fluttered closed at his touch. He felt a swell of victory.

Mirabel was not as impervious to his charms as she would have him believe.

I must proceed slowly then.

"You're right, as always." He sighed regretfully. "But do not kiss me again, Mirrie. For there is only so much self-control that a man can wield." Her eyes widened with surprise and Tristan chuckled. "I speak in jest." He tucked her arm beneath his elbow. "You are quite safe with me."

Mirrie's cheeks had stained with pink but her voice was quite level. "I have never doubted it."

They walked together back through the gardens and up the steps to the keep, only drawing apart when they reached the entrance hall.

"Will we go straight to my father's chamber?" he asked solicitously.

Her eyes went doubtfully to his boots. "Do you not wish to change?"

In truth, his stockings were damp and uncomfortable. But he also knew they had been longer at the lake than he had intended. His father would be waiting.

He glinted down at her. "I'm willing to suffer the consequences of my more impulsive decisions."

Mirrie poked him in the stomach, swiftly and unexpectedly. It did not hurt, but he doubled over with the shock of it.

"Stop flirting," she hissed.

Unable to hide his merriment, Tristan again took her arm and they proceeded up the winding staircase.

The dimness of the upstairs corridors was sobering after the brightness outside. The earl's manservant opened the chamber door with a deep bow for them both. As she turned to face his father, Mirrie dipped into a low curtsy whilst Tristan gazed about him.

Things seemed much as they had earlier that morn. The chamber now appeared bright and airy, smelling strongly of lavender which had been sprinkled into the rushes on the floor. His father sat up in bed, his golden hair combed and tidy, his bejewelled fingers folded together on the clean coverlet. Tristan's mother perched in a tapestried chair pulled closer to the bed. She was dressed in cream silk, and her bright eyes were turned towards him.

"Tristan," she said with pleasure. "And Mirabel."

"Come in, come in," his father beckoned. "We have much to discuss."

Tristan resisted the urge to stride forward. Instead he reached back for Mirrie's hand and they approached the canopied bed together. Her fingers felt cold within his and he squeezed them gently in encouragement.

Warm words followed, together with entreaties that the newly betrothed couple should sit and make themselves comfortable. Tristan fetched chairs, careful to attend to Mirrie's comfort before his own. All the while, he could see the usual spark of vitality in his father's face, and that mattered more than his easy acceptance of their news.

He had expected their announcement to be met with approval, but the evident joy with which Angus and Morwenna beheld Mirrie as their prospective daughter-in-law, surprised even him.

"I always suspected," said his mother.

"Did you?" Tristan asked in genuine wonderment, while Mirrie shifted uncomfortably and fixed her gaze on the fireplace.

"We will announce your betrothal at the midsummer ball," his father said, grandly.

Even Tristan blanched at this. Before he could gather his thoughts, Mirrie spoke up.

"Nay, please do not." Her voice was strong, though her face had turned pale. She looked down, seemingly unable to meet the many eyes gazing at her in surprise. "I only mean that coming so soon after your illness, it would not be right."

Tristan came to her rescue. "There would be much to arrange, certainly." He gestured with his hands, unsure exactly what that might entail. "And we are in no hurry to wed." Recalling his earlier conversation with Jakob, Tristan imbued his words with meaning.

"I am glad to hear it." His father's voice showed that he understood Tristan's implication.

Morwenna cleared her throat, dispelling the tension. "We planned to find you a bride at this ball, Tris. It does not seem fitting to go ahead now."

"What if I find Mirrie at the ball?" he suggested, pleased with the idea.

Mirrie spoke up. "But our betrothal has already been spoken of." Her voice was small. "News will surely spread."

"Gossip," said Tristan, dismissively.

"Gossip can hurt a family." His mother's curious gaze settled on him, but he did not allow himself to be discomfited.

"News also spread about your illness, Father." His voice carried around the frescoed chamber. "The midsummer ball should be an opportunity to celebrate your recovery and show to the world that the Earl of Wolvesley is well once more. At the same time, Mirrie and I will dance together. Be seen together." He took up her hand and impulsively pressed a kiss to the back of it. "We will be noticed." He paused. "And in the days to come, we will announce our intention to wed. Forsooth, we can throw another ball later for the official announcement."

This time it was his mother whose cheeks turned pale. "I do not wish to throw a second ball."

"Then the next celebration will be our wedding," Tristan corrected himself hastily. From the corner of his eye, he saw Mirrie flinch. "All of my sisters should return for it, should they not?"

"I am not sure Isabella will be able to leave her husband's side. He is ailing." His mother tightened her lips. "And of course, Frida's time draws near."

"I would want Frida by my side when our betrothal is announced," Mirrie exclaimed, seizing on this.

"All the more reason to bide our time." Tristan nodded sagely.

"But Esme can come home." His mother clasped her hands and turned to her husband. "There is no reason for her to stay away now."

"Indeed there is not." His father smiled benignly. "A family celebration then."

"A celebration of you," Tristan interjected.

His father laughed. "A celebration of my son's quick thinking, which led to my recovery. And of the life he will forge with a young woman we love as one of our own."

Everyone smiled, though he could see the strain in Mirrie's eyes. Tristan got to his feet.

"We should let you rest, Father."

Angus shook his head. "I grow tired of being treated like an invalid."

"You gave us all a terrible fright." Morwenna leaned over the bed and straightened his covers, tenderly.

"Your mother has me kept as a prisoner up here. What does the physician say?" His father's keen eyes swung to Tristan.

"It does not matter what the physician says," he answered, smoothly. "The man's methods all but killed you. I see it as my duty to dismiss him."

"Nay." His mother and Mirrie spoke as one, both of them looking up at him in concern.

"What is it?"

To Tristan, it was very simple. The physician should be dismissed. The man should count himself fortunate he received no worse consequences.

Mirrie spoke first. "'Twould be most unwise, Tris, to invite guests to Wolvesley with no physician here to treat them should they fall sick."

"Or fall at all," his mother added.

He could see the logic of this. "Very well." He reached for Mirrie's hand and drew her up beside him. "But immediately after the ball, I shall appoint a new physician."

It was the first time he had expressed such a strong opinion on the running of the castle. Tristan half expected a reprimand, but his father only nodded.

"I will leave that with you, my boy."

Tristan and Mirrie took their leave and withdrew from the chamber, both exhaling with relief as the panel closed behind them. He put a finger to his lips and led her to a wide window seat at the far end of the gallery before speaking.

"That was a triumph." He lowered himself onto the cushioned seat and tugged at her arm until she followed suit.

"A triumph of deception." She shook her head, smoothing her skirts with hands that still trembled. "My conscience does not grow any easier about this."

He crossed his long legs in a show of nonchalance. "Do you know what surprised me most of all?"

She tilted her head up at him. "What?"

Tristan kept his eyes trained on her face, which was beautifully illuminated by the window behind them. "My parents seem gloriously unconcerned about me marrying an heiress."

She opened and closed her mouth, looking at first wary and then displeased. "'Tis because they are kind, decent people. But that does not mean it is not in your interest to marry well."

"It is in my interest to be happy."

Mirrie blinked at him. "I want you to be happy, Tris,"

"And I want *you* to be happy." He meant it.

His parents had always enjoyed a happy marriage. He had long taken for granted the genuine smiles each bestowed upon the other, and the many, casual gestures of affection which passed between them. Now he realized, for the first time, how lucky they were.

"I cannot deny that I long for this ruse to be over." Mirrie looked down at her knees, her shoulders hunched.

Once this ruse was over, Mirrie would return to Ember Hall. It might be some time before he saw her again. The thought was not at all pleasing.

Seized by impulse, he again took her hand. "Come with me. There's something I want to show you."

She made a sound of complaint, but once Tristan had set upon a course of action, he was not easily deterred. They made their way to a low door in the northern tower.

A door that was rarely opened now.

"The school room?" Mirrie arched her eyebrows.

"The room which saw so much of our childhood." He twisted the handle and the door swung open with a creak. "After you." He stood to one side to allow her to pass, but Mirrie still looked uncertain.

"It's dark up there." She craned her neck around the corner, to where an old stone staircase twisted up to the tower room.

Tristan threw her a smile. "I never had you pegged as afraid of the dark."

She shook her head in exasperation. "Must you frustrate me with every word you utter? I would like to see you ascend narrow steps in long skirts without the ability to see where you should next place your foot."

He feigned penitence. "I see the problem. Allow me to go first. I shall open the shutters and all will be well."

He bounded up the narrow steps, remembering how steep the staircase had seemed when he was a small boy. Lessons had come easily to Tristan, as they had to all his siblings, and he had happy memories of the hours spent within these stone walls.

Though he also recalled hot summer days when he gazed out of the window and longed to be outside. And those long hours before luncheon, when he daydreamed of sneaking out to the kitchens.

The school room had not been used for years. Dust sheets covered the wooden desks and small chairs the six of them had once perched upon. A dim, grimy light filtered in through gaps in the shutters and the air smelled stale. It was a relief to throw open the long shutters, even though the dust this disturbed fell about him and made him cough. He waved it away and shouted down to Mirrie.

"You can come up now."

For a moment, he feared she had left him up here all alone. But then tentative footsteps sounded on the stair treads. He strode over to help her up the final steps.

"You wanted to show me an empty school room?" It looked as if Mirrie was aiming for a sceptical expression, but then a sneeze took her by surprise.

"I'm sorry," he said, quickly. "'Tis the dust. Here, come and stand by the window."

Whilst Mirrie recovered her composure, Tristan threw open the next of the shutters so the square-shaped room was bathed in light. This had once been a cosy, welcoming space. In winter days, a fire had flickered in the grate and their kindly tutor had read them stories from a rocking chair.

The rocking chair had since been claimed by the Seneschal for his own private chamber. Tristan couldn't blame him. As a child, he had longed for a turn in the rocking chair.

He was lost in nostalgia until Mirrie spoke up. "What was it that you wanted me to see?"

"Do you remember the rocking chair?" he asked.

She nodded. "I remember it all, Tris." Slowly, she swivelled around, dust motes dancing around her. "You would sit here by the window. And you would stare outside daydreaming when you should have been learning Latin."

"But you were the perfect student," he teased.

"Hardly. Your father would oft help me in the evenings. Otherwise I never could have kept up with you all." She bit down on her lip as if embarrassed at the memory.

"I never knew that," he said, softly.

"Well, I have never been one for flaunting my failings," she quipped. "Especially those that were not clearly apparent."

"You mean your skills on horseback?" he suggested, greatly daring.

To his relief, Mirrie smiled. "I do."

"Sometimes I would coax you onto the back of my pony when we were small. Do you remember that?" He chuckled at the memory. "We would all go riding in the woods and I hated to leave you behind. You told me you couldn't manage it, but I knew you could, if only you would put faith in yourself."

Mirrie turned away so he could not see her expression. "Aye. None of the others even tried to get me to join in. Perchance only you had the necessary powers of persuasion."

"Perchance only I suspected the true depths of your courage." She turned back to him at this, her eyes wondering, and he nodded in confirmation. "Yours is a quiet, steady sort of courage. It may not always be obvious to others, but 'tis all the stronger for it."

"Do you really think so?" The question was almost a whisper.

"I have long believed it," he said staunchly, determined to make her smile again. "I am accustomed to assessing courage in those who serve me. But skills on horseback do not count for everything. You oft would beat the rest of us in a running race. As you did again, this morn."

"That is my strength." She nodded firmly. "Running…and perchance dancing."

"We shall dance together at the midsummer ball." He closed the gap between them and offered her a small bow. "Shall we?"

"You mean dance? Now?" Mirrie put a hand to her heart. "I couldn't."

Tristan made a show of looking about him. "There is no one here to see." Before she could protest further, he took hold of her hands and raised them high, twisting his body so he stood sideways with his face angled toward her. "Pretend we are part of a Quadrille," he urged.

He thought she might refuse, so rigid was her body, but after a moment's hesitation, she mirrored his stance. Slowly, he began to walk her around in a tight circle, their bodies moving in unison even as her eyes were fixed firmly on a point somewhere north of his shoulder.

He came to a halt. "Why won't you look at me?"

"I am not in the mood for dancing," came her reluctant reply.

"We should practice before the ball." Tristan was not one to give up easily.

"There is time enough for that." She forced him to a standstill and met his teasing gaze with a sharp one of her own. "Why did you bring me up here? Not to dance, I am sure."

He regretfully released her. "Nay, you are right. Come, look at this." He beckoned her over to the covered desk nearest the wall and lifted up the edge of the dust sheet. "There." He pointed to an engraving on the rounded leg of the desk. "Do you know what that is?"

Mirrie bent beside him, her hands on her knees. She peered for a few seconds, before uttering a strangled sort of sound. "I think that you know the answer as well as I do."

He bent down beside her, elaborately tracing the initials that had been roughly carved into the wood. "M and T," he mused. "Could that stand for Mirrie and Tristan?"

He was teasing, aye, and it was a little unfair. But he did not expect her cheeks to flush quite so pink, nor for her to stand and reel away from him quite so quickly.

"You know very well that it does."

"I didn't." His voice still carried a trace of amusement, for his mind had not yet managed to join the dots of Mirrie's displeasure. "I only found it last winter." He put his hands on his hips and watched as she made a pretence of gazing from the window. "Did you carve our initials into your desk?"

She shook her head, so vigorously he thought he must be true.

"Who could have done it then?" He walked closer to her and leaned with elaborate casualness against the plastered wall.

"Jonah." She refused to meet his eye.

"Jonah?" This he had not expected. "Why?" He frowned with confusion.

Mirrie made another sound of exasperation. "Because he was teasing me, much as you are now. Both of you should know better. Especially you, Tristan, given we left the school room many summers since."

"Teasing you about what?" He was genuinely perplexed.

Mirrie stared at the floor until he began to think that she would not answer. But when she finally looked up, her eyes flashed with a new determination.

"Do you really not know?"

"I really don't." But oh, how he wanted to. He'd thought the initials might have been carved by Mirrie in some fit of childish fancy. But this seemed far more interesting.

Mirrie took a breath. "When I was younger, I held you in…some high esteem." Her eyes darted to his. "For a brief time."

"Held me in high esteem?" A smile curved about his lips. "Why Mirrie, do you mean—?"

"I might have believed myself a little bit in love with you." She stood with her arms and back straight, as if facing the dock.

The smile almost split his face in two. "Well, I never." He chuckled. "And Jonah knew this?"

She nodded grimly, her face resolute. "Frida too."

Tristan was enjoying himself immensely. "How come I never knew?"

Mirrie sighed, an unreadable emotion passing behind her eyes. "Because you rarely see what is right in front of you."

Far below them, an outer door slammed and a servant whistled as he went about his work. Mirrie and Tristan stood silently in the slanting sunlight, their eyes fixed on one another.

For a moment, Tristan felt unsteady on his feet, as if he stood on board a ship which rolled precariously upon the waves. Then the ship steadied, and 'twas as if the clouds parted and he basked in warmth, able to plot an onward course after so long wandering in the mists.

"Well, I see you now, Mirrie," he whispered.

CHAPTER THIRTEEN

S HE KNEW WHAT was about to happen, but she felt powerless to stop it.

In that moment, she didn't even want to stop it.

With one swift step, Tristan came to stand before her, placed his warm hands on either side of her face, and pressed his lips to hers.

His kiss was soft at first, but when she didn't pull away, he stroked one palm down the length of her spine and drew her closer, simultaneously increasing the pressure of his kiss. Mirrie was lost to the sensation of his hands holding her firmly and his mouth angled against her. Tristan's body was a wall of muscle, but his touch was gentle, easing away any tension inside her. Unable to help herself, she ran her hands up and over his broad shoulders. That seemed all the invitation he needed to brush the tip of his tongue against hers. Desire fizzed in her belly, making her feel both heavier and more alive than she had ever been before.

It was good and right to stand in the circle of his arms, safe from any storm. She raised herself on her tiptoes to press even closer, and Tristan made a noise at the back of his throat as his grip on her tightened.

That was when she came to her senses.

It took a massive effort of will to pull away from him. She staggered backwards, her breathing ragged and uneven.

"We mustn't," she said.

She didn't want to look at him, but her eyes moved upwards as if of their own accord. Tristan's bronzed face was flushed, his blue eyes dark with wanting. It was the first time she had ever seen him like this—as a man caught up in desire. The sight was powerfully arousing, but also a little frightening. She didn't know this version of him. But then he took a breath and the old Tristan returned.

"You are right, no doubt. Though it seems a shame."

Mirrie could hardly catch her breath. "I shall go back downstairs." She crossed her arms to stop herself from trembling.

"Nay, do not go." He pushed back a shock of golden hair and stood with one hand cupped around his neck. "I had the idea we were both enjoying it."

Darn him and his unshakable confidence.

"Was I mistaken?" he asked softly, his eyes holding her in a trap.

Mirrie bit down on her lip and tried to gather her thoughts.

Nay, he is not mistaken.

She could kiss him again, feel his hands upon her. Mayhap more besides. The prospect was powerfully tempting, especially when his full lips twitched upwards into a smile as if he could read the thoughts running through her mind.

But where would that lead them? To Tristan, Mirrie would be no more than another of his conquests. He would enjoy her and then leave her behind without another thought while he moved on to win over the next maiden. Whilst her heart would shatter into shards and never again heal.

She grasped for the right words to remedy this spiralling situation. "We risk too much."

"We do, for certain. You are right once again." He nodded as if in serious agreement. "I would not do aught to risk our friendship, Mirrie." He paused and sighed. "Though in truth, I cannot help but wonder if the risk might be worth the reward."

"Tristan, stop it." Her patience was at an end. "This is me

you're talking to."

"I know right well who you are, Mirrie."

"Do you?" She was cross now. "You don't know that I once waited all day for you to return from Lindum. I had on my nicest dress and hardly dared to move from the front steps in case it crumpled. But you arrived with some sister of a friend on your arm, and you didn't even notice me."

She was as surprised as Tristan at the force of this memory, bursting up from where she had buried it many years ago.

Tristan's eyes widened, but she wasn't finished.

"You don't know that every time you rode off to battle, I would spend hour after hour on my knees in the chapel, praying for your safe return."

You don't know that the main reason I accompanied Frida to Ember Hall was to get away from you. Because I realised long ago that you would never feel the same way about me. And it hurts. It hurts too much.

This last outburst went unspoken. She swallowed the words just in the nick of time, keeping them locked inside.

"You're right, I never knew those things." The glow of mischief left his eyes. "I feel I should apologise."

She tossed her head. "There is naught to apologise for. I know right well who *you* are. I have always known."

"And you have always held faith in me." It was a statement.

She pressed her lips together. "Almost always."

"Until now?" His tone was playful, but as soon as the words were spoken he held up his hands in apology. "Forgive me."

Mirrie resisted the urge to stamp her foot in anger. "My faith in you is challenged for good reason. It seems you have taken leave of your senses."

Tristan's voice rose to match hers. "On the contrary. It seems to me that I have just now learned what my senses must have been telling me for years."

I shouldn't ask. I definitely shouldn't ask.

"Which is what?" she demanded, knowing she played into his hands.

"That you are a beautiful woman, Mirrie." He made no move to come nearer, and somehow his words were more intimate precisely because of the physical distance between the two of them.

But she would not let him be her undoing. She had been protecting herself from Tristan's charms for years. One proper kiss could not break through her carefully constructed barriers.

"And you are a handsome man, Tristan," she echoed calmly. "But you don't need me to tell you that."

She had wounded him. She saw the flash of it in his eyes.

"Why are you so cross with me?"

Mirrie took a deep breath. "As I told you by the lake, you treat women like playthings." She held up a hand when he began to interject. "And I will not be one of them."

"You never would be," he protested.

"I am cross precisely because you don't see this for yourself." She wagged her finger at him. "You would risk all our years of friendship, and for what?" Despite her best efforts, her cheeks coloured as she thought about how she might finish that sentence.

"For the chance to see if we could be anything more. Whether that enquiry takes the form of another kiss, or perchance the courtship that rightly should have preceded this betrothal." Tristan leaned against the wall, his eyes fixed on hers. His sincerity delivered a hammer blow to the barriers around her heart. "Or am I truly too late? Do you no longer wait so keenly for my arrival, or pray for my safety?" He raised his eyebrows, questioningly.

"I will always pray for your safety." Mirrie's voice began to wobble. "And I anticipate your visits to Ember Hall with nothing but pleasure." She swallowed. "In the same way that Frida does."

"I see." Tristan smiled sadly, breaking the tension that had sprung up between them. "So you no longer believe yourself a little in love with me?"

"And Jonah no longer carves our initials into the furniture."

She deliberately made her voice light. "We all outgrow our childhood selves, sooner or later."

"That is a great pity." Tristan gave a dramatic sigh. "But if we cannot leave this room as lovers, we must depart it as friends." He held out a hand towards her, silently daring her to take it.

Mirrie did so, ignoring the jolt of awareness that struck her as soon as her fingers touched his.

"Friends," she repeated, with an emphatic nod.

"Unless you change your mind."

She tried to fix him with a scolding stare but saw immediately that he was teasing her. An impish smile chased across his chiselled features and his eyes were once again bluer than a summer sky.

"I shall let you know," she said, as breezily as she could manage.

He rewarded her with a grin before turning to close and fasten the shutters, returning the school room to darkness. Mirrie tried not to stare at his muscular arms reaching for the latch.

"Do you want to go down first?" he asked, his head turned away from her. "Before we lose the light."

It was a relief to walk away from temptation. At least, that was what Mirrie told herself as she crossed the bare wooden boards of the school room. It felt as if she descended to a colder, gloomier world. Every step down the stone staircase took her further from the memory of standing in Tristan's arms, his lips pressing against hers.

He desired me. She could not help but shiver at the thought. Whether she was right to rebuff his advances, she might never know. Part of her regretted it, wondering what might be happening to her at this very moment had she not backed out of his embrace.

And for what? Some misplaced notion of propriety? Or reputation? What value did her reputation hold for her when she would likely live the rest of her life as a spinster?

Standing at the bottom of the stairs, Mirrie was seized by a reckless impulse to run back up and throw herself into his arms. But it was too late. Tristan was already coming down behind her. He fastened the door and brushed the dust from his breeches.

"What a mess," he exclaimed ruefully. "I'm sorry. I didn't realise how dusty it would be up there."

She put a hand to her hair. "Do I look a state?" She dimly realised that it would not do to appear before the servants looking dishevelled.

The radiance of his smile was enough to make her knees weaken. "I told you just minutes ago that you are the most beautiful woman I have ever seen."

She pursed her lips and shook her head, even as her heart galloped beneath her kirtle. "You certainly did not."

"Well, words to that effect," he amended.

Mirrie dug her nails into her palms. "It would make me very happy, Tristan, if we never mentioned that conversation again."

Something flickered across his eyes, but his response was to bow low and take her elbow solicitously. "Can I remind you that when we sat on that window seat, over there"—he pointed as they passed on their way to the main staircase—"I told you that I wanted you to be happy?"

"Aye." She nodded her head but was not brave enough to meet his eye. "That is permitted." She came to a halt at the top of the sweeping stairs. "Where are we going?"

"To luncheon. I'm famished."

She did not think she could hold onto her composure during a long meal in the great hall. Her nerves were in tatters and she longed for some time alone.

"You must excuse me." She cast about in her mind for a reason to flee. "I had forgotten that I am to have a dress fitting ahead of the ball."

"That was arranged very quickly." He folded his arms and looked at her searchingly.

But Mirrie found she did not care if he believed her or not. "Aye. These things often are." She threw him an uncertain smile and turned tail, deploying all her remaining self-control to prevent herself from running headlong down the passageway.

She must put distance between herself and Tristan if she wanted to leave Wolvesley with her virtue intact.

But she was no longer sure if she cared about that.

SOME HOURS LATER, Mirrie had decided, somewhat regretfully, that it would not do to abandon her scruples. As a young woman who had made her life in the country these last years, she was no longer unduly concerned by notions of propriety. But she was very concerned by the condition of her own heart and soul.

Neither would come out of this unscathed, were she not to take steps to protect them, she reflected as she stood by the window in her bedchamber and gazed out over the paddocks. Her eyes kept focusing on the glinting surface of the lake, no matter how determinedly she turned them towards the trees. It was impossible for her to stop reliving what had occurred down by the shore.

When I kissed Tristan.

A chaste kiss. Nothing more. But 'twas undoubtedly the forerunner to all that had occurred afterwards, in the school room.

When things grew hot and tempting and decidedly less chaste.

Mirrie dug her nails into her palms and tried to get a hold of her errant thoughts.

Errant thoughts that had got her into this mess.

She wandered over to the dresser, drawn to a pretty vase of cornflowers that must have been placed there whilst she was out. The thoughtful gesture made her smile. Cornflowers had long been a favourite of hers. She loved the intricate detail and deep colour of their petals.

Mayhap because the blue was so close to the colour of Tristan's eyes.

Mirrie shook her head in frustration. For years she had managed her feelings for Tristan. Building barriers that she thought would last her a lifetime.

They had lasted less than three days.

She put a hand to her warm cheeks and walked purposefully towards her closet. Though she had lied to Tristan about a dress-fitting, it was true that she needed to find something to wear for the midsummer ball. Mayhap Molly could work her magic to update one of her old gowns? There were plenty to choose from.

She opened the door and was immediately assaulted by memories of the past. Long gowns of rippling silk trimmed with lace and fur, smooth to the touch and redolent of her youth. Growing up at Wolvesley meant a regular procession of balls and parties, and as she prepared for each, she would unfailingly think, *this is the time he will notice me.*

This dress.

This ball.

These jewels. *This* hairstyle.

So much agonizing hope followed days of devastating disappointment.

All of which had taught her a painful lesson; Tristan would never see her as anything more than a friend.

A good friend, aye. One that he might even profess to love *as a sister.* But his heart would never beat for Mirrie, the way her heart pounded for him.

She reached out to stroke the soft fur collar of a particularly beautiful gown of dusky pink silk. She had worn it for Beltane, she recalled. Tristan had danced with her and told her how pretty she looked. In those days long past, she had longed for time alone with him. Now she had such time in abundance, and it was exactly that which had brought her so close to danger.

She could no longer trust herself with him.

Even now, in the midst of her self-chastisement, part of her wondered where he was; what he was doing.

What might happen if she knocked upon his door?

She needed a witness to her actions; someone to keep her honest. Someone who already knew the depths of her feelings.

Or at least suspected them.

Mirrie paused for a moment, one hand on her closet door. If she wished to keep her virtue, nay, *her sanity*, she must act quickly.

She crossed to her writing desk, took up the quill and began to pen a message to Jonah.

CHAPTER FOURTEEN

T HE LADY WAS about to retire early, once again.

Tristan took a napkin from the Seneschal and cleaned his fingers, but all the while, his eyes were fixed on Mirrie, rising from her seat at the end of the table on the dais.

For almost a sennight now, she had done this. Arriving in the great hall just moments before his mother—almost as if she lay in wait behind a pillar. And leaving, just as soon as the sweetmeats were cleared away.

Mirrie curtsied to his parents and inclined her head towards him. Tristan nodded to her with equal dignity and a display of patience which cost his temper dearly. On the first night of this charade, Tristan had pushed back his own chair and courteously offered to escort her from the hall, but Mirrie had refused him.

Had *refused* him!

With impeccable politeness.

Tristan had always been a quick study. He did not believe in making the same mistake twice.

And so he sat and watched as Miss Mirabel walked graciously through the creeping tide of men-at-arms and disappeared through the high arched doorway. Just as she had for several nights now.

'Twas not even dark outside. God's bones, there was still at least an hour of daylight left to them. They could have walked in the gardens or played a game of cards. Trivial pastimes, the likes of which he had taken for granted all these years, along with Mirrie's ready smile and bubbling laugh.

All now denied to him.

His mother, dressed in a finely-embroidered gown of green silk, leaned towards him. "Mirrie denies there is aught wrong, so now I must ask the same question of you. Have you two exchanged cross words?" Her blonde eyebrows were raised towards Mirrie's departing back.

"We've exchanged no words at all," he growled.

Morwenna's look became severe. "What of your actions, then? Has aught occurred between you that should not have?"

"Of course not, Mother." He closed his mind to memories of their passionate embrace in the school room. After all, eye-opening as it was, he had done no more than kiss her. And they had spoken quite comfortably after, so it could not have been that which troubled her.

Looking puzzled, his mother sat back in her chair. She glanced sideways at his father, who was deep in conversation with the steward, then turned back to Tristan. "Mayhap she is anxious about the ball."

He threw her a look, just as the trio of musicians piped into a lively jig that could not have been more at odds with his mood. "Mirrie always looked forward to the Wolvesley balls." He drummed his fingers on the wooden trestle table. "Why should this one be any different?"

"Because of you," she replied softly. "'Tis one thing to desire the son and heir. Quite another to get him."

"Get him?" he echoed, his own eyebrows now shooting up beneath his thatch of hair. "What am I, Mother? A prize pig?" As if spurred on by his frustration, the musicians played faster, until Tristan wanted to roar at them to stop.

Morwenna hid her smile behind a napkin. "Oh, Tris, you know I didn't mean it like that." She dabbed at her lips, recovering her composure. "In any case, Esme and Jonah should be with us before dark. Hopefully they will bring Mirrie out of herself again."

Tristan made a non-committal noise. Jonah and Mirrie had always been close friends, although until that day in the school-room, Tristan had never suspected the two of them shared secrets behind his back. 'Twas ridiculous to experience envy towards his afflicted younger brother, but that was exactly the emotion surging through his veins.

It could not be borne.

He stood up abruptly, scraping back his chair and causing his father's conversation to cease. The earl glanced up towards him.

"Are you well, Tris?"

Tristan bowed. "I must take some air, Father. Is there aught I can do for you before I depart?"

Angus waved his hands in mock-exasperation. "Enough fussing, boy. I have your mother for that."

"You call it fussing. I call it love." His mother laid a hand over his father's. "And I won't be made to feel guilty over it."

"Quite right too, my dear." Angus lifted her hand and pressed it to his lips.

Such displays of affection between the earl and countess were hardly new, but tonight, Tristan had no stomach for them. He bowed again, then tripped down the steps from the dais and beat a hasty retreat from the great hall.

'Twas a great relief to hear the piping music fade once he reached the calm of the entrance hall. More soothing still to step out of the front door into a warm, welcoming evening. Birds twittered from the tree tops and horses whinnied from the paddocks, but these were merely background noises, giving him the space and quiet he needed to think. He took a deep breath and stood for a moment by the fountain, admiring the colourful reflections of the setting sun.

There was beauty enough here to fill his heart with joy, were it not already brimming over with frustration. He had ne'er known rejection to carry such a bitter sting, like a sharpened wedge tunnelling so deep inside him that he could hardly think of anything else.

Out of long habit, Tristan started walking towards the lake, but vivid memories of his last visit there with Mirrie made him swivel around and journey instead to the paddocks. He followed a faint rabbit path towards a group of grazing ponies, who swung their heads towards him and huffed out grass-scented breath over his extended palms. He rubbed their ears and talked to them gently, taking comfort in their kind, intelligent gazes.

It did not seem so long since he and his siblings had ridden on ponies like these, racing one another through the woods and acting out pretend battles with wooden swords and half-sized shields. Frida, he recalled, had been particularly dexterous with her wooden sword.

As he'd recalled up in the school room, on rare occasions, he had successfully persuaded Mirrie to join them, entreating her to sit up behind him on his fleet-footed pony with the reassurance that he would keep her safe.

Which he always had.

She would wrap her arms about his waist and hold on tightly as they galloped through the trees, squealing with excitement. She had enjoyed it, despite her trepidation, just as he'd known she would.

But left to herself, Mirrie would choose to watch their escapades from a distance, keeping herself tucked away, safe from the prospect of harm.

Much as she was doing right now.

Mirrie was going to great lengths to avoid being alone with him. Was it because she was avoiding temptation?

Tristan teased out the tangles in a particularly coarse mane as the pony grazed contentedly. The more he thought about it, the more he was sure this was right. He couldn't deny a grudging acknowledgement of the sense in this. It showed great self-discipline, but then, she had always been one for forethought and rationality.

Tristan gave the ponies a last pat before moving away. It didn't matter what he did or where he went, his thoughts endlessly circled back to Mirrie.

Hell's teeth, how was it he had only just noticed how pretty she was? Not in a sisterly way, but in a way that seemed designed with him in mind. They had always been friends, good friends. He had long thought of her as one of a worryingly small group of people who he could rely on to be unfailingly honest with him. In his sphere, flatterers and panderers were frequent, even amongst those he counted among his closest companions. Truth-telling was a rare gift.

And Mirrie had given it in abundance.

Tristan's evening walk had done him no favours at all. He was more out of sorts on his return than he had been watching Mirrie walk away from him in the great hall. Only one resolution shone through the tangled mess of his thoughts.

I must woo her.

And what better occasion than the midsummer ball, on the morrow?

Deep in contemplation, Tristan was oblivious to the bustle and excited chatter coming from the stable yard. 'Twas not until Esme barrelled into him, brightly-coloured ribbons flying out behind her, that he realised his siblings had arrived.

"Are you not going to greet us, Tris?"

"Esme." He embraced his sister, who seemed to grow more lovely with every day that passed. "Did you have a pleasant journey?" He noticed the carriage that had come to rest in the yard. Trunks were being unloaded from the back and Jonah's blond head bobbed about in the crowd of grooms and stableboys who had rushed out to help.

"Indeed we did not. One of our horses went lame at Belford and we were obliged to take shelter at Rossfarne Castle for what felt like an age. We should have been here in time for dinner."

"I am sure some food will be found for you," Tristan observed. "Why did you come by carriage? 'Tis much quicker to ride over the moors." He bent closer to her ear and lowered his voice. "Don't tell me that Jonah pleaded some frailty? He can ride as well as you or I."

"Nay, brother, 'twas not for Jonah's sake we took the carriage." Esme raised her finely shaped eyebrows. "We had company," she added in a whisper.

"Who?" Tristan was intrigued.

Esme took his arm and turned them both around in time to meet Jonah and a tall, brown-haired man who was walking uneasily by his side.

"Allow me to introduce my brother," she chirped prettily. "Lord Tristan de Neville, this is David Bryce. He's a physician recently come to the village near Ember Hall."

David Bryce bowed to Tristan. "It is my pleasure, my lord."

"Mr Bryce." Tristan nodded. The man's smile was wide, but it could not hide the tremor of anxiety in his hands, nor the sheen of perspiration on his brow.

Not a keen traveller, he concluded.

"Tris." This from Jonah, who dipped into the smallest of formal bows.

"Jonah." Tristan's greeting was equally lukewarm. "We do not oft see you at Wolvesley for these occasions."

"I thought to make an exception." Jonah inclined his head. "Also to bring David. I heard from Mother that there were some issues with the castle physician?"

"Aye, that is true enough."

The small group began walking towards the keep, through early evening shadows which lengthened around them.

"Does Father continue to recover?" Esme asked, taking his arm.

"He is almost back at full strength." Tristan gave her a reassuring smile.

"I am happy to hear it, my lord."

Tristan cast a glance at the physician. "Did you come prepared to treat him?"

He sensed Jonah's displeasure at the question, but could not guess why he bristled. Mr Bryce, however, answered readily enough. "I am always prepared for a patient."

"David is here as our guest." Jonah self-importantly cleared his throat. "He is a friend of Ember Hall. Frida and Mirabel both hold him in high esteem."

"You are too kind," muttered the physician.

Tristan threw him a smile, hoping to set him at ease. The man was as nervous as a hound expecting a beating. "That is praise indeed. My sister Frida does not readily place her trust in any physician."

Mr Bryce seemed to walk taller. "I have been pleased to treat little Miss Flora to Lady Frida's satisfaction."

"Excellent," Tristan replied, but his mind had taken flight elsewhere and he hardly heard as Jonah took up the mantle of extolling Mr Bryce's skills and experience.

Instead, he found himself recalling a conversation from the last time he visited Ember Hall.

Did Jonah not speak of a physician who had intentions towards Mirrie?

Tristan's pace increased as his memories sharpened into focus.

The physician's name had been David.

And this same man was now here, at Wolvesley Castle.

"You have a most marvellous home, milord," the physician said, resting a hand on his breast as his gaze swept around approvingly.

Tristan nodded; his thoughts not easily budged. Did a lowly physician really imagine he could court Mirrie?

His Mirrie?

Tristan nodded, making an outward show of attention as Jonah continued to list Mr Bryce's many virtues as a physician.

"It is possible he could take a second look at Father?" Jonah concluded.

Tristan's smile remained fixed in place. "You must ask Father yourself. I'm afraid he may be a little weary of physicians now." He fixed Mr Bryce with his gaze. "But by all means, make your enquiries. I will leave you in my brother's capable hands." He made a show of bowing to Jonah. "I have matters to attend to. You will find your way, of course?"

It was not really a question, but Esme answered it impatiently. "Jonah has not been back at Wolvesley for some time, Tristan. But have no fear. You go about your business, whatever it may be. I will play hostess while a servant fetches Mother." She took both men's arms in a proprietorial gesture and marched them in the direction of the great hall.

With relief, Tristan turned towards his father's solar, the room he was beginning to think of as his private retreat. Angus had not yet picked up the reins of earldom, and Tristan was enjoying taking on the duties in his stead. They gave his days shape and purpose.

But now, he had no intention of working, he merely wanted to be alone so that he could think more of his quest to woo Mirrie.

The stakes had just risen that little bit higher, and Tristan loved nothing more than a challenge.

CHAPTER FIFTEEN

MIRRIE HAD NEVER forgotten how magnificent Wolvesley Castle looked on the occasion of a feast or ball, but on this day, the opulence and grandeur held a special significance for her.

Firstly, because she had never before opened a Wolvesley ball by dancing with Tristan.

Secondly, because once events had taken their course, she might never see such splendour again. *Not for some time, anyway,* she corrected herself.

With that in mind, she paused for several seconds atop the sweeping staircase, breathing in the heady fragrance of wildflowers which had been wound about the pillars and scattered in vases about the entrance hall. Down the marbled corridor to the great hall, she could hear the excited chatter of assembled guests, together with the first melodious trills from a group of musicians that had been especially selected for this occasion. Liveried servants wore crisp, freshly laundered tunics paired with highly polished boots, their faces taut and professional as they offered up goblets of mead carried on silver trays. Mirrie did not allow her eyes to linger long on the giggling group of young ladies who had just ascended the steps to the keep. She knew that each and every one of them would be more attractive than she. Each and every one would be more fashionably attired.

Each and every one would wield a more proper claim to Tristan's attention than she ever could.

Her insecurities could rise up and ruin the evening, if she allowed them to.

"Lovely, isn't it?" Mirrie startled to find Esme by her side, linking an arm through hers. "I always think at these moments that 'tis as if the castle is holding its breath, waiting for something to happen," she added, dreamily.

"That's mighty fanciful, Esme," Mirrie commented, though she had been thinking along similar lines herself.

"Well, 'tis not only Jonah who has an appreciation of the finer things in life." Esme waved her free hand airily. "And we cannot all be practically-minded, like our dear Frida."

"No indeed." Mirrie did not try to hide her smile. Beside her, Esme was as bright and beautiful as a butterfly. No one could ever accuse the younger de Neville sister of being practically minded. Big-hearted and fun-loving; aye. But not the one you would choose to have by your side in a crisis.

But this was a ball, not a crisis, Mirrie told herself, even as her heart lurched for want of Frida's steadying company.

"You look lovely too, Mirrie." Esme's big blue eyes looked at her searchingly. "Wherever did you find that luscious gown? I feel quite plain in comparison."

Esme was resplendent in a gown of alternate deep blue overlaid with panels of gold silk. She would not have looked plain beside a peacock.

Mirrie looked down at the dusky pink dress, originally tailored for her many years ago, but updated and refreshed by Molly, who had worked night and day to make it suitable for tonight. She had expertly replaced the fur trim with delicate lacework and lengthened the skirts to achieve the flared cone-shape which was the height of fashion, even if it was also the height of impracticality. The bodice, tightened by Molly's determination and backed up by whalebones, made it difficult to take anything more than shallow breaths. This would have to be a night of low emotion and even lower exertion.

"'Tis an old one from my closet," she answered honestly.

"You know as well as I do, that I shall have little need for fine gowns after tonight," she added in a whisper.

Esme pursed her lips as they began to descend. "I have never been so clever as Frida or Isabella, but one thing I've learned over the years, Mirrie, is this." She paused dramatically, one dainty foot hovering in mid-air. "One simply never knows what is going to happen next."

Mirrie had been hoping for something more profound, but she covered her disappointment with a smile. "You are entirely correct." She nodded with all the emphasis that her restrictive gown and heavy headdress would allow.

They reached the bottom of the staircase and turned towards the great hall. Here, the swell of sound from music and conversation seemed so much louder. There was a rush of bodies, bright colours and almost tangible excitement. Mirrie breathed as deeply as she could, grateful for Esme's arm still linked with hers.

"Lady Esme de Neville and Miss Mirabel Duval," the Seneschal boomed.

Esme smiled and nodded, taking admiration from the crowd as her due, whilst Mirrie tried to hide her unease. She had not been expecting to make such a grand entrance, nor to receive such a reaction to it. The nearest guests sank to the floor in deep curtsies and low bows, leaving only a handful of high-ranking earls and countesses still standing.

And Tristan.

Her breath caught at the sight of him.

He was attired in an emerald-green tunic which glittered with gold thread. His hair swung about his shoulders like burnished bronze, his breeches were spotless white and his leather boots fit snugly about his muscular calves. When he walked towards her, she froze like a deer facing a hunter's arrow.

"Mirrie," he bowed as low as a servant approaching the earl. "And Esme." His sister received a pat on the shoulder. "How lovely you both look."

"Indeed we do," Esme responded breezily. "'Twas ne'er in

doubt." Her eyes skittered over her brother's and scanned the crowd behind him. "Excuse me, both of you, there are people I must say hello to."

"Is she looking for someone in particular?" Tristan murmured in her ear. He had come to stand by her side, somehow taking her arm in the process.

Mirrie still felt frozen into position. With great effort, she lifted her gaze to seek out Esme. "I can no longer see her."

"She disappeared in a trice." His lips twitched. "I begin to suspect my little sister has a secret lover here at Wolvesley. 'Twould explain why she was so cross when I told her she must leave for Ember Hall."

Mirrie was so aware of Tristan's proximity—of his masculine fragrance of sandalwood soap mixed with leather, of the way his powerful shoulder muscles rippled beneath his tunic—that she had little space left in her thoughts for Esme.

She nodded vaguely, before realising that more was expected of her.

"Esme is surely old enough to know her own mind." She stepped sideways, moving from the path of two splendidly-dressed young ladies who were deep in conversation.

Tristan's smile became rather fixed. "True enough, no doubt. But I fear my sister does not share the good sense and self-discipline necessary to make *knowing one's own mind* such a virtue."

Mirrie's mouth hung open. Surprise made her uncaring of curious eyes. "Are you cross with me, Tristan?"

He turned his shoulders, shielding her from the crowd and giving them at least the illusion of privacy. "'Tis a role reversal, is it not?" He looked down sombrely before his lips twitched. "I speak in jest, Mirrie, surely you know that?"

Her heart sank a little. For a brief moment she had glimpsed the possibility of change.

"But I have missed you, these last days," he whispered against the top of her head. "I have gotten the impression that *you* might be cross with *me*."

She could not help her gaze travelling upwards until it clashed with his. "Not cross," she managed, trying not to stare at the fullness of his lips.

Lips that pressed against mine with such passion.

"Not happy, either." He shrugged his shoulders with an appearance of pragmatism, before clasping both her hands inside his. "'Tis true, we wandered somewhat from the path of friendship." He held her a prisoner of his blue eyes until she felt a blush rise up to stain her cheeks. "And we found ourselves somewhere unfamiliar."

Is that a hint of nervousness? Not in his voice, nor in his eyes, but in a slight tremor that passed from his fingers to her.

He cleared his throat. "Perchance we need to work together, Mirrie, to find out where we are." His voice deepened. "And where we might go next?"

It was as if the noise and bustle of the great hall faded away to nothing. There was just Tristan, holding her hands, saying unexpected things.

She could only nod. Her mouth had turned too dry for her to speak.

"So you will not run from me, after the ball? You will stay close so we can talk?"

Now she saw urgency and sincerity in his eyes. Real, not imagined. She would ne'er have imagined this.

"So we can be truthful," he whispered, leaning so close she could see a faint line of stubble on his bronzed cheeks.

"I would like that," she managed to say. "After the ball. Not here."

God's bones, she could not have this conversation in front of so many witnesses. Not when she was also expected to dance and dine and smile.

Tristan waved to a servant and took two goblets of mead from a tray.

"To us." He passed one to her and held the other high.

"I do not think we should make such a toast," Mirrie said quickly. She did not think she should partake of too much mead either. She knew well enough how potent the brews were at Wolvesley.

"To our success in opening the ball." Tristan drained his goblet with a flourish. "My mother has been gesticulating at me e'er since you and Esme entered the room."

Mirrie was instantly flustered. "Then we should take our positions." Her hand trembled as she pushed her goblet, still full, back onto the tray of the bewildered servant.

Tristan winked. "Without delay."

He led her to the centre of the large dance floor. Usually this space was cluttered with tables and chairs, but all had been pushed back for the evening to allow space for dancing. The vast fireplace had been left unlit, but in place of blazing logs, blood-red roses had been arranged amidst the granite stone. The musicians paused, waiting for Tristan's nod, and the assembled guests fell to silence. Mirrie felt her limbs tingle with a feverish mix of nerves and excitement. This was all she had dreamed of and more.

She was about to dance with Tristan.

And Tristan wanted them to talk together, *truthfully*.

Even as her heart galloped, Mirrie bade herself to remain calm. She had been here before. So many times she had believed Tristan to be on the cusp of a declaration or e'en just a realisation that his feelings echoed her own. So many times she had been disappointed.

But only a fool would deny the beauty and wonder of this single moment in time. When Tristan's hands held hers. When his blue eyes shone with excitement, looking only at her. When their bodies moved as one, in time to the lilting melody of the musicians.

The crowd exhaled in collective approval as they picked up speed, Tristan's hip against hers as he lifted her in a spin. Mirrie felt a smile stretch across her lips. She had always loved dancing and Tristan was the perfect partner—perfectly in time; perfectly accurate in his steps. His nimble feet were always where they should be; his strong arms always ready to provide support.

All too soon, the music came to an end. Tristan bowed and she dipped into an answering curtsy, as applause rippled through the crowd. His lips brushed against her cheek, so lightly she could have imagined it.

"We did it," he said.

She smiled. She had no words left inside her.

"Come." He offered her his arm. "We should go and find refreshment."

Mirrie felt as if she were in a waking dream. Together, they walked through the crowd to a long table filled with drinks. He poured her a goblet of wine and she took it, uncaring of anything except Tristan's smile and how it seemed meant for her alone.

Can this be the moment I've so long been waiting for?

Just then, a tall, dark-haired beauty melted away from a group of guests stood by the hearth and walked proprietorially towards them.

"Tristan," she said. "Dearest. How grand you look in all your Wolvesley finery."

For a terrible moment, Mirrie thought this might be Juliana, returned to Wolvesley in a gown fit for a princess. But whereas Juliana's eyes held wisdom, this woman's eyes seemed devoid of any real feeling. The pearls around her neck shone with more warmth than the insincere smile she bestowed.

Mirrie immediately felt diminished. Dismissed even.

"Mirabel, this is Lady Susannah Grey. I trained alongside her brother at Lindum."

Of course you did, thought Mirrie.

Outwardly she smiled and dipped into a small curtsy.

"'Tis a pleasure to meet you," she said.

The woman's cool eyes raked over Mirrie's re-fashioned dress. "Likewise." Her attention then turned fully to Tristan. "You must come and talk with us, Tris. Jakob is insisting he won the joust at Forbisher last summer and I just know that isn't true."

A beat passed during which Mirrie truly believed that Tristan would refuse. But with naught more than an apologetic smile, he took Lady Susannah's proffered arm and was soon swept up in the chattering group. Before he disappeared from view, Lady Susannah placed a possessive hand on his shoulder, as if staking her claim. Tristan did naught to move it.

Mirrie thought she might be sick. She was glad to have refused the mead, otherwise the rolling in her stomach might have caused her e'en more embarrassment. She felt rather than saw dozens of curious, calculating eyes swing in her direction and once again wished that Frida was by her side.

If not Frida, then Isabella—who would detract from Mirrie's shame with her pure, unparalleled beauty.

Or Esme, who would bring a smile to her lips with some frivolous remark.

Or Jonah, who ne'er passed up on a chance to comment on Tristan's ill behaviour.

Mirrie dared to raise her eyes and look around in some desperation, but not a single ally was near. A peal of laughter from the group by the fireplace seemed entirely directed at her.

This cannot be borne.

Holding her head high, she slipped through the thronging crowd and out of the great hall. Tears prickled at the corners of her eyes as she marched down the marbled corridor, remembering how happy and excited she had been to parade in the opposite direction so very recently.

Not e'en Mirrie, with her low expectations of life and love, had anticipated a fall so swift and severe.

She steadfastly ignored the inquisitive gaze of Alfred, Tristan's manservant, who was waiting in the entrance hall. But the presence of so many maids at the foot of the stairs made her alter her planned course; instead of racing for the sanctuary of her bedchamber, she turned out of the front door and all but ran down the stone steps towards the fountain.

With her sobs masked by the splashing water, she gripped the stone basin and allowed her emotions to surface. Her shoulders shook and the ribbing in her bodice nipped at her flesh, but Mirrie's sadness was too raw to be easily subdued.

It had all been so much worse than she had feared.

Ne'er should she have allowed Tristan to break down the barriers around her heart.

She could only blame herself. He had promised merely an honest conversation, not a declaration of commitment. 'Twas her own fancies that had conjured the romance between them. And her own overblown emotions that were now summoning near hysteria over such a trifling event. But when Tristan turned away from her, toward the beautiful, wealthy woman, it had underlined to her the hopelessness of wishing for more.

Tristan was not meant for her.

And he never would be.

"Stupid woman," she muttered aloud, straightening her shoulders and dabbing at her eyes with her gloves. She could not return to the keep with red eyes and blotchy cheeks. Just how much of a laughingstock did she want to be?

The night air was blessedly warm, with a slight breeze that mussed her hair like a caress. She had no cause to return immediately; no wish, for sure, to re-enter the great hall. She could walk about the grounds. Or she could simply stay here, releasing her woes to the cold reflections of the fountain.

Mirrie leaned over to better judge her reflection. The night was too dark for details—lit only by stars and the blazing torches affixed to the outside of the keep—so the shimmering pool of water showed the blurred outline of an elegantly dressed young woman. An attractive young woman, even. One who might deserve a dance with a handsome man.

She removed a glove, dipped her hand into the cold water and swirled it around until her reflection dissolved and reformed. Then she splashed some of the water onto her hot cheeks, feeling better for it. Gradually, she came to be more herself; composed and controlled. She dried her hand on her skirts and replaced the glove, thinking more of practicality than appearance.

Much as she would like to stand out here forever, staring into the forgiving waters, she could not.

A more sensible plan would be to announce she had a headache and officially retire to her chamber.

Mirrie took a breath and turned back towards the keep, staggering backwards against the granite bowl of the fountain when she realised she was being watched.

"Forgive me," said a male voice. "I did not mean to startle you."

Mirrie put a hand to her heart. The man stood in the shadows and though she recognised the voice, she could not immediately place it.

"To whom do I speak?" she asked.

"'Tis only I, David Bryce." He came down the final steps until his face was faintly illuminated by a wall torch. "I was wondering if it was you standing there."

David. The physician from Ember Hall. Mirrie relaxed. He would mean her no harm.

"It is," she said without thinking. She gave a little laugh. "I mean, 'tis Mirabel."

"I know," he said softly. "Are you well, Mirabel?"

"Indeed." She squared her shoulders, grateful for the dim light which would hide her reddened eyes. "I was only partaking of the night air."

"'Tis a beautiful night." He came to a halt, a few paces from her side.

"Are you enjoying the ball?" she asked.

"Wolvesley Castle is as grand and welcoming as I could e'er have imagined. Grander even." He turned a little so he was looking back at the keep. Lights blazed in the windows whilst music and laughter spilled from the wing containing the great hall. "In truth, Mirrie, I ne'er could have imagined you came from such a place as this.

Mirrie gave an unladylike snort. "I can guess exactly what you mean."

"Can you?" He swung around to face her so abruptly that she reared back against the stone.

She reached for her composure. "Only that I am sure you have noted that I am happiest at Ember Hall, in surroundings much less grand."

David came closer. "May I?" He reached for her hand.

Mirrie let him take it, though trepidation was beginning to squeeze at her heart. The granite stone was cold against her dress and the spray from the fountain had begun to wet her hair. It felt like time to go inside.

"Mirabel, I hope you know that I have long admired you," David said in a rush.

Aye, she knew. Or at least, she had suspected it. But for long days now she had thought of naught but Tristan.

Mirrie swallowed, buying herself time. "I thank you for it."

"I am only a physician and must look to the practicalities of life. But now that I know your situation, I believe we might build a worthy life together."

Mirrie's heart seemed to become lodged in her throat. Here was the declaration she had longed for, but the wrong man was speaking the words. He squeezed her fingers, but she felt no spark between them.

She closed her eyes. This was all too much, coming so soon after the tumult of the ball. "I am tired, David," she said tersely. "Forgive me, can we speak more of this in the morn?"

"We can speak whenever pleases you." His brown eyes shone with earnestness. "I would devote the rest of my life to pleasing you, Mirabel, if you will allow me."

His face loomed closer and Mirrie was suddenly aware that he intended to kiss her, right here by the fountain. The very idea made her nauseous all over again. She ducked to the side and pulled her hands free of his grip.

"Good night," she said, pretending that no awkwardness existed between them.

"Until the morn," he called after her.

Mirrie picked up her skirts and returned to the keep, her eyes turned away from the servants and a group of guests milling in the entrance hall. As if sent by divine assistance, Molly met her at the foot of the stairs.

"May I be of help, miss?" the maid enquired.

"I have a headache, Molly. I must retire for the evening. Kindly get a message to the countess."

Molly bobbed into a curtsy. "Very well, miss."

Relieved, Mirrie began to climb the stairs, entirely oblivious of Tristan's eyes boring into her back.

CHAPTER SIXTEEN

TRISTAN FELT AS if he had been punched in the stomach. Though he was usually proud of his quick wit, it was taking a darned long time for him to make sense of anything he had just seen.

Mirrie, *his Mirrie*, standing by the fountain, kissing the dratted physician Jonah had brought from Ember Hall.

Tristan dragged a hand through his hair, shocked to find he was trembling.

He could not deny the truth of his own eyes. Though, the more he thought on it, the more he seized on the notion that he had not actually seen them kissing. He'd seen the man, David Bryce, *lean in* for a kiss, and at that very second Tristan had wheeled away from his position on the front steps and careered back inside the keep, as unsteady as a drunkard.

Mayhap the maids thought him well into his cups, for none of them approached him. He was left alone to replay the conversation he had not wanted to hear.

"I would devote the rest of my life to pleasing you, Mirabel, if you will allow me."

Tristan leaned back against the frescoed wall, hoping that by steadying his breathing he might tame the pounding in his head.

How did this happen?

One moment, she had been dancing with him, quite happily he'd thought. The next, she was walking from the great hall in a huff.

"Methinks your friend is jealous from the loss of your attention," Susannah had said, snidely.

He'd been ready with some quip about Mirrie's sweet temper, but then he realised that she was quickly disappearing down the corridor. Realization dawned; Mirrie had walked out on his mother's ball. All because he had turned his back on her for a moment to talk with some friends.

He was struck abruptly with awareness that in walking away from Mirrie, he had been rude, plain and simple. But it had been a shock to see Susannah. And not a nice one. Especially when his attention and intentions had been so thoroughly focused on Mirrie. In the heat of the moment, he had reacted impulsively in the hopes of keeping the situation from getting out of hand.

Susannah was not a woman who would tolerate coming second. And so, to deal with her more efficiently, he had made of show of treating her like the most important person in the room.

'Twas only a pretence. And only for a moment. Had Mirrie waited, as he'd expected her to, he'd have been back at her side before the next dance began.

"Bloody women," he muttered.

It was then he heard hurried footsteps and he looked up in time to see Mirrie speaking in a lowered voice to Molly, his mother's maid. Mirrie then ascended the stairs, whilst Molly trotted off to the great hall.

Tristan didn't wait long before he started after Mirrie, his long legs taking the familiar steps two at a time. He didn't care that people were watching him from the entrance hall.

He would not be made a cuckold in his own castle.

He caught up with her just before she turned the corner into the corridor that led to her bedchamber. Up here, the noise of the ball hardly permeated. It was as if they had entered a small, private world, where candles emitted a flickering light and peace prevailed.

"Mirrie," he called.

She paused for a moment, before ploughing on without even

glancing behind her. Tristan increased his pace, sensing instinctively that if she reached her bedchamber, she would bolt her door against him, and there would be no chance to speak with her before morning. Mirrie also broke into a run, but she was hampered by long skirts and he was more determined to meet his goal.

"Why are you running from me?" He put a hand on her door handle to prevent her from turning it. His breathing was fast and heavy, which only increased his exasperation.

Mirrie was also breathing hard. Her eyes were pink, he noted, as if she had been crying.

"I am running because I hoped to avoid this conversation." She folded her arms and took a step away from him.

"And why have you been crying?" he asked steadily.

She looked away and tightened her lips, causing his frustrations to give way entirely to concern. Nothing mattered more than Mirrie's happiness.

"Because I am a fool."

A beat of silence fell between them. Tristan shook his head. "Nay, you are no such thing."

Mirrie glanced up at him and the pain in her hazel eyes made him wince.

"I am sorry if I was the one to make you feel that way," he added, in a rush. "Why did you leave the ball? I thought we were going to talk."

Mirrie's laugh was the last thing he was expecting to hear. "I apologise, Tristan. I should have been more specific."

"What do you mean?" He fought against lowering his brows, choosing instead to flatten his back against the smooth wood of Mirrie's door and stretch his legs in front of him. "Tell me," he prompted.

She chewed on her lip, gazing at the floor to the left of his booted feet. "When you asked if we could talk, I thought you meant straight away."

He didn't follow. "We were about to dance."

Mirrie's face screwed up with impatience. "After the dance."

"You are cross because I took a moment to say hello to an old friend?" He raised an eyebrow.

"I am cross because you left my side to keep company with your mistress."

Her words struck him like an arrow through the heart. He opened his mouth to deny it, then closed it again.

Mirrie knows more of the world than I realised.

Mayhap she knows more of me *than I would like.*

"Heaven help me." She sank to her knees, hugging herself as if she had been wounded. Her voice wobbled. "I was right."

Tristan was filled with contrition. He sank to the floor beside her. "Susannah was once my mistress, that is correct," he said, humbly. "But not for some time now."

Mirrie sniffed, keeping her face turned resolutely away from him. "I believe she would like to be reinstated."

He couldn't keep from chuckling at her dry tone, but he quickly sobered. "That may be true. But these things require the consent of both parties." Greatly daring, he reached out and ran a finger down the curve of her cheek, causing her to turn to face him.

"And you do not give your consent?"

"I do not. Not to her. Not ever again." He shuffled closer to her, finding her hands amidst her rumpled skirts and intertwining their fingers. As always, a frisson of connection fizzed through him as his skin made contact with hers.

Mirrie's gaze held him steady. "Why not?"

"Because of you." 'Twas a relief to say it. "Because of you dear, sweet Mirrie. You are all I can think of now."

It no longer mattered that she had allowed another man to pay court to her. He cared naught for Mr David Bryce, physician. All that mattered was that he speak the truth of his heart.

But with her parted lips hovering inches from his own, Tristan would have had to be a saint to resist leaning in for a kiss. And Tristan had ne'er pretended to be a saint.

Placing one hand firmly behind her head, he leaned closer and claimed her mouth with his own. As before, the rightness of it flooded his senses. Mirrie moved against him, causing new flames of desire to ignite inside his belly. She smelled of lavender and something wild and sweet that he couldn't place. He closed his eyes and allowed the sensation of their lips brushing against each other to take over. It was all he needed. All he wanted. Until the moment he felt her hands stealing around his shoulders, then he wanted more.

Tristan wrapped his free arm around her waist and pulled her closer, slanting his mouth against hers and delving deeper. With every stroke of his tongue, he felt her yielding, until she was heavy and languorous against him, half sitting on his lap. Her hips brushed against the hardness of his desire. He ran his hands down her sides, pausing briefly at the undersides of her breasts and he ached to explore them without her dress in the way.

But it would not do to undress a lady out here in the corridor.

He pulled back, with effort. His hands were still dancing over her body. "Shall we go inside your chamber?"

Mirrie looked at him. From her position, her head was almost on a level with his. He thought he could see through her beautiful eyes right into her soul.

So busy was he, looking into her eyes, that he did not see her hand coming towards him until it was too late. Mirrie delivered a stinging slap across his cheek, before struggling to her feet.

"What was that for?" he demanded, more surprised than angry.

Mirrie shook her head violently. "I cannot talk to you." She lunged for the door.

"Oh yes, you damn well can." He sprang to his feet with the reflexes of a trained warrior and slipped inside the door before she could slam it shut.

"What is this now?" She flung her hands, palms facing upwards, towards him. "Will you ravish me against my will?"

"Of course I will not." He wanted to shout, but he forced

himself to hiss the words instead, not wishing to cause her further embarrassment by risking them being overheard.

Mirrie's eyes blazed. "You should not have followed me in here. But you care for no one but yourself and the immediate pleasure of the moment."

He blinked, not understanding. His cheek stung. "I don't know where I am with you, Mirrie. One moment you kiss me, as if you want me. The next you turn me away."

"And you are not used to being turned away."

For a moment her voice broke, and he thought her tears would be his final undoing. But then she straightened, staring him down with a type of hardened resolve he was more accustomed to seeing on a battlefield than in a woman's eyes.

"That is the only reason you take such an interest in me, Tristan. Because I am perchance the only woman you have ever wanted, who you have not had."

"God's blood, Mirabel. How will we ever know what we could be, if you will not allow us to try?"

Mirrie put her hands on her hips. "And trying means us coming in here. Kissing. And more." Her voice quavered. "Up there on the bed, where you will take your pleasure and leave me with a babe in my belly?"

"Nay." Shocked, he moved towards her. "I would never do that."

"'Trying,' to me, means conversation and getting to know one another, all over again. It means something finer and deeper than physical desire." She tore her eyes from his and rubbed at her temples. "It means telling the truth."

"Which is what I promised to do before we danced together." Tristan took a breath, trying to calm his emotions.

"Right." Mirrie nodded, as if she too were gathering her wits. "Shall I tell you something that is true, Tristan?"

"Please do." He folded his arms and looked at her expectantly.

Mirrie sniffed and walked over to the window. All was dark

beyond, but she made a show of looking out anyway. She shivered, despite the warmth of the evening, and he was about to search the chamber for a cloak or shawl, when she finally spoke up.

"It was true, what Jonah said back at Ember Hall," she said, dully, turning to face him.

"Jonah?" Tristan's eyebrows shot upwards. 'Twas the last name he wanted to hear. "What does he have to do with this?"

"You don't remember, do you?" Her tone was reproachful, but she took a few steps closer to him and rested her weight against the back of a carved wooden chair.

Tristan longed to sit down, but the only place was the bed and that did not seem appropriate. "Enlighten me, please."

Mirrie took a breath. "It was Esme who started it. She was talking about people's characters and how they are unchangeably fixed."

Tristan had no immediate memory of the conversation, but couldn't escape the idea he was not going to like whatever was coming next.

He scratched at his head, knowing he couldn't escape it. "And what did my dear brother say to that?"

Mirrie looked up, as if conjuring the memory from the air. "He said that you would always be impulsive and rash." She paused, wrapping her arms around herself. "And that I would forever be waiting upon you."

A beat passed. Tristan's first reaction was to feign amusement, but his smile died on his lips as Mirrie's words re-played inside his head. There was no avoiding the rush of pain that followed. "Is that what you really think?"

Mirrie's lips tightened. "Aye."

Tristan held up his hands. "After all I have done. Fighting. Negotiating. In France and in Scotland." His legs felt strangely weak, and his chest was growing tight. "That is your opinion of me."

Mirrie looked as if she might come toward him but changed

her mind. "There is no doubting your discipline on the battlefield, Tris. Nor your courage, nor your loyalty to your country." She floundered. "'Tis one of the reasons you are held in such high esteem, why heads turn when you walk into a room." She smiled, ruefully. "We all rely on you to do what is right."

His breathing became easier. "I am relieved to hear it."

"But off the battlefield, 'tis another matter entirely."

He raised his eyebrows. "I am the same man."

"You do not act as if you are." Mirrie's voice wobbled with emotion. "'Tis as if you leave your self-control in the armoury. You are impulsive. You take your pleasures without thinking of the consequences."

He gasped for air, like a fish caught on a beach. "That is a cruel assessment."

She bit down on her lip but met his gaze squarely. "'Tis fair."

He shook his head, trying to order his muddled thoughts and mount a defence, but deep in his bones he knew that Mirrie's words had the ring of truth.

You leave your self-control in the armoury.

In a way, he did. 'Twas a way to pick up the reins of domestic life after seeing horrors on the battlefield. To drink and feast and aye, *take his pleasures* so that the roaring in his ears—of battle cries and clashing metal, of injured men and dying horses—would begin to fade. A habit formed when he was but a youth. One that had become engrained.

He shook his head again, attempting to dislodge the blood-red images taking root in his mind.

"Mayhap you are right, Mirrie," he said, his voice was sharp with remembered pain. "Thank you for bringing this to my attention. I shall endeavour to do better."

Mirrie made a sound between a laugh and a cry. "I beg you not to make promises you cannot keep."

"Who says I cannot keep my promises?" Tristan's bewilderment turned to anger. "Do you have such little faith in me?"

Mirrie walked back over to the darkened window, her shoulders hunched. "Of course I have faith in you. All of England keeps faith in you."

He longed to move closer to her but felt forbidden from doing so. "But do you only have faith in me as a knight? Or as a man, speaking to you as simply and honestly as I know how?"

It took all his inner strength to keep his voice from trembling. So much depended on her answer. But as Mirrie's gaze remained fixed on the darkened lawns, he realised that she was not going to grant the reprieve he sought.

The injustice stung, like a blade slicing through his ribs. Tristan bade himself remain calm. "I am sorry to be such a disappointment," he declared. "For my part, I have always kept faith in you, Mirrie."

He left the bedchamber and didn't look back.

CHAPTER SEVENTEEN

MIRRIE AWOKE FEELING that she could not face the morn. 'Twas another beautiful day; she could see the sun peaking behind the shutters. But every bit of her body ached with a pain that was not only physical. A deep weariness, sadness even, had taken root in her soul; a weariness that was better suited to the shadows of her bedchamber, than to the brightness outside of it.

She would languish in here for as long as she could get away with.

Mirrie pulled the covers over her head and sighed, willing sleep to come and reclaim her so she did not have to replay the events of last night in her head.

I slapped Tristan.

And David all but asked for my hand.

She could not help but groan out loud at the mess of it all. How had such tangles formed around her, so quickly? As a child, she had once become caught in vine weed whilst swimming in the lake. One moment all had been well, the next, she felt her ankle ensnared in something rope-like that she could not escape, no matter how she twisted and tugged.

'Twas Tristan who saved her, diving down beneath the surface with a sharp stone to cut her free.

She shook away the memory. It would certainly not be Tristan who saved her from this particular tangle. He was the root cause of most of it.

A knock sounded on her bedchamber door and Mirrie held herself still and quiet, hoping that whoever it was would simply walk away. She closed her eyes as the door swung open and tentative footsteps approached the bed.

"Miss Mirrie?"

Was she to be denied any peace at all?

"Yes," she croaked.

"I have a message for you, miss."

Mirrie opened her eyes to find Molly standing by her bed. "Who is it from?" she mumbled.

If it is from Tristan, I want naught to do with it.

"I dunno, miss, 'twas waiting for you in the hall. I thought I would bring it up, together with something to break your fast." She gestured to the night stand behind her, which bore a tray of foodstuffs and a pitcher of ale.

"My insistence on not having a maid assigned to me has caused your own workload to increase." Mirrie shook her head regretfully, then winced at the pain.

"Never mind that, miss. Will you read the message now?"

"I'll take it." She held out her hand for the parchment, but the rest of her stayed resolutely under the covers.

"Let me just open the shutters," the maid said, comfortably.

"Nay, please do not." Mirrie saw Molly's surprise and added, "I have a headache."

Molly tutted. "A headache which will only worsen if you try to read in such poor light."

Mirrie could not argue with that. She pushed herself up onto the pillows and shaded her eyes as brightness streamed into the chamber. Molly stood almost exactly where Mirrie had been when she refused to tell Tristan she had faith in him *as a man.*

She swallowed down a rising swell of grief. "Thank you, Molly."

The experienced maid took the hint. "I'll leave you now then, miss."

Mirrie unfolded the parchment and recognised Jonah's hand

with a burst of emotion she told herself was relief.

Dearest Mirrie,

Is this all my fault? I fear it may be. Come and talk to me. Please. I'll be waiting in the old bakehouse.

J

Mirrie sighed with exasperation and crumpled the parchment in her hand. The last thing she needed to be tasked with was assuaging Jonah's conscience.

She swung her legs down to the floor, averting her gaze from hairpins scattered on the dresser; mementos of the ill-fated ball. The last time she'd dressed in this chamber, she had needed the assistance of two maids to make her as elegant and feminine as possible.

Looking elegant and feminine hadn't worked out too well.

She decided against ringing the bell for Molly or one of the other maids to come and help her dress. Instead, she rummaged in the closet until she located the shapeless woollen gown she'd worn for that long-ago ride from Ember Hall. 'Twas not really that long ago, she ruminated. It only felt like it. Next came braccae, which she'd worn to ward off the cold several winters past. Her hair, she made an attempt at combing, but then left loose to tumble wilfully over her shoulders.

By all that was holy, it felt good to abandon her pretence at airs and graces and go about Wolvesley dressed as her true self.

Mirrie didn't pause to break her fast. Her stomach was still in knots from last night, and any food or drink would only increase her nausea. But she held her head high as she tripped down the stairs and out into the freshness of another midsummer morn. Servants nodded to her as she passed; not one of them seemed to stare at her outfit or giggle behind her back.

She should have done this long ago.

She passed the fountain, noticing that the almost unbearable glare of bright sunlight in its foaming waters had, this morn, softened into something paler. Overhead, fluffy white clouds were gathering around the sun. Mayhap they would finally have some rain.

Rain would match my mood.

Mirrie let her arms swing by her side as she walked along the side of the keep to the cluster of low-ceilinged wattle-and-daub outbuildings, that included the old bakehouse.

She came to a halt in the doorway and folded her arms across her chest. "This is a curious place for a meeting."

Jonah was perched on a little stool which Frida used to sit upon to chop herbs and grind pastes. The old bakehouse had not been used for its original purpose for many years. But before her accident and subsequent move to Ember Hall, Frida had taken over the little room and used it as a store for her herbs and healing salves. The fusty air still carried the tang of comfrey and mint, even though Frida had ensured every last jar was transported along with her other belongings to Ember Hall. The wooden shelves now stood empty. In fact, Mirrie thought them a little forlorn.

Jonah sat beside the only window, which was rather grimy. Mirrie had no wish to venture further inside and risk getting cobwebs caught in her hair, but Jonah beckoned her with a frantic gesture she could not ignore.

"Close the door behind you," he insisted. His blue eyes were even wilder than usual.

"What is this about?"

"I want to make sure we're not overheard." He shot her a look. "For your sake, Mirrie."

She leaned back against a cleanish patch of wall and folded her arms again. "I am not aware that I have anything to be ashamed of."

Despite the steadiness of her words, inside she quailed in case word had gotten out about her and Tristan's kisses last night. Just about anyone could have seen them.

"I would never suggest otherwise," he answered smoothly.

He dragged a hand through his hair, a gesture horribly reminiscent of his older brother. The two were more alike than they would ever admit. "I meant about David."

"Oh." Mirrie was momentarily nonplussed, but this soon turned to exasperation. "Why did you bring him here? Did you not think things were complicated enough?"

"Aye." Jonah nodded gravely. "That is what I want to apologise for. 'Twas all my idea, after all."

"It was." Mirrie nodded as the memories clicked into place. A surge of anger took hold and she found herself deepening her voice in a mocking parody of Jonah. "Tell Mother and Father you've already found true love. You've missed life at Wolvesley, Mirrie. Why not return on Tristan's arm and tell the world you love him?"

"Well, I never said *that*," Jonah commented mildly, arching his eyebrows.

"It's a mess." She covered her hot face with her hands.

"I'm sorry." She could hear sincerity in his voice. "I admit, part of me thought that if you and Tristan spent enough time together—" He left the sentence unfinished.

"You thought wrong," she said in a small voice. "But then, why bring David here?" She flung her arms wide, flinching when her fingers dislodged a spider.

"I shouldn't have." Jonah leaned closer. "But you wrote to me, Mirrie, saying how bad things had become." He shrugged. "So I thought, why not?"

A beat passed, in which Mirrie tried and failed to control her rising temper. "Why not?" she repeated.

Jonah began to tick things off on his fingers. "You're a beautiful woman. You've always wanted children of your own. And next winter you will be six and twenty."

"All of that is true, Jonah." She sighed. "And all of that is irrelevant."

"David would give you a home and a family."

Mirrie covered her face with her hands again. "I know that."

"Mayhap his interest in you was piqued when he learned the identity of your guardian, and mayhap he is more than a little motivated by coin. But such considerations could be said to be a credit to his rationality. His tendency to think things through carefully." Jonah opened his hands. "A trait he shares with your good self."

Her stomach churned as if she might be sick.

"Jonah," she warned.

"When you calculate the sum of it, David Bryce is a good man. A reliable man."

"I know that, too," she shouted. "He is reliable and steady and all of the things that Tristan is not."

There was a scuffle from outside the window, like footsteps. Mirrie's blood ran cold. Was someone listening? She leaned forward to see, but Jonah held out a hand to keep her back. "'Tis just a group of stableboys," he whispered. But he hauled himself up from the stool, as if their conversation was at a close.

"So you will accept David's offer?" His tone was matter-of-fact.

Mirrie looked at him as if he was mad. "I will do no such thing."

"But you just said he was reliable and steady." Jonah pursed his lips.

Frustration surged inside her. "I don't want a man who is reliable and steady. I only want Tristan."

A beat passed, giving Mirrie more than enough time to regret her outburst. Jonah's gaze went once to the open window, then settled on her face. "Despite all he has done to anger you?"

"Tristan is all I have ever wanted." She felt weak as a kitten as the sustaining anger slowly drained away from her. "But things between us are impossible." Her hands wrung together. "It would be better if I returned straight away to Ember Hall. Can we do that, Jonah? Please?"

She was asking a lot, but Mirrie rarely asked anything of anyone. Surely just one of the de Neville siblings could prioritise her interests this one time?

"Whatever you want." Jonah took her hands, but a frown clouded his brow. "But are you sure you're doing the right thing? I am no expert in love, but I understand that compromise is important. We cannot always have what we want."

Mirrie nodded, shakily. "I know what I'm doing," she assured him. "'Tis a funny thing, Jonah, but on this point, I believe Tristan has been right all along. No one should marry for less than love."

TRISTAN WALKED AWAY from the old bakehouse without any clear idea of where he was going. It had been a foolish idea, he ruminated angrily. He should have known better than to put his trust in Jonah.

He kicked at a fallen branch, taking satisfaction in seeing it skitter into the long grass.

Jonah had gone out of his way to lead Mirrie to a declaration of feeling for the physician. 'Twas as if he had wanted Tristan to be listening outside, for the whole purpose of humiliating him.

His quest was accomplished. For Tristan had ne'er been more humiliated.

Nor angry. Nor seized with such a fierce desire to break something.

He walked until he reached the lake. Then he followed the winding path all the way around the perimeter, paying no attention to the birdsong or the rippling reflections. He was in no mood for the glories of nature. On his way back to the keep, he found Jonah sitting on a low stone wall, apparently waiting for him.

"You left too soon," his younger brother announced, without preamble.

Tristan folded his arms and regarded him. They had never

been close. But nor had he ever before considered Jonah his enemy.

"What did I miss?" He kept his tone neutral.

Jonah was twisting a blade of grass in his long, slender fingers. "She said she loved you."

Tristan's eyebrows shot up. "She said those exact words?"

His brother squirmed on the stone wall. "Mayhap not those exact words." He frowned in concentration. "She said you were all she has ever wanted. And that she would not marry for less than love."

Tristan let out a low laugh. "I agree on that score."

"I tell you, if you had not dashed away, you would have heard her declare her feelings for you." Jonah shaded his eyes from the sun and looked up at him. "Do I need to say more to convince you?"

"Nay." Tristan widened his stance. "But I am not convinced."

Jonah sighed. "Well, 'tis your loss, brother. Mirrie wants to return to Ember Hall, right away."

Sorrow clutched at his heart, but anger tossed its claws away. "With you at her side, to offer comfort?"

"There is no cause for jealousy between us," Jonah said, equably. "Yes. I will return alongside her. I would not allow her to make the journey alone."

"What about your physician?"

"David?" Jonah pursed his lips. "I cannot answer for him. Mayhap the man will not want to share a carriage with a woman who so recently spurned his advances."

Tristan raised a hand to stop him. "Mirrie spurned his advances?"

Jonah shrugged. "I cannot say. All I know is what I already told you. Mirrie has said she is not willing to marry for less than love. And for some reason, brother, she persists in loving you and no other."

His words fell like summer raindrops on Tristan's shoulders. They were irritating but easy to ignore. Jonah knew nothing;

could tell him nothing. He had far better return to Ember Hall and stop meddling in Tristan's life.

He nodded with a show of formality to his brother. "I wish you a pleasant journey."

Jonah cocked an eyebrow. "Is that a dismissal?"

Tristan would not be goaded. "You are welcome to treat it as such." He turned with deliberate slowness to face the lake.

"Very well." There was a pause, filled with scuffling noises indicating that Jonah was heaving himself upright. "I would say that it was nice seeing you, Tris, but that would be a lie. Try not to upset anyone else."

By the time Tristan had framed a suitable response, Jonah was already walking away. Walking with as much speed as he could manage, Tristan noticed. A wry smile curved his lips. Was his younger brother worried that he would chase him down and deliver a punch for his troubles?

It's a little bit tempting.

Instead, he picked up a different path to the paddocks and walked slowly, being in no particular rush to arrive anywhere. He had learned little from Jonah. The snippets his brother had claimed as fact, Tristan was not willing to believe.

He had already been made a fool of once. Twice.

He shook his head. If Mirrie wanted to marry the physician, the *reliable and steady man*, then she was welcome to him.

There was naught he could do to stop her, after all.

He crested a hill and for the first time, knew a sinking feeling when the granite battlements of the keep came into view. Those solid walls had always been a place of sanctuary. Of happiness.

Mayhap things would go back to normal when Mirrie returned to Ember Hall?

But the prospect brought him no lurch of anticipation.

Tristan's temper had soured further by the time he reached the castle gardens. He was in no mood at all to encounter Mirrie's physician lurking by the rose bushes.

The man straightened up when he saw Tristan, dipping into a

bow and having the grace to look discomfited.

"I was just admiring the rose bushes, my lord."

"Indeed." Tristan squared his shoulders. "And are you an expert at horticulture, Mr Bryce?"

"Nay, not at all. Only insofar as knowing what herbs and plants can be put to use in my professional field."

"Ah, yes." Tristan began walking back to the keep. To his immense irritation, David Bryce kept pace with him. "Your professional field. You are a physician, are you not?"

"I am, my lord."

"And do you enjoy your work?"

"Very much."

Tristan halted. The beginnings of an idea were taking shape in Tristan's mind. "Yet you live close by Ember Hall. Is there much call for a physician so far north?"

David Bryce tightened his lips regretfully. "Alas, not so much."

"We have great need for a new physician here at Wolvesley." Tristan kept his voice light. "But I assume you have obligations to keep you further north. Family, perchance?"

"No family, my lord." The man simpered. "'Twould be an honour indeed to work at Wolvesley."

Tristan smiled. What he was about to do was wrong, mayhap. But cross as he was with her, he still had a role to play as Mirrie's protector.

If this man had intentions towards Mirrie, Tristan would do well to test the strength of them.

"'Tis a demanding role." He pretended to pause to think. "We would need to see if you would suit."

"Of course." The physician nodded eagerly.

"The salary, of course, reflects the post." He named the sum, which he knew would exceed the man's current earnings.

David Bryce's eyes opened even wider.

Tristan began walking again. They had all but reached the steps of the keep. He glanced at the fountain and the memory of what he had witnessed there last night caused him such a surge of rage that he almost dunked Mr Bryce headfirst into the pool.

Instead he swivelled around, pretending to enjoy the view. "Would that be amenable to you?" he asked, calmly.

"Very much, my lord."

Tristan wanted to get away from this man, but his test was not yet complete. He put his hands behind his back and forced himself to walk steadily up the stone steps.

"And would an immediate start be possible?"

"I am at your disposal." The physician smiled again. Evidently the prospect of so much coin had put him in an excellent humour.

"Are you sure?" He frowned in a pretence at concern. "I know that Miss Mirabel and Lord Jonah plan to return to Ember Hall later today. Do you not wish to accompany them? To gather your belongings, or say your goodbyes?" He lingered long over the last suggestion.

But Mr Bryce appeared still caught up in contemplation of the promised coin. "There is naught to return for," he announced. "If it pleases your lordship, I will begin straight away."

"It pleases me." Tristan waved to the passing Seneschal. "This man will see you settled in." He raised his eyebrows and the Seneschal bowed his acquiescence. "Please excuse me, gentlemen, I have business to attend to."

Tristan had never walked away from anyone with such speed.

As much as Mr Bryce's avarice left him cold, he calculated Mirrie's foolishness as the greater crime. The woman had accepted advances from a man who weighed her against coin and found her lacking.

As far as Tristan could see, he had provided her with a lucky escape.

Later that morn, when Jonah and Mirrie departed in the carriage, he did not join the rest of his family in waving them off.

He told himself that he hardly even noticed them leave.

CHAPTER EIGHTEEN

Frida's bedchamber was a haven of peace. The polished wooden furniture seemed to glow in the sunshine whilst a warm breeze brought the fragrance of summer grass in through the open window. Frida sat up in bed, looking tired but happy.

"She's such a dear little thing." Mirrie hovered over the walnut cradle and gazed into the sleeping face of Frida's new baby.

"Aye, but she has a good pair of lungs on her. You mark my words, you'll be wanting to head back to Wolvesley Castle for a bit of peace before the sun rises on the morrow."

Callum's ready smile belied his words. He stood by Frida's side, one hand on her shoulder, beaming down at his little daughter, born on midsummer's eve.

While Mirrie had been arguing with Tristan, Frida had been far more fruitfully engaged. And now that Mirrie was back at Ember Hall, enmeshed once more into the daily fabric of domestic life, she had trouble convincing herself that the whole Wolvesley interlude had not been some dangerous dream.

"What will you call her?" Mirrie extended a gentle finger and stroked the baby's small, rounded cheek.

Frida and Callum exchanged glances.

"We thought we might call her Mirabel," Frida said, tentatively.

Mirrie knew a rush of joy, a marked contrast to the self-flagellation and despair she'd known recently. "Truly?" She put a hand to her heart, unsure if she had heard correctly.

"Truly." Frida nodded emphatically and reached for Mirrie's hand. "After my dearest friend."

"Oh, Frida." Happy tears brimmed at the corners of her eyes.

"But we'll call her Merry for short, so as not to confuse folk." Callum twinkled at her.

"Perfect," Mirrie breathed. She summoned a smile, determined to keep at bay any strong emotions which might threaten her hard-won composure. "Are you sure this is not some ruse to ensure I take my turn in caring for the babe?"

"Of course not." Frida's blue eyes opened wide with denial.

Mirrie squeezed her hand. "Good. Because it is not necessary. I would be honoured to share in her up-bringing, whatever she was named."

Especially as I am unlikely to have any babies of my own.

Pushing the intrusive thought away, Mirrie leaned over and kissed her friend. "I should let you rest."

"I'll come with you, Mirrie." Callum patted his wife's arm. "You will call me if you need anything, dearest?"

"I will." Frida smiled serenely at both of them, as they picked their way out of the bedchamber.

They walked down the wide staircase together. The hall was quiet around them, as if giving Mirrie time and space to think.

"Callum, may I speak with you a moment?" she asked, seizing the moment.

"Aye, lass. Whatever is it?" The big highlander looked at her in concern.

"Nothing ails me," she reassured him. They had reached the bottom of the stairs and she checked to ensure the great hall was empty.

It was, bar a familiar hound slumbering in a patch of sunlight.

"Shall we sit, for a moment?" she suggested.

"Whatever you wish." He followed her into the hall and lowered himself into an adjacent chair. "You have me apprehensive."

"There is no need." She smoothed her skirts over her knees, thinking again how much more comfortable she was in the plain woollen work gowns which she habitually wore at Ember Hall. It had not suited her to be dressed in finery; a doll masquerading as the prospective bride of Lord Tristan de Neville. She sat up straight in the tapestried chair and met Callum's enquiring gaze. "I would like to take on more responsibility in the running of the estate."

His brown eyes widened with surprise. Mirrie swallowed down her nerves and spoke on before he could react further.

"Frida will be increasingly taken up with the children, as is only right. And there is more I could do, out on the land, I'm sure of it. I know I'm only a woman—"

She trailed off as Callum's face broke into a broad smile. "You mistake me, lass. What you saw then was relief. I thought you might be after telling me that you wanted to return to Wolvesley Castle."

"Nay." She pursed her lips and shook her head firmly. "That is the last thing I want."

"Very well." Callum linked his hands together and cleared his throat. "Your request is timely, as it happens. I've recently received word that my father is ailing." He paused and put a hand to his head, but not before she had seen his kind brown eyes awash with emotion.

Mirrie looked away to give him time to recover. Through the open windows she could spy the blushing pink petals of climbing roses. If she concentrated, she could even discern their heady perfume wafting through the hall.

But that only put her in mind of her conversation with Tristan, by the rose gardens at Wolvesley, and she fixed her gaze on the wooden floor instead.

"Your father is the Laird of Kielder, is he not?" she prompted, gently.

"Aye. He has responsibility for a great deal of land and a great many lives within it." Callum scratched at his bushy beard. "And I am his only heir."

Mirrie sat silently for a moment, digesting this. "You are returning to Scotland?" She tried hard to keep her voice level.

"Not yet. But I believe that time may come."

"Does Frida know?" she whispered.

Callum nodded. "We keep no secrets from one another." He sat forward with a display of fortitude. "Methinks I spoke of this too gravely. 'Tis not all bad. Our countries have known an uneasy peace since the Bruce's death."

"But much is still unknown about the intentions of the young king." Mirrie twisted her hands together, thinking of the innocent baby upstairs along with Flora and Christopher, the babe's two young siblings.

Callum inclined his head. "I can see your worries, Mirrie. And I can see the sense in them. But you forget one thing." His tone grew jocular.

"And what is that?" Mirrie smiled in return.

"I am brother-in-law to Tristan de Neville. England's greatest knight. Scotland's greatest ally." Callum sat back in his chair with a chuckle.

"Ah, yes. How could I forget?" Mirrie made a show of tidying her hair until she had her face better under control.

I can ne'er escape Tristan. His name and memory dog my heels.

"As to your wish to take a greater role in the life of Ember Hall, I can only thank you with the greatest sincerity. You have always been a hard worker; 'twas one of the first things I noticed about you."

They shared a smile, both remembering Callum's first visit to Ember Hall when he masqueraded as a knight under Tristan's command—when in fact, his orders had come from Robert the Bruce himself.

Much had changed since then. But Frida and Callum had loved each other passionately, undeniably, from their very first meeting. Loved each other despite all the challenges they faced. And that love, ultimately, had triumphed over all.

Their story was not Mirrie and Tristan's story.

Mirrie took a breath. "I should like to take on more responsibility with the land. Mayhap with bringing in the harvest."

Callum looked at her closely. "'Tis hard, physical work. There is much you can do away from the harvest."

"I need to do something new and different," she interrupted. She crossed her arms and tried to project strength and resolve. "Do not ask me why."

"Very well," he nodded slowly, his long fingers drumming on the arm of his chair. "But allow me to say this, Mirrie?" His voice gentled.

She looked away from him. "What is it?"

"Should your wishes ever change." He shrugged his muscular shoulders. "Should you decide, perchance, that your happiness lies elsewhere than Ember Hall, you must give me your word that you will grasp that future with both hands."

A weary smile tugged at her lips. "That is most unlikely."

"Sir Callum Baine claiming the hand of Lady Frida de Neville was most unlikely," Callum pointed out. "We none of us know what the good Lord has in store for us. All I ask is that you do not feel beholden to us here. Whatever happens in Kielder, we shall manage."

She straightened her shoulders and met his concerned gaze. "You have my word."

"That is all I ask." He stood up and clasped her shoulder in a brotherly gesture. "We have all missed you, Mirrie."

She patted his hand, her eyes clouding with tears. "As I have missed all of you."

And I shall never leave you again, she vowed.

TRISTAN HAD SCARCELY noticed the decorations for the midsummer ball being set up, but he seemed unable to escape them now.

Whenever he walked down the main staircase, the wild flowers strewn about the marble pillars in the hall made his fists clench in frustration.

"God's bones, Mother. When will this mess be cleared away?" he burst out one morn.

Morwenna had been on her way to his father's solar, but now she turned to face him. "I had asked specifically for them to remain in place until the petals begin to wilt." Her voice was mild. "But as they put you in such a perverse temper, I will order their removal this very day."

Tristan put a hand over his eyes, immediately contrite but still grappling with waves of frustration. "If the sight of them pleases you, then pay me no heed."

"You are my beloved son. I pay you every heed." Morwenna took his arm. "Come, let us not waste the day indoors. Walk with me in the gardens."

He had little choice but to accompany her out into another lovely day at Wolvesley Castle. The sky was bluer than the sea and the fountain sent up jets of sparkling water which caught the rays of the sun and refracted them back in all the colours of the rainbow.

But Tristan's temper was not appeased.

"Forgive me, Mother, but I cannot walk with you for long. I have much to do before luncheon."

"Tell me more. Perchance I can help." She smiled up at him, the very picture of serenity, robed in a simple gown of pale blue with her blonde hair neatly plaited about her head.

Tristan swallowed down his instinctive refusal. For all his mother's quietude, he knew her life had not been easy. And after his father's recent ill health, Tristan should know more than anyone not to take either the presence, or the support, of his parents for granted.

They were walking, by long habit, on the winding path which led up through the paddocks. Morwenna had always been happiest and most relaxed around horses. Tristan also felt some of the weight on his shoulders decreasing as he greeted his favourite charger.

"He's looking well," Morwenna commented, running her pale hands over his sleek, black neck.

"I imagine he is bored, as I am," Tristan retorted.

Morwenna made no attempt to hide her smile. "Is it the battlefield you both miss? All that blood and danger?"

At this moment, he would quite happily take the ugliness of a battlefield over the unfathomable machinations of his own mind.

Although he could never miss all the death and destruction that battle brought, even when one fought on the winning side.

He sighed, momentarily lost in thought. "There is something to be said for the clear singularity of purpose one feels at such a time."

"Truly?" Morwenna raised her eyebrows. "You do not enjoy this hard-won period of peace we are enjoying? A peace you had such a hand in creating?"

"Of course." The uneasy peace now existing between England and Scotland was not something he would ever dismiss. "Peace, prosperity, stability. They are the very things we fight for."

"Just so. And speaking of prosperity, I should tell you that your father has read through your proposal to introduce a three-field system. He believes you are right. 'Tis a way to increase our harvest."

"I am pleased to hear it." Tristan smiled at his mother and regretted his earlier outburst. He patted the horse's shoulder and accepted him nuzzling at his pockets. "I should take him for a gallop over the moors."

"Aye, that might be one way of improving your temper."

"And another?" Tristan eyed his mother speculatively over the horse's ears. She rarely made pointed observations if there was not something serious that she wished to say.

"Son, tell me what is troubling you."

Where would I even start?

"'Tis the market traders," he hedged. "Some time ago I had the idea of introducing a covered market to Wolvesley. I spoke to Father about it as soon as he recovered, for this is the perfect time to build the stalls, before winter sets in."

Morwenna was nodding slowly. "I can see the benefits of such a plan."

"So could Father. So could the traders," he added quickly.

"Where lies the problem?" Morwenna resumed their walk, holding up her skirts as the ground rose into a slight incline.

"The carpenters cannot source the correct wood. The traders cannot decide where they would like to base themselves." Tristan folded his hands behind his back to prevent himself from flinging them around like a child in the midst of a tantrum. "In short, everything has gone wrong."

Everything went wrong on the day that Mirrie left.

"These things can take time, Tristan."

"And it is damnably frustrating." The words escaped him in a growl.

Morwenna turned to face him. They had crested the hill and now stood with the beauty of Wolvesley woods unfolding beneath them. A slight breeze rustled the branches of the ancient oak trees and the silvery song of a ruddock floated through the warm air.

"Now tell me what is *truly* troubling you." She arched her blonde eyebrows. "I doubt the logistical challenges of sourcing wood can put my eldest son in such a foul temper."

Under her watchful gaze, he felt his anger turn to desolation.

"Could it be, Tristan, that it is someone close to all our hearts who has disturbed your equilibrium?"

"Jonah put me out of sorts. He always does. But he is gone now," Tristan muttered.

His mother sighed loudly. "You well know that I do not speak of Jonah." She shook her head in exasperation. "The two of you are more alike than either of you would ever admit. In more ways that e'en I first realised." She fell silent, her eyes fixed determinedly on the tree tops as if she had said more than she intended.

"What do you mean?" Tristan grudgingly gave in to his curiosity.

"You resent Jonah because of his cleverness. He resents you because of your strength. Is that not enough?"

"Nay, Mother. That is not what you meant at all."

She put her head to one side. "Very well. If you insist. I believe a certain young lady has come between you."

One name floated across his mind. "Mirrie?"

"The very same."

"Why should she—?" Tristan stumbled. He had given his parents a very poor explanation for Mirrie's hasty departure from Wolvesley and, to his surprise, they had accepted it with little questioning.

"It was clear to a great many of us that Jonah had a special place in his heart for Mirrie when you were all growing up," Morwenna said, fondly. "It was hard for him, to give that up."

Some response was expected of him, but he could not properly form it.

"But he put his feelings to one side, because of you."

"Why would he do that?" Tristan was nonplussed. "I never asked it of him."

"You had no cause to. I doubt you were e'en aware of how he felt." Morwenna put her hands in the small of her back and tilted her face towards the sun. "The ways of love are eternally strange. Jonah would have given heaven and earth to Mirrie. But Mirrie has only ever had eyes for you."

Tristan's pulse picked up speed, although he kept his expression neutral. "I saw some silly graffiti in the school room." He plucked at some long grass and shredded it in his fingers. "But it was youthful nonsense. Mirrie may have felt that way about me for a short time when we were children. She admitted as such." *And Jonah knew it too,* he realised, with a pang of self-awareness. "But 'twas naught serious."

Morwenna smiled at him gently. "Is that what she told you?"

He nodded.

"I would not call Mirabel a liar. But perchance she was forced to make certain statements to protect her dignity, or, more likely, the friendship that exists between you. Perchance she rightly sensed that you were not ready to hear such a declaration."

Tristan felt himself on uncertain ground. "You are telling me that Mirrie has long had feelings for me?" He flinched at the awkwardness of asking such a question of his own mother.

She met his gaze. "Aye, that is the truth of it."

"Well, she has put them away from her now." He scratched at his head, frustration swirling in his gut once more. Hadn't he asked, *nay begged*, Mirrie to give their fledgling relationship a chance?

"Such feelings are not easily put away. Methinks Jonah knows this as well as anyone else."

Tristan groaned out loud, then flung himself down onto the springy grass. "'Tis all a mess, Mother."

She carefully lowered herself down beside him. Not talking. Giving him the space he needed to think it all through.

"If Mirrie has such feelings for me, why did she agree to come here and act the part of my betrothed? Why did Jonah suggest it?" He took a breath. "'Twas all a ruse, Mother, agreed upon before we departed from Ember Hall. I'm sorry for it. But there it is."

He waited for the axe to fall, but Morwenna only nodded slowly. "I know."

He frowned, incredulously. "For how long have you known?"

"That day in your father's bedchamber. When the two of you showed such resistance to announcing your betrothal at the ball, 'twas then I began to work it out."

"Are you not angry?" He could not reconcile what she was saying with the calmness of her delivery.

"I would be hypocritical if I were." She paused to send him a rueful smile. "I consider myself culpable in the deceit, Tristan."

"How so? You were not e'en at Ember Hall when we conjured the plan." He rolled onto his side so he could study her more closely, feeling more curiosity than anything else.

She stroked back his hair. "But 'twas I who sent you there. 'Twas I who made sure your head was full of our insistence that you find a bride."

Tristan blinked in amazement. "I wondered at your sudden insistence on marrying me off."

"I knew you would find Mirrie waiting there for you. Beautiful, kind Mirrie," she added, emphatically. "She would be the perfect bride for you. But only if you began to see her in that light."

He had no words. He rolled onto his back, put his hands behind his head and gazed up at the blue sky. Fluffy white clouds floated aimlessly above him, much like his thoughts. He could not decide if he were angry or amused at his mother's meddling.

After all, she had only pointed him in the direction of Mirrie. He had done the rest.

"*Have* you begun to see her in that light?" she asked, softly.

He answered honestly. "I don't know how I feel." He threw her a rueful smile. "Except out of sorts with everyone and everything."

"Well, that is the important question you must answer before anyone else's heart is further compromised. Certainly before you visit Ember Hall again."

"I have no plans to visit Ember Hall," he said stiffly.

Morwenna pressed her lips together. "It is your sister's home. Some day you must go back there. And you have hardly been happy these last days, Tristan."

He plucked at a handful of grass and let it fall.

"Tristan?"

"Aye, you are right." He sat up and clasped his hands around his knees. He had felt as if a part of him were missing ever since Mirrie rode away from Wolvesley.

And perchance he felt slightly lighter of heart just for acknowledging that.

"You must try to work out *why* you are so out of sorts. I am unused to seeing my handsome son with such a scowl on his face," Morwenna said lightly.

"I will endeavour to appear more cheerful." He dropped some of the grass over her lap and she brushed it away with a chuckle before turning to him with a serious expression.

"And then you must decide if you truly love Mirrie. And if the answer is yes, I ask you this. What are you going to do about it?"

He fixed his gaze on the distant treetops. "That is precisely the problem, Mother. For if I have learned one thing these last days, 'tis that our friendship is very dear to me, and I would do naught to risk it." He took a breath. "And if I have learned a second thing, 'tis that my actions all too often do exactly that."

Morwenna watched him closely, a small smile playing about her lips. "But?" she supplied.

"But I find myself craving her company." *And her smile. And her laugh.* Tristan added silently, struggling to articulate these new, deeply held emotions.

"Then you must talk to her." Morwenna nodded firmly, as if it was all so very simple.

"But if I get it wrong again..." Tristan deliberately left his sentence unfinished.

His mother reached out and patted his shoulder. "You must curb your instinctive impatience. Take things slowly with Mirrie."

"You mean, careful conversation? Slow walks through the woods?" He raised an eyebrow.

She nudged him with her elbow and laughed. "I mean no hasty decisions. No grand gestures. Court her as if she is a new acquaintance."

"But I know Mirrie as well as I know anyone in this land."

"Which is why this transition will be hard, for you both. The question is, are you willing to try?" Her voice rose with emphasis.

A beat passed. Tristan tilted his face toward the sun and closed his eyes.

He was willing to *try*. But was he willing to face rejection *again?*

He thought the answer must be yes, for there was no alternative that he could see.

Chapter Nineteen

MIRRIE PLACED THE last bread roll in the over-stuffed hamper and nodded to the two waiting farm boys.

"You can take it now."

"Thank ye, miss."

Though small, the boys were well used to working in the fields and between them they hefted the heavy hamper out of the kitchen and onto the waiting cart with enviable ease. They then hopped on the back of the cart and settled in for the ride back to the hayfields. Mirrie pretended not to see them each swiping a hot heel of bread from the basket.

Mirrie wiped her hands on a cloth and looked about the untidy kitchen. It was hotter than ever in here, with the bread ovens first fired up since before dawn. Agnes had rolled up the sleeves of her stained tunic to reveal forearms made muscular through hours of kneading and beating.

"Is there aught else I can do?" Mirrie asked the long-time cook of Ember Hall.

"Nay, miss, you should take a well-earned rest." Agnes pushed back the tendrils of long grey hair that had escaped her plait. "I'll whip up a last batch of cakes for the evening meal."

"Methinks there will be many mouths to feed this night." Mirrie crossed to the sink and rinsed her hands, enjoying the rush of cold water on her warm skin. "'Tis likely everyone now bringing in the harvest will come back to the hall."

"God willing, this harvest is a good one." Agnes fanned herself with a floury hand. "Sir Callum said the barn stores are filling up nicely."

Mirrie nodded. She had counted the sacks of corn herself, just last night. Lammas Day was not long past, but already they had more animal food set aside than at the end of last summer's harvest.

"God willing," she echoed Agnes's plea. If the skies turned to rain, much of the crop could still be ruined. But there was no sign of that. Yet.

"Be off with you then, miss. You look fit to drop," Agnes said, turning away to fetch butter from the cold store.

Mirrie was not affronted; she had long grown used to the cook's abrupt manner. But she had no intention of going upstairs to rest. Instead, she slipped off her apron and stepped out into the sun-drenched warmth of the courtyard. Here she paused for a moment, enjoying how the golden rays of light caught the honey-hued ancient stone. Pink roses nodded lazily in the gentle breeze and the only sound was the haunting mewl of a curlew, circling high overhead. Such peace and calm after the fiery heat of the busy kitchen was a balm to her. However, she only allowed herself a short time to enjoy it.

'Twas just days since she had sat in the great hall and asked Callum if she could play a greater role in the running of Ember Hall. And helping to bring in the harvest was the hardest and most important job of all.

Mirrie glanced down at the palms of her hands, which were already blistered after long hours wielding a pitchfork out in the fields. Frida had insisted she spread honey over her chapped skin, and bind her hands in bandages overnight. Now, Mirrie slipped on a pair of thin cotton gloves she had brought down from her bedchamber. They would offer little protection, but would be better than nothing.

"Good morn, Miss Mirabel," shouted one of the grooms, coming out of the stables with a pitchfork swinging from his hands.

"Good morn, Alaic," she replied.

Alaic returned to the barn and Mirrie set off for the hayfield with a bounce in her step and a smile that was halfway to being genuine. Within minutes she would be joining a busy group of workers comprising farm-workers and villagers, all working together to bring in the harvest. She enjoyed the feeling of unity and purpose; and long hours outside helped banish the shadows of doubt that had taken root in her heart.

Whenever Mirrie was alone, with little to occupy her hands or her mind, her thoughts would invariably return to Tristan. A little voice would pipe up, asking her if she was sure she had done the right thing.

Should I have left Wolvesley without taking the time to talk to him?

She couldn't help looking over her shoulder whenever she heard a man's heavy, booted footstep or gravelly laugh. Sometimes it seemed inevitable that Tristan would come looking for her at Ember Hall. Sometimes it seemed more likely she would not see him again for months, if not years.

She did not know which of these outcomes was the least disturbing.

And where was David? That other suitor who had been so eager to claim her hand at the midsummer ball? He too had disappeared, like a summer mist.

Mirrie snorted as she picked up her skirts to jump over a fallen log. Whatever charms she had wielded that night must have faded away to naught. And looking down at her loose-fitting grey tunic, she could see why.

But it was so very freeing to tell herself that she did not care. To scoop up her hair into an unfashionable, untidy knot and roam about with neither a bonnet nor gloves—except to protect her tender flesh from hard, manual work.

To be amongst people who did not judge her. And did not mislead her either.

Aye, it's good to be home.

She rounded the last corner and came in sight of the vast hayfields which were filled not only with their own farm workers, but also villagers, including women and children. It took the whole community to bring in the harvest and was a time of hard work and togetherness. She put a hand over her eyes and scanned the labourers until she spied Callum, forking cut hay into a waiting wagon with impressive strength and accuracy. But he paused in his work when he saw Mirrie and was quick to flash his customary wide smile.

"Have you come again to join us?" He pushed a shock of dark hair away from his eyes.

"If you will have me?" she smiled back.

"We will be stopping for lunch within the hour, if you would prefer to join Frida and some of the other women in laying out the food?" He gestured towards the nearby cart which had brought provisions, all packed by Mirrie, up to the fields.

"Nay." She shook her head. "I would prefer more manual work."

"'Tis all important, Godly work," he pointed out, his dark eyes fixed on her.

Finding me wanting?

"I should prefer to work up a sweat and forget my troubles." She raised her eyebrows meaningfully. "Must we quarrel over this yet again?"

"I am in search of no quarrel. Here." He held out his own pitchfork with a wink. "You carry on with this. I will go down to the end of the field and press on with the scything."

"Thank you." Her cheeks had pinkened, partially from the noonday sun, and partially from her outburst. She could not escape the notion that she was still acting in some sort of ruse and consequently, that she risked discovery and censure at every turn.

But that was true, she thought, as she grasped the fork firmly and dug it into the hay. She had kissed Tristan, Frida's brother. And not one of these good people knew that.

'Twas one thing keeping her feelings for him a secret. 'Twas quite another to stay silent about all that had passed between them.

And all that *could* have passed between them.

There were times when the little voice in her head regretted that not more had happened in the school room of Wolvesley Castle.

Or in the corridor outside my bedchamber.

Mirrie pressed her lips together, hoping to silence these errant thoughts with hard, physical labour. Over time, she had learned how to swing the fork just so, to lift the maximum amount of hay without spinning of balance or dropping the bulk of it. It took all her concentration though, and she did not even hear the cry ring out for everyone to down tools and gather together for some much-needed food and drink.

A shadow fell over her, as she poised at the apex of her next swing.

"Will you not partake of refreshment?"

Her first thought was that the speaker was Callum, but as her fork dug through the cut hay, she realised the voice was deeper and more refined.

A voice which made her breath catch in her throat and her skin prickle with awareness.

Mirrie felt perspiration running down her forehead; her hair, she knew, was slick with sweat.

The last person she wanted to see right now was Tristan.

"I will stop in a while. I must finish this row first," she replied, not even glancing towards him.

Why did he come?

Tristan oft helped bring in the harvest at Wolvesley. But never before had he joined them at Ember Hall.

"But everyone else has stopped."

She raised her eyes to the grassy knoll where the cart had halted earlier. Rugs had been spread all around, and tired workers now sat together, eating and drinking. No one spared her any attention.

"If you do not go now, all the nicest cakes will be gone," he urged, his voice low.

She shrugged, still determined to not look in his direction. "Agnes is already baking more. Besides, I am guided by more than my belly."

She thought he would stay and argue further. She was disappointed to hear him walk away.

But disappointment was a familiar companion; one she was used to living beside. She flexed her fingers and re-positioned her sore hands on the handle of the pitchfork. A long row of cut grass stretched before her. It was now more important than ever that she finish it. She would take refreshment later.

She straightened up when the ache in her shoulders became unbearable, surprised to see another worker down at the end of the field, where the grass was still uncut. This worker was tall and strong, grass flew up with every swing of his scythe. He worked methodically and accurately, legs braced, bronzed shoulders bare to the sun.

Exertion had already made her heartbeat quicken, now it began to gallop. Her hands slipped on the fork and she stumbled on the uneven ground.

This would never do.

Tristan was working his way toward her. Soon he would be at her side. Talking to her, *looking at her*, and she was not prepared for such a conversation.

He had kissed her. She had slapped him. Then she had left without saying goodbye. And he had let her.

Too much had passed between them for politeness to be observed in a hayfield. Especially when her dress stuck to her sides with perspiration.

Mirrie didn't pause to consider her actions. She left her fork laying atop a pile of chopped grass, and turned away.

She couldn't return to the house; he would only track her down there. Nor did she want to walk past the happy group of workers picnicking atop the rugs. Instead, she ran lightly down the side of the hayfield and through a shady copse of trees, her long legs pounding wildly beneath her as she descended a steep slope. The ground here was often muddy, but the prolonged warm, dry weather made dust fly about her as she rounded the final corner and emerged into Ember Cove.

The hard ground turned to shingle, which was difficult to walk on. She pressed on, breathing hard, heading for the welcome shade of the cliffs. As soon as she reached them, she sank to the ground, uncaring of how the miniscule stones would stick to her tunic. She stretched out her legs and leaned aching back against the coolness of the stone, letting her head roll back and her eyes feast on the glittering expanse of the sea.

She forced her thoughts to quieten, so all that filled her head was the gentle rushing of the waves on the shingle beach and the mournful calling of the gulls.

The air was fresh and clean. There was no one here but herself. Mirrie reached forward to tug off her boots, relieved to rid herself of their weight.

If only she could plunge into the inviting sea, to wash away the dust of the day along with all her woes.

But she could not. Walkers on the cliffs above could look down upon Ember Cove and see her. She would have to be satisfied with cooling off in the shade.

So be it.

Mirrie was used to resigning herself to less than what she truly desired.

She sniffed at the sudden wave of self-pity.

Why should she always be the one to sit in the shade?

The rhythmic rolling of the waves seemed to call to her, inviting her down to the shore. She walked forward, drawn by the sparkling water and the promise of cool release. When a large wave rolled towards her, soaking the toes of her stockings, she merely smiled and shuffled further in. Her feet sank down into the shingle, anchoring her in place. The sea rose around her ankles and a salty breeze caressed her hot face.

Why should she not have this pleasure? And more besides?

She opened her arms and tilted her face to the sun, closing her eyes as the cold waves rushed back and forth. The sound was hypnotic, as was the pull of receding water of her calves and the feeling of shifting shingle beneath her toes.

Her cares began to lessen along with the ache in her shoulders. She allowed her mind to relax; her body to be one with the waves.

She did not hear Tristan walking slowly towards her, across the beach.

When he cleared his throat, her eyes flew open in surprise.

"What a wonderful idea, Mirrie. There is naught better than paddling in the sea on a hot day. Do you mind if I join you?"

CHAPTER TWENTY

H E KNEW WHAT she would say in response.
"'Twould not be proper, Tristan."

So when instead she nodded slowly, surprise caused his heart to still.

"I was thinking the very same thing. The water is so soothing," she said, closing her hazel eyes once more, her face upturned towards the sun.

Tristan was nonplussed. He put his hands on his hips and watched the waves running up the shore. He stood a few paces diagonally behind her, still attired in his work boots and breeches. He had pulled on his shirt before following her to the cove, though he had left it unbuttoned. A warm breeze buffeted his bare chest, sending whispers of temptation through his body.

But he had come to Ember Hall to talk to Mirrie, not to tease her. Nor to resurrect the awkwardness that had almost brought their cherished friendship to an end. He kept his distance for he dared not touch her. One touch could cause his physical longings to rise up once again and overwhelm his rational self.

Making him the fool she thought him, rather than the worthy man he sought to be.

"I owe you an apology," he said.

She did not react, not even with a flicker of emotion. She stood like a woman frozen in time, her simple smock floating out around her calves, her beautiful hair cascading down her back in a loose plait that cried out to be released. Tendrils had escaped to frame her heart-shaped face, flushed from the sun and her hard work in the fields. He had scarce believed it when Callum pointed him towards Mirrie: a woman wielding a pitchfork with all the skill and dexterity of a young man.

But then, Tristan had always had faith in Mirrie's abilities. She was stronger, braver and more capable than she realised.

Although, he could not accuse her of short-sightedness. Not when he had failed to see what had been right before his eyes, ever since their youth.

"I should not have let you leave Wolvesley without saying goodbye."

She gave the slightest shrug of her slender shoulders.

"I should not have let you leave at all," he amended.

She turned towards him now. "You do not own me, Tristan. I can leave a place without your permission." Her eyes skittered over his face, leaving him almost breathless.

He paused to choose his words more carefully. "I only meant that we should not have parted with so much left unsaid between us."

Her gaze lifted over his shoulders, focusing on the granite cliffs at the edge of the beach. "I am sorry for what I left unsaid. You infuriate me, it's true. But when all's said and done, there is no one I trust more." She sighed. "I have always had faith in you."

"You have?" His eyebrows climbed beneath his hair.

"Of course. You are a loving son and brother, as well as a mighty warrior. And a peacemaker to boot."

He was both humbled and surprised by her words. But whereas once he might have made light of her praise, now he was driven to express himself with sincerity.

"Your opinion matters to me, Mirrie. It matters a great deal."

Her gaze clashed with his, honest and unflinching. "You must know by now how I feel."

"How must I?" He took a step closer, against all his better judgement, as if he was drawn by a magnet. When she flinched away, he reached out his hand and softly touched the side of her face. "Tell me, Mirrie. How can I know this, when you are so eager to discount any tenderness you felt for me in the past—and point out my shortcomings in the present?"

Nay, he should not have touched her. Now he wanted more. But he forced his arm to drop. To stand apart from her and not reach out again.

"Perchance I am aware of your shortcomings, simply because I am aware of you, Tristan. All of you. Good and bad."

God's blood, his mother was right; he could see it now. Mirrie loved him. Not because he was heir to the Earl of Wolvesley. Nor for his wealth, not even for his reputation as a knight of the realm. She loved *him*. Faults and all.

The realisation made him breathless; 'twas a gift he was not sure he deserved.

But one thing he knew for sure. He would not allow it to slip through his fingers.

"As I am aware of you?" he said, closing the gap between them and slowly, carefully, placing his hands about her waist. He stood directly behind her, holding her as gently as if she was made of spun glass. He wanted her to lean against him, so he could wrap his arms about her and drop kisses on the exposed nape of her neck. But he would not, could not move. Not until she gave her permission.

She shook her head, letting it drop forward so he had no hope of divining the expression in her eyes. "You have seen me, yet not seen me, for nigh on twenty summers." Her voice held a tremor.

She spoke the truth.

"I cannot deny it. I have been a fool. But I see you now, Mirrie."

She made a noise he could not identify.

"I see you when I wake. I see you before I go to sleep. You haunt my every waking moment. I am like a blind man who suddenly can see the light." He spoke directly from his heart, his words tumbling over one another.

She shook her head again, but he could see some of the tension had gone out of her. "You speak with the legendary charm of the de Nevilles."

His breath caught as she leaned against him, just as he had wanted. Small waves rushed over his boots, no doubt ruining the leather, but he did not care.

"I must use the gifts God gave me." Slowly, greatly daring, he moved aside her plait and dropped his lips to where her neck met her shoulder. When she did not resist, he held her tighter, and kissed her there again.

Now she sighed heavily and lolled against him. "I should not allow you to do this."

He stilled. "If you say the word, I will stop."

Part of him wanted her to stop him, for he had come here to talk, as his mother had urged and as Mirrie herself had wished. He recalled her words in her bedchamber at Wolvesley.

"Trying, to me, means conversation and getting to know one another, all over again. It must be something finer and deeper than physical desire."

Back in Wolvesley, he had decided to take his mother's advice and formally court the young woman who had stolen his heart.

But the trouble was, Tristan's physical desire for the woman in his arms was finer and deeper than aught he had ever known before.

He traced a line of kisses to her shoulder, nudging his lips beneath the loose material of her tunic. Then he retraced his path, paying special attention to her jawline and nibbling gently on her earlobe. Mirrie responded to him with equivalent sensuality to that soaring within him, clutching at his hand as it curved over her belly and bracing her shoulders against his chest as the withdrawing tide pulled at their feet.

He helped her step up the shore, away from the dragging waves, and turned her towards him. Her eyes were half closed with pleasure, her body still pliant in his hands.

"I am falling in love with you," he said.

Words he had ne'er said to another. A sentiment that had ne'er before come to his mind.

She opened her eyes and tilted her chin so she was looking directly at him. He cupped her cheeks and held her gaze; and he saw doubt written across her lovely face.

"Truly." He firmed his stance against the shingle. "Mirabel Duval. I believe I am in love with you."

Her lips parted and he seized the opportunity to claim her mouth with his own, pulling her to him with urgency and running his hands the length of her spine. He knew a surge of victory when she responded to his kiss, wrapping her hands around his shoulders and pressing herself against the hardness of his bare chest. His tongue probed past her lower lip, delighting in her small gasps of pleasure. In another moment, he met her tongue with his, exalting in the jolt of connection which reverberated through them both.

He was hardening with desire for her. With the way her slim hips were crushed against him, she must feel it, through the thin fabric of her tunic. Just as he could feel the softness of her curves. His hands skimmed over her breasts and he groaned as the liquid need inside him grew stronger.

She felt right in his arms. Just as she was right in his life. She was the part that made him whole. The part that helped everything to make sense.

His mother was right, about this as about everything. Life had been naught without Mirrie.

"You must decide if you truly love Mirrie. And if the answer is yes, I ask you this. What are you going to do about it?"

He heard her words clearly, above the crashing of the waves and the calling of the gulls. And suddenly, he knew exactly what he was going to do about it.

He had come here to talk, so that he and Mirrie could begin to get to know one another, all over again. But such a courtship was unnecessary, for he already knew her, truly and deeply. Just as she truly knew him.

He broke apart from their kiss and held her away from him so he might look properly into her hazel eyes. Eyes that had darkened with desire, just like his.

Her breath came heavy and quick, just like his.

"Mirabel," he said, "will you marry me?"

SHE HEARD HIM as if in a dream. Everything had become languorous and slow; her limbs heavy with desire. It was the easiest, most natural thing in the world to lean against his sinewy strength and be swept away by his kisses.

But this question was unexpected and it made her agitated. She was not ready for it; could not put her faith in it.

"Nay, Tristan." She wanted more of his kisses, more of his hands against her body. For the first time, she was quite clear-thinking about that.

"Why not?" His deft fingers drew circles on her shoulders so she wanted only to close her eyes and succumb to the pleasure of his touch.

"Because of who I am and who you are." Impatiently, she rose on her tiptoes and pressed her lips to his, wanting more of what he had so freely given.

Why should she deny herself?

But he was withdrawing from his kisses. His hands spanned her waist and his breath was hot against his ear.

"That is no good reason."

His words were calling to a more sensible, rational part of her; the part she wanted to put away so as to give in to the sensuous pleasure building within her core.

"Don't," she said. "Please. Just kiss me."

He growled low in his throat and pulled her to him once again, kissing her so deeply it felt as if her mouth was welded to his. His hands stroked her body, stoking the flames already igniting inside her. She ran her hands over the taut muscles of his chest, then up over his shoulders, dipping beneath the soft fabric of his shirt. *This* was what she wanted. To be as one with the man she adored; standing so close not a breath of air could separate them. So close that she could feel his need for her, hardening against her belly.

"Marry me," he said again, one hand cupping her breast and making her breath come even faster.

In response, she kissed him harder, standing on her tiptoes and crushing her lips against his. Leaning into his touch, even though she knew it was forbidden.

"Stop asking," she gasped, the very moment he pulled back.

He gazed down at her with fire in his eyes. She thought he might argue, but instead he scooped her into his arms and held her close against his chest as he carried her up the shore. He laid her down on the shingle and hovered over her, the breadth of his shoulders shading her from the midday sun.

"I want you, Mirrie. I want you now and I will want you still on the morrow and on the morrow after that. Each day, for the rest of my days."

Need was pooling inside her, like a surging itch she could not scratch. Her hands grasped his shoulders, instinctively pulling him down against her. "And I want you."

He blazed a trail of kisses down her throat until his lips met the top of her tunic. His warm hands stroked her breasts until she longed for him to tear the tunic from her body. Instead, he began to unbutton it with almost unbearable slowness, kissing and caressing the newly exposed flesh and causing her to squirm beneath him. She closed her eyes, willingly surrendering herself to his touch and to the pleasurable sensations pulsating through her.

He tugged at her shift and she lifted her hips so he could pull it free; the warm whisper of wind across her belly alerting her to the fact she was entirely unclothed, Naked, before and beneath him. His blue gaze devoured her, head to toe, and she felt no shame, only a deep burning desire. Though for what, she could not say. She only knew it felt right to be in Tristan's arms. For Tristan's hands to be on her body; his lips worshipping the most sensitive parts of her until she wound her fingers in his hair and moaned out loud.

"Marry me, Mirrie," he said again, his expression dark with desire.

"I cannot." Her body trembled so it was an effort to form the words.

"Why not?" His hand was travelling down from her belly to where she wanted him most. But he paused, waiting for her answer.

She arched her back, pressing herself against him, craving more. But Tristan only stroked back her hair and looked deep into her eyes, one hand softly brushing against her inner thighs.

"Why not?" he repeated.

"Because I could never be a countess." Her answer came in a rush of breath. It was no more than the truth. A fact, like day following night.

He kissed her as his fingers neared their mark and she moaned again with unexpected pleasure, opening herself up to his touch and the soaring sensations that snatched at her breath as he slowly stroked her very core.

"Tristan," she gasped.

"I wish you could see yourself as I do, for there is naught you cannot do, Mirrie." His lips settled around on her breast as his fingers moved inside her, turning her to liquid. He moved up her body and pressed a kiss to the nape of her neck. "I have faith in you. I always have."

She raked her fingers along his back, wanting to claim him as her own as he whispered the words she had longed to hear. "I love you."

"I love you, too."

Another truth. She had loved him almost all her days. For a terrible moment he moved away from her, but when she forced her eyes to open, he was back, holding her to his naked body. Their limbs entwined and nothing had ever felt so good and so right. He moved above her, his knee gently drawing her legs apart, his hips settling into place. She gasped as he entered her, knowing only a moment's pain before pleasure took her in its grip once again. Tristan filled her wholly. His mouth covered hers, swallowing her cries, before he pulled back his head.

"Marry me."

Her hands clawed at his shoulder as her hips bucked against him, instinctively wanting him to move inside her, but he thrusted deep and then stayed still.

"Marry me," he said again, nudging his hips just enough to stimulate her from the inside in a way that sent her close to the edge of a precipice she had never known existed.

"Aye," she gasped, releasing all she had to the desire staking claim of her senses. "I will marry you, Tris."

There followed a long stretch of what she could only call bliss. Their bodies rocked together and Mirrie soared over the precipice, wrapping her legs around him as she shattered into pieces. He called out her name, eyes squeezed shut, then slumped against her so for a while she bore his full, muscular weight.

She could not move. She did not want to move. He was pinning her to the ground and she thought she had ne'er been in a place that felt so right.

Then he rolled to his side and pulled her towards him, kissing her lips and her forehead, embracing her closely. And naught had ever felt better than that.

"Mirrie. You have made me the happiest man in all of England."

She snuggled against him, enjoying the warmth of his flesh and the sun on her limbs. She had no words, but it did not matter. She only wanted to prolong this moment, when she had all she had dreamed of and more besides.

He traced his finger down her cheek. "You are wise and good and beautiful, but I must tell you, you are wrong about one thing."

"Oh yes?" She raised an eyebrow inquisitively. "What is that?"

"When the time comes, you will make a remarkable countess."

A flicker of unease unfurled in her belly. Her fears, so long held, could not so easily be put aside. But she reminded herself that Tristan knew the responsibilities and requirements of his position.

And Tristan has chosen me.

She recalled his words, just now: "I have faith in you. I always have."

In the school room at Wolvesley he had claimed to see the true depths of her courage.

She closed her eyes so he would not see her tears of joy.

"I will try," she whispered, breathing in his unmistakably masculine scent.

"You will succeed." He kissed her shoulder. "Just as you succeed at all else."

She settled herself against him, comforted by the rhythmic beating of his heart.

"I am glad I persuaded you to say yes."

She smiled, her face still pressed against his chest. "You were most persuasive."

His hands stroked her back. "I will be sure to remember the best way to negotiate with my wife."

"Do not presume that I will give way in all things," she said, with mock seriousness.

"I have yet to introduce you to all the methods at my disposal," he replied, with a chuckle that sent a thrill of anticipation through her.

But what had been agreed between them was a serious matter, and mayhap they should not jest so soon. She arched back her head so she could look him in the eye.

"Did you come to Ember Hall intending to ask me to marry you?"

He held her gaze, tenderly but honestly. "I came here with

the hope of courting you. I have to say, I did not plan to propose."

His admission left her cold. She pulled away from him and flinched at a cool breeze wafting over them. "When did you decide?"

"When we were standing over there." He nodded towards the sea.

Agitation settled upon her. She sat up and was all too aware of her nakedness. She looked around for her shift and pulled it towards her, covering her breasts.

"What is wrong?" His hand went to her arm and she could not help pulling away.

"It was a question asked on impulse?"

"And nonetheless meaningful for it." He sat up beside her, so she must avert her eyes from his sculpted form. Tears brimmed at her eyes again and this time she could do naught to stop them rolling down her cheeks. "Mirrie." His face creased with concern. "I spent long days and longer nights thinking of you. Of us. Of how we could proceed. I thought that you would not want to rush into anything."

But I rushed headlong into your arms!

She pulled the shift over her head and tugged it down over her body, feeling stronger the moment she was decently covered. "You should not have done it," she muttered. "*We* should not have done it. I do not blame you, Tris. I was equally willing."

"What are you saying?" Bewilderment chased through his eyes.

"I cannot marry you on a whim."

"'Tis no whim." His voice rose in consternation. "'Twas a decision reached after much soul-searching, believe me."

"I cannot believe you. Not when you are known for thinking only of the moment." It was difficult to pull on her tunic with hands that shook like saplings in a storm.

"I know that I am in love with you."

They were the words she had longed to hear, yet she could

not put her trust in them.

"When we stood over there." She too pointed to the sea. "Before we both lost our wits. You said that you *believed* you were in love with me."

He put his fingertips to his temples and winced. "Aye, you're right. I was finding my way, Mirrie. I'm no expert when it comes to declarations of the heart."

The sincerity in his voice was almost her undoing.

"Can we not find our way, together?" His blue eyes looked at her beseechingly. He was all she had ever wanted. Offering her all she had ever dreamed of. But Mirrie's insecurities, now awakened, would not be so easily quietened.

"'Tis too late for that." Fully attired, she got to her feet, brushing the shingle from her clothes and praying that her trembling legs would hold her upright.

"Mirrie, where are you going?" He reached for his shirt.

"I am going away from you."

At least, if she could manage it. The uneven ground coupled with her emotional distress meant the odds were stacked against a graceful departure. She furiously rubbed the tears from her eyes. Blurred vision was the last thing she needed. She took one step forward, then another, putting distance between herself and the man who had broken her heart. But she had scarcely made any progress to speak of before he caught up with her. His strong arms held her fast, so she could not escape.

"I do not understand." He was clad only in his shirt, which was loose and unbuttoned.

She could not argue with a man in a state of undress. But she had no choice. He would not let her go.

"A proposal of marriage should be properly thought through." She sniffed but met his gaze with a challenging one of her own. "It should not be cobbled together just to give you an excuse to slake your lust."

His hands dropped from her arms and she all but staggered to one side.

"That is what you think this is?" he asked quietly. "Nothing more than lust?"

"That is what I fear." She put a hand to her heart, wanting to keep the grief inside.

"That is how little you think of me?" Tristan's voice cracked. "Mercy, Mirrie. What must I say to make you believe me?"

"I don't know." Grief made her double over in physical pain.

"Would you have preferred a steadier and more reliable proposal, perchance by the fountain at Wolvesley?" His voice rose with emotion.

"Do not speak of David Bryce," she breathed. "That is not fair."

Tristan took a deep breath. "Where is he now, this physician of yours?"

She straightened her back. "I cannot tell you."

"Aye, well, I can tell you." He dragged a hand through his dishevelled hair. He accepted a post at Wolvesley. He chose coin over you, Mirrie. Mayhap coin was all he was ever after."

"Why would you be so cruel?" she whispered, looking past him to the waves breaking on the shore. A view that had once brought her solace but now would forever serve as a reminder of her foolishness.

"I am not cruel. I am a man made of flesh and blood and desire, struggling with emotions I have ne'er felt before." He took another shuddering breath. "You say I am impulsive. Reckless even. Aye, I have been in the past. I'm the first to admit it. But I have ne'er made false promises. Not to anyone." His voice dropped to a near whisper. "Why, in heaven's name, would I start with you?"

The sincerity shining from his eyes was beginning to reach her. Mirrie clutched her arms around her chest, not knowing what to do. For a moment, the only sound was the rushing of waves onto the shingle.

Tristan shook his head, his gaze hardening. "Forsooth, being impulsive is no crime and does not render my feelings any less valid. Certainly, I would never be moved to propose to a woman, any woman, once I had a glimpse of her potential wealth."

"I have no potential wealth," she countered, though it hurt her to speak.

"And once your physician discovered that, methinks he would have rescinded his proposal and moved on. Just as he was quick to cut all ties with you once I offered him a well-paid position."

She digested this, oblivious to the calling of the gulls and the crashing of the sea.

"*You* offered him the position?"

"Aye. The very day after the ball."

"So that is why I have not heard from him." She gave him no chance to reply. "And did you consider my feelings in this at all?"

"I saved you from a man who puts coin before love." His voice rose against the waves.

"You moved him out of the way for your own ends," she screeched back, uncaring of losing her decorum.

He shrugged his shoulders. "I see you are determined to think badly of me, whate'er I say or do now."

She turned away, unable to fight any more. "You look to control me, like a soldier in a well-planned battle sequence. Like you control all else in your life. For the betterment of yourself."

She heard his intake of breath and knew she had wounded him.

"That is unjust."

She forced her legs to move forward, to take her away from further harm.

"Goodbye, Tristan," she said over her shoulder.

This time, he did not come after her.

CHAPTER TWENTY-ONE

TRISTAN LEFT ENOUGH time for Mirrie to flee, then he forced his leaden limbs back to Ember Hall.

He would take his horse and leave. At this time of year, darkness would not fall for many hours yet. He had time enough to ride back to Wolvesley Castle.

Even if that were not so, he reasoned he must leave. There was naught now to stay for. And the fierce energy that had carried him over the moors to this remote northern outpost, was now entirely deflated.

He dragged his booted feet through the shingle, feeling his usual optimism shrivel and die.

He had come here to mend the rift that had sprung up between him and Mirrie; and to see if their relationship might be set onto a different path. But now they were further apart than ever before.

Tristan knew a hot wave of frustration. What else could a man do but profess love for a woman and ask her to marry him?

Naught.

He clenched his hands into fists as the shingle turned to compacted earth and rose up into a steep incline before him.

She had once been a puzzle he was determined to solve. Now she was the woman who had hurt him, without good cause. One who would not see reason; who refused to be budged. He had never before thought of Mirrie as stubborn, but now he saw that the label suited her well.

Tristan put his hands on his knees and took a deep, steadying breath. Anger was beginning to rise up inside him, twisting his thoughts into something dark and ugly.

He must remember that Mirrie was hurting too. She had shed tears; her distress was palpable.

He would have offered comfort, but she would not accept it.

He ran a hand through his hair, conscious of his dishevelled appearance as he passed the hayfields, still abuzz with bustle and hard work. No one spared any attention to the ill-dressed lord, walking with such great weariness that he could hardly raise his hand in greeting. And for that at least he was grateful.

He reached the courtyard without meeting another soul. The place appeared deserted; everyone was lending their strength to the bringing in of the harvest. *Good.* He could make his departure with no further delay. He had already spied the inky black ears of his charger when someone said his name, stopping him in his tracks.

"Tristan."

He turned to see Frida looking none too pleased. Her hands rested on her hips and her mouth turned down in a thin line. Usually his elder sister radiated calmness and serenity, but not today.

"Frida." He stood where he was, his arms hanging by his side. "I am glad to have seen you before I leave. Glad also to find you and the babe so well." In truth, he had spared his new niece little more than a cursory glance before rushing off to find Mirrie, but she had struck him as a healthy, pretty little thing, and he was not quite so caught up in his own affairs to forget that.

Frida made a disgruntled sound. "Thank you, but I am not here to talk about the babe."

"What then?" He opened his palms in a show of ignorance, though he knew it could only be one thing.

"Mirrie," she said, walking closer and fixing him with a hard stare. "What has happened between you?"

Tristan found himself wishing for a courtyard full of workers. "You have seen her?" he hedged.

"Just now." Her voice quavered. "Tristan, if you have done what I think you have done…" She trailed off.

He broke her gaze, looking instead at the pink roses climbing outside the front door of the hall. "I might as well say it. I seduced her."

"Oh, Tris." Her hands covered her mouth.

"And then I asked her to marry me," he added, the fact of it still causing him pain.

Frida relaxed her stance but looked more bewildered than before. "And she refused you?" Disbelief rippled through her words.

"She accepted me, at first." He shrugged. "But as I understand it, the lady has now declined my offer." He tried to keep his expression neutral and his emotions tightly locked inside.

"Tristan," she said again, shaking her head so her silvery blonde hair streamed behind her. "When will you get this right?"

He laughed without humour, the sound bitter and harsh. "I begin to think I never will." He turned back to his charger. "But do not worry, Frida. I will be gone before Mirrie sets foot outside again."

"She has not yet come in," his sister retorted impatiently. "What do you mean, you are leaving?"

"There is no reason for me to stay."

"You are running away?" He heard her light footsteps running to catch up with him.

"I am returning to Wolvesley," he corrected her, pausing to meet her gaze before opening the stable door. "I will not stay where I am not wanted."

Frida seemed to expand with rage. "So that is it? You will go away, give up, leave Mirrie devastated?"

He leaned on the half wooden door, weariness washing over him along with the scent of hay and horse. "What else would you have me do?"

"Fight for her." Frida stepped closer, looking as if she might land a punch herself. "For the first time in your life, Tristan, fight for something other than land or glory."

His ire sparked. "That is unfair. I fight for peace and the safety of my family and country."

"And now I am asking you to fight for the woman you love." Frida laid a hand on his arm, holding him tightly when he would pull away. "That is, if you do love her, Tris. Truly."

"I love her." The words almost ripped him in two.

"Then find a way to win her." She stepped back, her arms folded provocatively. For Frida, it was all very simple.

"I have already tried." He reached out to pat his charger, who came to investigate the commotion at his door. "I tried to tell her the truth of my heart but she would not hear me."

"Then you must try again." Frida nodded decisively.

"I doubt that Mirrie would want to see me."

His sister huffed out a breath. "So what happens now? You say you love her, but you will ride off and live the rest of your life without her?"

"Don't say that." He pressed his lips together, unable to countenance such a future. Not now that he knew what true happiness felt like.

"Only cowards run away," Frida stated. The gleam in her eye showed she knew she had struck a blow.

Tristan clenched his fingers around the stable door. He never could stand being called a coward.

But this was new territory for him. He had faced many battles in his life, but none that struck so deeply into his soul.

"I opened up my heart." He rested his head on his hands. "In response, she told me I was reckless, cruel and motivated only by lust." He groaned into his palms. "Ye Gods, this makes me sound as petulant as a child. Is this what love is, sister? Something that hurts and makes one doubt one's own mind?"

Frida considered this. "At times, aye. But love can also bring out the best in a person. And that is what must happen now. You must dig deep." She leaned over and tapped at his chest. "In here."

He ruminated on this. "I would fight for her. I would do anything."

But Frida shook her head. "No swords, no grand gestures. Just you, Tris. You need to convince Mirrie to have faith in you."

"As a man." He thought of that long-ago conversation in Mirrie's bedchamber "Where is she now?"

Frida smiled in triumph. "She was heading for the standing stones the last time I saw her." She fixed him with another stare. "Please try and choose your words with more care, this time."

The path to the standing stones was familiar from childhood. Tristan's feet knew the way, leaving his mind free to roam. He recalled racing his siblings over these hills, when naught was more important than his small wooden sword, his trusted pony and the enticing smell of honey cakes wafting from the bakehouse.

When he would have never believed anyone who told him there would come a time he would clash with Mirrie. That she would strike a blow at the very foundations of his self-belief. For her steadfast refusal to credit him with reason and rationality had indeed made him question what kind of man he was.

What kind of man he wanted to be.

His men-at-arms had always followed him implicitly into battle. He had commanded mighty armies; been entrusted with perilous negotiations with the most powerful figureheads in England and beyond.

But what good were his skills as a warrior if the woman he loved did not trust him as a man?

"You must decide if you truly love Mirrie. If the answer is yes, what are you going to do about it?"

His mother's challenge had seemed, on the face of it, so easily met. But now he realised that this was no quick skirmish, swiftly executed with minimal planning. This was mayhap the riskiest campaign of his life.

And the stakes were as high as the chance of failure.

Frida had always loved the standing stones; seven granite monoliths rearing towards the sky in an uneven circle atop the cliffs. She had spoken of an ancient energy radiating from them, but to Tristan they had represented no more than a place to play. He would dare his sisters to jump from the tallest stone, thrilled to demonstrate his own strength and bravado.

He supposed they were as good a place to come and think as any other.

At least, that was what Mirrie appeared to be doing. At first, he could not see her. Then he made her out, leaning against one of the highest stones and gazing out at the sea. It was only the wind whipping at her tunic that drew his eye. She seemed as one with the landscape, merging into the hard stone in her desire to hide away from him.

For she knew he was there. His battle-honed instincts told him as much.

But she would not look at him, and this stung him more than her emotional refusal to be his wife. For time had passed, but her anger and upset still persisted. Like the calling of the gulls and the crashing of the waves beneath them.

Like his own anger and upset which still flooded his veins, making it almost impossible to think clearly.

He scuffed his boots in the long grass, unfamiliar with such a strong sensation of awkwardness. He knew not what to say, nor how to say it.

Mirrie was the one to finally break the silence. "Did you come here to find me?"

"Aye." He nodded. "Frida told me where you were."

He hoped he was not breaking a confidence.

"I am not sure I have anything else to say to you, Tristan."

Her voice was clipped and steady and this also caused him grief. For Mirrie had always spoken to him with warmth, as if he was someone important in her life.

He cleared his throat. "Allow me to speak, please?"

He waited for her small nod of permission. Her face was drawn and he thought he had never before seen her so cold and remote.

And I am the one who has done it to her.

Nay, he didn't fully understand all the reasons why. But he would take responsibility anyway. He would do whatever it took to make Mirrie smile again.

To make her believe in him again.

"We have spoken much about the importance of truth between us. I must tell you this, I spoke the truth when I told you I love you. I spoke the truth when I asked you to be my wife. There was no recklessness. No flirting. No intent to disarm you. I spoke from my heart." He put his hand to his chest.

Mirrie looked down at the grass, but not before he had seen tears shimmering in her eyes.

"But I understand that you doubt me." He left a beat for his words to fall, nodding with resignation when she still did not react.

"I understand that I need to demonstrate my feelings with more than kisses and passion," he tried again. "I must prove myself worthy of you."

God's bones, how he hated to beg. But he would do this and more.

When she finally spoke, her voice was unnaturally high. "There is no question of worthiness."

He dared take a step closer. "What then?"

She held up a hand, warding him away. A hand he could no longer naught but heed.

"The question is one of consideration." She bit down on her lip. "Of serious intent."

Tristan straightened his shoulders. "Very well. That is all the instruction I need."

Now he had caught her attention. "What do you mean?"

The plan formed in his mind as he spoke. "I will leave Ember Hall right away. Like you, I have naught else to say. But I will return in a sennight and once again ask you to marry me. If you refuse me, because you still doubt my serious intent, then I shall try again a sennight later. And so this will go on, for as long as it takes for you to accept that this is no mere whim of mine."

He made her a formal bow.

"Farewell, Mirabel."

Her hazel eyes opened wide, but he did not wait for a response before turning on his heel and marching away from the standing stones.

He had laid out the plans for this battle. It was one he intended to win.

CHAPTER TWENTY-TWO

S EVEN DAYS HAD never passed more slowly.

Mirrie tried not to count them, but her errant brain did so anyway. It mattered not how hard she worked in the hayfields, or how exhausted she was when she finally fell into bed of an evening, a feverish excitement gripped both her body and her heart whenever she thought of Tristan and his promise.

She had not known him ever to break his word.

Some days it was all she could do not to sob with painful anticipation.

But on the seventh day, her emotions took a more fearful turn. *What if he does not come?*

She served her time bringing in the harvest. The long grass had all been cut and turned. Now was the time to fork the remainder into the big hay carts to be transported to the safety of the barn. It was hard, physical and monotonous work, but she relished the chance to fix her mind on a task so simply defined. When the sun beat down and her blisters stung and her back ached, the endless circling of her thoughts relaxed just a little of their hold on her.

But all too soon, the afternoon shadows began to lengthen and the long lines of workers headed indoors. Mirrie could not bear to be idle. Instead, she made her way to the standing stones, where Tristan had made his final vow.

A vow I should have at least acknowledged.

At the time, she had been silenced by a potent blend of sorrow, anxiety, self-pity and surprise. Now she berated herself for not speaking up and telling him she would count on him keeping his word.

Standing in the centre of the circle was a tall man with a crown of golden hair. Her heartbeat quickened before she realised, a moment later, it was Jonah.

"You do not oft come all the way up here," she greeted him.

"I had an idea I might find you here." He leaned his hands against a waist-height stone and hefted himself onto the level surface of it. "I wanted to talk to you." His wasted leg hung crookedly below him, but he looked comfortable enough. Indeed, with his highly embroidered tunic, polished boots and imperious stare, he was every inch his father's son.

And Tristan's brother.

Apprehension rippled through her. Did Jonah know something she did not?

"We talk most days," she countered lightly, making a show of plucking daisies from the long grass.

"I wanted to talk in private."

Mirrie gave up. She flung herself down on the grass, stretched her legs out in front of her and met his searching eyes. "What about?"

A smile curved at his lips. "What else but my brother?"

She twirled the daisies, trying to keep herself calm.

"I have an idea what happened between you," he said softly.

She put a hand to her flushed cheeks and hung her head, but he only chuckled.

"Fear not, Mirrie. I most certainly do not want to talk to you about *that*." He shifted on the stone, shading his eyes from the slanting sunlight.

"Please do not embarrass me. I suffer enough."

"I have no wish to do so." His voice was grave. "What I meant was, I have an idea that Tristan asked you to marry him. And a strong suspicion that you refused him."

She nodded. Up to now, the only person she had told was Frida. And Frida, she knew, was no gossip. But Ember Hall was a small household and Jonah had known her since childhood.

"My second strong suspicion is that you are not happy about this?" He left the question hanging.

"How could I be?" she burst out.

"Exactly that." For a moment she thought he might jump off the stone, but he only leaned towards her. "You have loved Tristan almost all your life. Why ever did you refuse him?"

"You know why." She swallowed. "You said yourself that he is impulsive. He speaks first and thinks later. How can I trust anything he says?"

Jonah pursed his lips. "Because to the best of my knowledge, my brother has never before asked a woman to marry him."

A sob escaped her.

"Even Tristan, for all his fancy talk, would hesitate to make such an offer if he did not mean it."

His words stirred hope in her breast, until she recalled the exact circumstances of his asking.

"He was… I mean, we were…" She chewed on her lip. The sentence was impossible to finish.

Jonah held up a hand. "My brother is no innocent amongst women. Trust me on this."

"That is hardly reassuring." She turned her face away.

"Hardly news, either. Come now, Mirrie. You know Tristan, good and bad. He has taken a long line of willing women to his bed. None of them e'er became his betrothed. And not for want of wrangling, I'll wager."

"Jonah. I don't know what to do." It was the first time in her life she had felt so lost.

"I myself have called him impulsive. But oft-times, I daresay that which we label impulsive behaviour is but an example of his quick decision making. And you must see that quality is a strength." He lowered his voice. "It perchance saved my father's life, this last month. And I've no doubt that many a battle has been won because of it."

Emotion was welling up inside her, like a dam that was sure to burst.

"Would you want to change him?" he asked softly.

"Nay." She wrapped her arms about her chest. "'Tis as you say. I know him, good and bad."

And I love him, good and bad.

"Well then." Jonah leaned back and tipped his face to the evening sun, giving her time and space to process her rambling thoughts.

"How come you are so ready to defend him?" she asked, as the thought occurred to her. "You are hardly his greatest ally."

Jonah smiled. "I feel the time has come to put my childish envy of Tristan to one side. Does he exasperate me? Aye, and I've no doubt he will continue to do so. But he is also a man I am proud to call my brother."

He shuffled forward and lowered himself to the ground, wincing as he did so.

"Do you need help?" She sprang to her feet, ready to extend her hand.

"Do not fret, sweet Mirrie. I can manage this and more." He winked at her. "I am endeavouring to mend my long-time reputation as *the Scowler*. And I find that walking in these beautiful hills helps to heal my body and soul so that my smiles come more readily."

Mirrie put her hands behind her back, trying to keep her expression neutral. "I for one never called you that."

"Nay, but I know it was a common refrain amongst Frida and Tristan." He thought for a moment. "I even heard it from Esme's lips. Though Isabella rarely took her attention from her looking glass for long enough to notice anyone or anything else around her."

She pulled a face. "Your assessment is harsh."

"But fair?" He raised a questioning eyebrow.

"Fair." She allowed herself to smile. "No one has called you the Scowler for some time."

"So my methods must be working." He clapped an arm about her shoulder in a brotherly way. "I will return to the hall. Pray, think on what I have said."

"I will." She nodded.

How could I do anything else?

Impatience gripped at her limbs, but she could think of no place else to go. She hadn't dared venture down to the cove since she had met with Tristan down there. The memories would be too close, too painful to endure. She could not bear the chatter and bustle of the great hall, filled with labourers come in from the fields. Nor did she wish to leave the safety of the estate so late in the day.

She could only sit with her back to the hard stone, her hands wrapped around her legs, her mind whirling relentlessly round and around the same refrain.

Had she spoken too harshly to him?

Frida had told her that she should make Tristan fight for her love. *But does he really love me that much?*

Mirrie put her head in her hands, part of her acknowledging that 'twas her own insecurities she battled against. Insecurities that had clawed at her skin when she contemplated the very real prospect of becoming a countess. Insecurities that had made her doubt a declaration of love and a proposal of marriage from the man she had long adored.

I must learn to have more faith in myself.

Tristan had always expressed faith in her. From the time when they were children, and he was urging her to join in with their pony-back games. He had seen strength in her that others overlooked.

She remembered his words down on the beach and thought her heart might split into two.

"I wish you could see yourself as I do, for there is naught you cannot do."

The next moment, she had rounded back on herself. Did she

not have the self-respect she was born with? If she was to marry and build a life with any man, could she not expect, at the very least, for him to respect her opinions? *And keep his word?*

And at this thought, the tears sprang to her eyes once again, for the sun was slipping inexorably towards the sea and it was surely too late for Tristan to arrive.

Slowly, the realisation sank like a stone in her belly.

He was not coming.

She sat on the grass until the ache in her back grew unbearable. Then she walked back to the hall, stooped over like an old woman who had lost all faith. Darkness had all but fallen by the time she turned into the courtyard, and she thought her eyes were deceiving her when a horseman turned in at the gate.

She stood on the cobbles and waited for him, hope daring to unfurl deep inside her.

It was Tristan. She knew by his height and bearing. She even knew his horse—the feisty charger he rode into battle. An unsuitable mount for a genteel journey with his sister, Esme, in tow. But the only choice if he rode alone.

And he was alone.

She was conscious of the bright lights shining behind her as everyone gathered in the great hall. Chatter and music filtered through the ancient stone, and tempting aromas from the kitchen drifted through the front door which had been left open against the prolonged heat of the day.

But she only had eyes for Tristan.

He rode up right beside her, then halted his horse and sprang lightly down to the ground.

"I'm sorry I am late." His voice carried through the near dark, like a whisper on the wind.

"We fixed no specific time."

He breathed heavily. "You had a right to expect me whilst the sun was up, at least."

He was right. She should not deny it. "What detained you?"

"You remember I spoke to you of erecting a covered market

at Wolvesley?" He slipped the reins over his horse's head. "Progress has been painfully slow. But today, at last, the first posts were erected. Forgive me, Mirrie, but I could not leave until I had seen the job done. It was my idea. My responsibility."

"You are here now," she said, softly.

She thought he smiled, though it was difficult to make out his expression. "I must see to my horse." He began to lead him towards the stables.

"No, wait." She shook her head in confusion, but the words were said now.

"What is it?" He paused, his horse whickering with disapproval.

"I cannot stand to wait a moment longer."

"For what?" His warm hand was on her cheek.

She closed her eyes at his touch. Her pulse galloped. "Will you make me say it?"

"Nay." His words came in a rush. "'Tis only that I hardly dared to hope you would speak to me. Much less that you would be waiting. And wanting to hear what I had to say."

"I am waiting." She swallowed. "And I am wanting."

He hooked his arm through the reins so he could take both of her hands in his. "I have a question for you, and it is one I have thought long and hard over."

Her heart soared and her whole body trembled. "I would like to hear it."

He stepped closer, so she could hear the raggedness of his breathing and feel the heat from his body.

"Mirabel Duval, will you do me the honour of becoming my wife?"

She nodded, emotion forbidding her to speak.

"I would rather hear your answer than guess at it."

"I will." She flung her arms about his neck, rejoicing in the moment his arms closed around her. "I will marry you, Tristan."

"Despite all my faults?"

"Even because of them." She could not wait for his kiss. She stood on her tiptoes and claimed it for herself, closing her eyes to savour the sensation of his mouth on hers. His cheeks were raspy with stubble. His powerful body was her port in a storm, now and forever.

"I will spend the rest of my life working to be the man you deserve," he whispered in her ear.

"You are already that and more." She cupped his face. "I love you, Tristan."

He swung her around so her feet flew in the air and the horse startled in surprise.

"I love you, Mirrie. With my heart and my head and every bone in my body."

"That is mighty lucky." Happiness made her giggle. "I recall you were most keen to marry for love."

He set her gently down. "Aye. You see I was right about that." His voice was playful.

"You are impulsive and rash. But you are most always right, Tristan. That is one of the things I love about you."

His hands caressed her shoulders. "If I am most always right, 'tis only because I have always had your wisdom to guide me." His voice had grown serious. "I am naught without you, Mirrie."

She tipped back her head to make out the brightness of his eyes, gazing down in hers. "Then I had better stay close."

He ducked down for another kiss. "I am counting upon it."

CHAPTER TWENTY-THREE

Year of our Lord 1330
Ember Hall, Northumberland

THE SILVERY SONG of a ruddock accompanied them as they passed through the corn meadow. Blue skies overhead promised another day of beautiful sunshine, but the temperature had not yet climbed high enough to invite discomfort. Nonetheless, Mirrie was pleased to have abandoned her fine gown in favour of a simple linen tunic, belted at the waist and loose over her shoulders. Perchance her attire was not befitting her station as Lady Mirabel de Neville. A station that, slowly but surely, she was beginning to inhabit with confidence. But for today, ensconced in the familiar surroundings of Ember Hall, she was happy to just be Mirrie.

Beside her, Tristan ran his hand over the brightly hued crops, nodding in admiration. He too was dressed simply, in breeches and a crisp white shirt, with his heavy locks of hair shining more golden than the sun.

"It will be another good harvest," he pronounced, looking about with satisfaction.

"My husband, the farmer." Her lips turned up into a smile.

He grabbed at her hand and swung it. "See how I was right about the land rotation?"

"I never doubted it," she assured him, linking her fingers with his and squeezing.

"I will be right about Esme, too." He nodded sagely, helping her onto a small wooden stile. "You will see. Mother will have

238

identified a suitor for her. She has an uncanny knack of knowing what is right for us, even before we know it ourselves."

Mirrie paused atop the stile, taking the opportunity to look down upon her handsome husband, which was not a view she oft had chance to enjoy. His blue eyes crinkled into a smile as he slipped his hands around her waist.

"Your mother is wise indeed," she agreed, soothing his thick hair back from his forehead. "I am still surprised at the role she played in our courtship."

"Aye, whilst you fretted about deceiving her."

"Quite rightly so." Mirrie rested her hands lightly on his broad shoulders. "Deceit is a strong word, Tris. I would not say your mother deceived either of us."

"'Twas more that she opened my eyes." He rested his forehead against her belly and sighed with contentment. "I cannot help but wonder who she has in mind for my sister. Esme has been indifferent to all suitors so far."

Mirrie made a noncommittal noise before jumping down from the stile. She shaded her eyes as she took in the timeless view of wispy white clouds above a sparkling sea.

"You think I am wrong?" Tristan came up behind her, wrapping his arms about her waist.

She leaned back against him, enjoying his height and strength. Over the last months, he had become her rock.

"I fear you are mistaken," she corrected him.

Tristan laughed lightly, his lips tracing a faint line of kisses along her shoulder.

"Do not do that." She wriggled away, unable to keep from giggling. "Else we shall never reach the cove."

Hand in hand, they walked down the stony path, their paces evenly matched. Hardly a breeze stirred the long grass at either side of them, and the sea was calm and still, with the shallowest of waves breaking to foam softly on the shore.

Mirrie thought the water had never looked so inviting.

"Tell me the truth about Esme," he urged as they rounded

the corner and took their first steps onto the shingle.

"I do not wish to speak ill of your sister."

"She is your sister too." He smiled down at her. "What has she done that is so terrible?"

"Naught that I know." Mirrie gripped his hand tighter to steady herself on the uneven ground.

"Then what do you suspect?"

She sighed. "'Tis more a fear that your bright, beautiful sister—*our* bright, beautiful sister," she corrected herself, "shows such indifference to marriage simply because she has already given her heart to another."

"Surely that is a blessing?" He frowned.

"Only if the man in question is worthy of her." Mirrie stopped and caught at his other hand. "Tris, let us not speak of this now. Esme is safe under the protection of your parents. No harm can come to her. Ignore my misgivings."

"I am your husband. I shall never ignore your misgivings."

His sincerity made her smile. "And that is only right."

But Tristan was still frowning. "Mirrie, I know you to be wise in matters of the heart. And sensitive to the moods and actions of others. If you truly think that Esme is courting some disaster, please do tell me."

"Not disaster." She looked out at the sea for inspiration. "Only innocent mischief, mayhap. Esme is a woman determined to follow her heart wherever it leads her. After all I have learned these last months, I can only admire her pursuit of happiness."

Tristan seemed unconvinced, but Mirrie had not brought him here to talk of his sister.

"You know better than I how the mighty de Nevilles can quickly turn any situation to their advantage," she added, lightly. "And dear Esme has that ability in abundance."

"I cannot deny it." He brushed his thumb across her cheek. "What she lacks is prudence and a clear grasp of consequence."

"Ah, but she has me for that."

"What would any of us do without you?" He dropped his lips

to her forehead, sending pinpoints of awareness prickling through her.

Was it only last summer they had stood almost in this exact spot and first professed their love for one another? Though the occasion had ended in heartbreak, she still treasured the memories of each twist and turn on their journey to happiness.

"I oft wonder, to be sure," she said with mock primness, before twirling around and settling herself on the shingle beach. As Tristan raised a surprised eyebrow, she stuck out an ankle and rotated it. "I have a job for you, husband."

He hid his smile in a low bow. "I await your orders."

She leaned back on her hands. "Remove my boots."

His shadow blocked the sun as he dropped to his knees and carefully, efficiently, removed first one boot and then the other. Mirrie had deliberately not worn stockings this morn. She dug her toes into the damp shingle and felt the cool relief of it.

"What now?" he asked, his voice raspy and deep.

"Help me up." She held out her hand and allowed him to raise her up again. His hands caught at her waist and she knew that if she wanted to do this, she must do it now.

In another minute, Lord Tristan de Neville would chase all rational thoughts from her mind.

"That is all, thank you," she said, waving her hand in dismissal and walking away from him, towards the gentle sea.

"Where are you going?" he called after her.

She turned with a smile, opening her arms wide. "To bathe."

She stepped into the shallows without hesitating, closing her eyes in exhilaration as cold water chased around her calves. Gulls cried overhead and the sun shone down like a blessing. She took another step and lurched downwards as the shore dipped away. Her tunic was soaked now. There was naught for it but to stretch out her limbs and let the waves wash over her.

A whoop from behind alerted her to Tristan, who had pulled off his shirt and was plunging in beside her. Foam splashed up as he dove beneath the surface, emerging seconds later to shake himself dry. Droplets of water clung to his bronzed skin and his smile was wicked as he reached for Mirrie.

"What a clever idea," he murmured, sinking down to his knees and grasping her waist.

"I thought so."

He kissed her softly, tasting of salt. "But you should have removed this." He tugged at her sodden tunic.

"Why, Tristan." She widened her eyes in mock horror. "Someone might see."

"Then let us stay beneath the cover of the water." He pulled her towards him. "Where I can keep you all to myself."

They had been married six months, but that time had done naught to dull the fire between them. Mirrie thought there would never come a day when she did not melt at his touch or the whisper of his lips on hers. Soon the heat from their bodies mingled with the gentle tug of the tides, and her cries of pleasure joined the calls of the gulls high overhead.

"There is something I must tell you," she said, when they had both caught their breath. Waves ran up and over Tristan's muscular body. He laid back in the shallows and smiled up at her.

"What is it?"

She caught his hand in hers. "I am with child."

He sat up in a rush, water sluicing from his hair and shoulders. "Truly?"

She nodded. "Is this happy news?"

"How could it be anything but?" He held her shoulders and gazed at her reverently. "I am the luckiest soul in all the land."

Mirrie wrapped her arms about him and pressed her lips to his. She would not tell him he was wrong. But she knew that in all of England, there was not one person, man or woman, who was luckier or happier than she.

THE END

About the Author

Elizabeth grew up in a rambling old farmhouse high on the Yorkshire moors, where a sense of history was never far away. She studied English at university, specialising in mythology and folklore and often bemoaning the lack of sword-wielding heroines. After graduating, she spent several years moving between northern France, southern Germany and London, where she worked in travel publishing and PR.

She now lives a stone's throw from her childhood home, with her husband, children and a feisty black cat who enjoys interrupting her writing. She plots most of her novels while walking in the rugged Yorkshire countryside, finding endless inspiration in the rolling hills.

www.ingramcontent.com/pod-product-compliance
Lightning Source LLC
Chambersburg PA
CBHW072113300726
48975CB00003B/795